touchy subjects

W9-CHX-332

ALSO BY EMMA DONOGHUE

FICTION

Stir-Fry

Hood

Kissing the Witch

Slammerkin

The Woman Who Gave Birth to Rabbits

Life Mask

Landing

LITERARY HISTORY

Passions Between Women:
British Lesbian Culture 1668–1801

We Are Michael Field

ANTHOLOGIES

The Mammoth Book of Lesbian Short Stories (ed.)

Poems Between Women: Four Centuries of
Love, Romantic Friendship, and Desire (ed.)

DRAMA

Ladies and Gentlemen

EMMA DONOGHUE

touchy
subjects

stories

A HARVEST BOOK • HARCOURT, INC.

Orlando   Austin   New York   San Diego   Toronto   London

Copyright © 2006 by Emma Donoghue

All rights reserved. No part of this publication may be reproduced
or transmitted in any form or by any means, electronic or mechanical,
including photocopy, recording, or any information storage
and retrieval system, without permission in writing from the publisher.

Requests for permission to make copies of any part of the work
should be submitted online at www.harcourt.com/contact or mailed
to the following address: Permissions Department, Harcourt, Inc.,
6277 Sea Harbor Drive, Orlando, Florida 32887-6777.

www.HarcourtBooks.com

The Library of Congress has cataloged the hardcover edition as follows:
Donoghue, Emma, 1969–
Touchy subjects: stories/Emma Donoghue.—1st ed.
p. cm.
I. Title.
PR6054.O547T68   2005
823'.914—dc22   2005026170
ISBN 978-0-15-101386-9
ISBN 978-0-15-603261-2 (pbk.)

Text set in Bulmer MT
Designed by Cathy Riggs

Printed in the United States of America

First Harvest edition 2007
A C E G I K J H F D B

This book is for Finn Claude Donoghue Roulston,
with a big wet kiss.

Contents

DESIRE

DEATH

BABIES

Touchy Subjects

Sarah's eyes were as dry as paper. Jet lag always made her feel ten years older. She stared past the blond chignon of the receptionist in Finbar's Hotel. Twenty to one, according to the clock on the right. One take away eight was minus seven. No, try again. Thirteen take away eight was five. Twenty to five, Seattle time. Morning or evening? Wednesday or Thursday?

She shut her eyes and told herself not to panic. A day either way would make no difference. *Please let it not make any difference.*

"Ms. Lord?" The Germanic receptionist was holding out the key.

Sarah took it and tried to smile. There were four different clocks behind the desk, she realized now. The one she'd been reading was New York, not Dublin. So here the time was a quarter to six, but according to her body clock it was . . .

Forget it.

Bag in hand, she stumbled across the marble floor towards the lifts.

A young assistant porter in Edwardian stripes brought up her double espresso ten minutes later. Sarah felt better as soon as she smelt it. She even flirted with the boy a little. Just a matter of "That was quick," and a tilt of the eyebrows, just to shake herself awake. He answered very perkily.

Even if, to a boy like that, thirty-eight probably seemed like ninety. *Every little hormone helps.*

Her heart thudded as the caffeine hit home. She dragged the chair over to the window; sunlight was the best cure for jet lag. Not that there was ever much sunlight to catch in Ireland, but at least it was a clear evening. Her eyes rested on the long glitter of the river as she drained her espresso. Time was you couldn't even have got a filter coffee in Dublin; this town had certainly come on. You could probably get anything you needed now if you paid enough. She winced at the thought: too close to home.

Knotted into the starchy robe, she flexed her feet on the pale red-and-black carpet and considered the dress spread out on the bed. She knew it was comical, but she couldn't decide what to wear. This was a big night, most definitely, but not the kind of occasion covered in the book on manners her mother gave her for her eighteenth birthday. (Sarah still kept it on her cookery-book shelf in Seattle; guests found it hilarious.) Whatever she wore tonight had to be comfortable, but with a bit of glamour to keep her spirits up. Back home, this sleeveless dress in cream linen had seemed perfect, but now it was creased in twenty places. Like her face.

Sarah was tempted to keep on the dressing gown, but it might frighten Padraic. She wished she knew him better. Why hadn't she paid him a bit more attention at all those Christmas do's? She was sure there was a chapter on that in her etiquette manual: *Take the trouble to talk to everyone in the room.* Last year her entire corporation had undergone a weekend's training in power networking, which boiled down to the same thing, with motives bared.

Work the party. You never know when someone might turn out to be useful.

Was she using Padraic? Was that what it all amounted to?

No more bloody ethical qualms, Sarah reminded herself. This was the only way to get what she wanted. What she needed. What she deserved, as much as the next woman, anyway.

The dress was impossible; it would make her look like cracked china. She pulled the purple suit she'd traveled in back on; now she was herself again. Cross-legged on the bed, she waited for her heartbeat to slow down. Six twenty. That was OK; Padraic was only five minutes late. All she wanted was to lie down, but a nap would be fatal.

There was that report on internal communications she was meant to be reading, but in this condition she wouldn't make any sense of it. She stretched for the remote and flicked through the channels. How artistic the ads were, compared with back home in Seattle. Sarah paused at some sort of mad chat show hosted by a computer. Was that Irish the children were talking? How very odd.

Please let him not be very late.

The Irish were always bloody late.

Padraic was relieved that Finbar's Hotel was way down on the quays opposite Heuston Station, where he was unlikely to bump into anyone he knew. He stood outside for a minute and gawked up at the glistening balconies. He remembered it when there was only a peeling facade, before that Dutch rock star and his Irish wife had bought it up. What would it cost, a night in one of those tastefully refurbished rooms? It was a shame all the yuppies had to look down on was the Liffey.

The first things he noticed when the doors slid open were the white sofas, lined up like a set of teeth. Ludicrous—they'd be black in a month. Padraic grinned to himself now to relax his jaw. Greg in marketing had this theory about all tension and pain originating in the back teeth.

Padraic was the kind of man who always wore his wedding ring, and it hadn't occurred to him to take it off. But as he stood at the desk and asked the receptionist whether Ms. Lord had checked in yet, he thought he saw her eyes flicker to his hand. He almost gave in to a silly impulse to put it behind his back. Instead, he tugged at the neck of the Breton fisherman's jumper he had changed into after work.

The receptionist had the phone pressed to her ear now. She sounded foreign, but he couldn't tell from where. What was keeping Sarah? What possible hitch could there be?

Poor woman, he thought, for the twentieth time. *To have to stoop to this.*

"Padraic?"

He leapt. He felt his whole spine lock into a straight line. Then he turned. "Máire, how *are* you! You look stunning! I don't think I've seen you since Granny's funeral. Didn't I hear you were in England?" The words were exploding from his mouth like crumbs.

His cousin gave him a Continental-style peck on the cheek. "I'm only back a month."

Her badge said MÁIRE DERMOTT, RECEPTION MANAGER. He jabbed a finger at it. "You're doing well for yourself." If he kept talking, his cousin couldn't ask him what he was doing here.

"Oh, early days," she said.

"It all looks fabulous, anyway," he said, wheeling round and waving at the snowy couches, the bright paintings, the rows of tiny lamps hanging like daggers overhead. He edged away from the desk, where the receptionist had got Sarah on the phone at last.

"So how's Carmel?" asked Máire. "And the boys?"

Padraic was about to give a full report on his respectable family life when the receptionist leaned over the desk. "Excuse me, Mr. Dermott. If you'd be so good as to go up now, the room is 101. And please tell Ms. Lord that the champagne is on its way."

He offered Máire a ghastly smile. "Friend of Carmel's."

His cousin's face had suddenly shut down. She looked as snotty as when they were children doing Christmas pantomimes and she always made him play the ox.

Padraic gave a merry little wave of the fingers. "Catch you later," he said, backing away.

On the way to the lifts Padraic glanced into the establishment designated as the Irish Bar, which looked just like the one he and Carmel had stumbled across in Athens. He pressed repeatedly on the lift button, then put his hand against his hot face. It was god's own truth, what he'd told his cousin about Sarah being a friend of Carmel's. But it was also, under the circumstances, the worst possible thing to say. His father's side of the family were notorious gossips. Once again, Padraic Dermott had dug himself a pit with his own big mouth.

Sarah was standing in the door of room 101, her heart ticking like a clock. When she saw him coming down the long corridor she felt a rush of something like love. "Hi!" she called, too loudly.

"Hey there!"

They kissed, as if at a cocktail party. Padraic's cheek was a little bristly.

"Come in, come in! I'm thrilled to bits to see you!" She knew she sounded stage-Irish; she was overcompensating. She didn't want him to think she was some transatlantic ice queen who'd forgotten how to travel by bus.

Thank god there were armchairs, so they didn't have to sit on the bed. Padraic hunched over a little, hands on his knees, as if ready for action. She tried to remember if they'd ever been alone in a room together before.

"How was your flight?"

"Oh, you know." Sarah yawned and shrugged. "How's business these days?" she asked.

"Not bad," he said, "not bad at all." She could see his shoulders relax a little into the satin-finish chair. "We're diversifying a good bit. Lots of opportunities."

"I'll bet," she assured him.

"And yourself?"

"Well, I got that promotion." She added a little rueful smile. Not that he would have any idea which promotion she meant.

"Of course you did!"

Did she detect a touch of irony? Surely not. "And the lads?" she asked.

"Doing great," he told her. "Fiachra's in the senior school this year."

Sarah nodded enthusiastically. "I brought them some stuff . . ." Her voice trailed off as she nodded at the heap of presents on the sideboard. She didn't mean to play the rich Yank, buying herself a welcome.

"Ah, you're very good." Padraic was craning over his chair to see the presents.

Then a silence flickered in the air between them.

"D'you ever see anything of Eamonn these days?" His tone was ostentatiously light.

"Not really," said Sarah. "He's in Boston."

"Mmm. I just thought—"

"That's nearly as far from Seattle as from Dublin."

"Right."

Padraic was looking as if he wished he hadn't mentioned

Eamonn's name. She hadn't sounded touchy, had she? She hadn't
meant to, if she had. It was just the general twitchiness of the occasion. Padraic just sat there, looking around at the furnishings.
And then, thank Christ and all his saints, a knock on the door.

The boy in stripes brought in the champagne on a tray. Was
that a hint of a smirk on his face? Sarah squirmed, but just a little.
In her twenty years away from Ireland she had taught herself not
to give a shit what anybody thought.

Five minutes later, Padraic's hands were still straining at the
wire around the cork. Sarah thought for an awful moment that
she'd have to ring down and ask for the boy to be sent back up.

"Excellent!" she said, when the pop came, very loud in the
quiet room. The foam dripped onto the table. "Ooh, doesn't it
make a mess!"

And then she realized she sounded just like that nurse in the
Carry On films, and the laughter started in her throat, deep and
uncouth.

Padraic looked at her, owl-eyed, then started laughing, too.
His face was red. He filled both glasses to the brim.

"I swear, I didn't mean—," she began.

"I know you didn't."

"It was just—"

"It was," he said, knocking back half the glass and wiping one
eye.

Sarah felt a bit better after that little icebreaker. She offered to
refill his glass.

"Better not," said Padraic, all business now. "You know what
Shakespeare said."

She tried to think of all the things Shakespeare ever said.

"'Drink,'" he explained. "'It makes a man and then mars
him . . . provokes the desire, but takes away the performance.'"

"Really?"

Padraic added, "It's the only quote I ever remember."

Sarah nodded. Privately she was sure Shakespeare had never said any such thing; it sounded more like Morecambe and Wise. It was time she took charge of this conversation. "Listen," she began in the voice she used at meetings. Was she imagining it, or did Padraic sit up straighter? "Listen," she tried again, more gently, "are you sure you're OK about this?"

"Absolutely," said Padraic.

"No, but really, you've only to say." She let the pause stretch. "It's a lot to ask."

"No bother."

Typical bloody Irishmen, can't handle any conversation more intimate than buying a paper. Sarah pressed her fingertips together hard and tried again. Her voice was beginning to shake. "I hope you know I wouldn't be here if there was any other way."

"I know that, sure."

"I can't tell you how grateful I'll be—I mean, I am, already." She stumbled on. "The only thing is, I get the feeling Carmel kind of talked you into this?"

"Nonsense," he said, too heartily. "I'm more than happy. Glad to be of use."

She winced at the word.

"Well now." Padraic got up and straightened the sleeves of the shirt he wore beneath that ridiculous striped jersey. "I suppose I should get down to business." From his jacket pocket he produced a small empty jar that said HEINZ PEAS & CARROTS FOR BABY.

Sarah stared at it. "How suitable." Her throat was dry.

He peered at the ripped label. "Would you look at that! I grabbed the first clean jar I could find that wasn't too big," he added a little sheepishly.

Compassion swept over her like water. "It's perfect."

They stood around as if waiting for divine intervention. Then

Sarah took a few light steps towards the bathroom. "Why don't I wait—"

"Not at all," he said, walking past her. "You stay in here and have a bit of a nap."

She heard the key turn in the bathroom door.

A nap? Did he seriously think she could sleep through what might turn out to be the hinge of her whole life?

Padraic knew he was being paranoid, but just in case. Sarah might think of some further instructions and burst in on him in that scary suit with the pointed lapels. Anyway, he'd never been able to relax in a bathroom without locking the door.

The jar looked harmless, standing beside the miniature elderflower soap. He tried perching on the edge of the bath, but it was too low; he feared he might fall backwards and damage his back. *Dublin Businessman Found Committing Lewd Act in Luxury Hotel.* All right for the likes of George Michael, maybe, but not recommended for a career in middle management. And his cousin Máire would never forgive him for the publicity.

He tried sitting on the toilet—with the lid down, so it would feel less squalid, more like a chair. He leaned back, a knob poked him between the shoulderblades, and the flush started up like Niagara. He stood up till the sound died down. Sarah would think he was wasting time. Sarah would think him a complete moron, but then, he'd always suspected she thought that anyway.

Now, these weren't the sort of thoughts to be having, were they? Relaxing thoughts were what were needed; warm thoughts, sexy thoughts. Beaches and open fires and hammocks and . . . no, not babies. Would it look like him, he wondered for the first time, this hypothetical West Coast child?

He hadn't been letting himself think that far ahead. All week he'd been determined to do this thing, as a favour to Carmel,

really, though Carmel thought he was doing it for her best friend.
He'd been rather flattered to be asked, especially by someone as
high-powered as Sarah Lord. He couldn't think of any reason to
refuse. It wasn't your everyday procedure, and he wasn't planning
to mention it to his mother, but really, where was the harm? As
Carmel put it the other night, "It's not like you're short of the
stuff, sweetie."

Still, he preferred not to dwell on the long-term consequences.
The thought of his brief pleasure being the direct cause of a baby
was still somehow appalling to Padraic, even though he had three
sons and loved them so much it made his chest feel tight. He still
remembered that day in Third Year when the priest drew a diagram on the blackboard. The Lone Ranger sperm; the engulfing
egg. He didn't quite believe it. It sounded like one of those stories
adults made up when they couldn't be bothered to explain the
complicated truth.

Padraic sat up straighter on the glossy toilet seat. He did ten
complete body breaths. It was all he remembered from that stress
training his company had shelled out for last year. Three hundred
euro a head, and the office was still full of squabbles and cold
coffee.

He unzipped his trousers to start getting in the mood. Nothing stirring yet. All Very Quiet on the Western Front. Well, Sarah
couldn't expect some sort of McDonald's-style service, could she?
Ready in Five Minutes or Your Money Back. She wasn't paying for
this, Padraic reminded himself. He was doing her a great big
favour. At least, he was trying to.

He zipped up his trousers again; he didn't like feeling
watched. If he could only relax there would be no problem. There
never was any problem. Well, never usually. Hardly ever. No more
than the next man. And Carmel had such a knack . . .

He wouldn't think about Carmel. It was too weird. She was

his wife, and here he was sitting on a very expensive toilet preparing to hand her best friend a jar of his semen. At the sheer perversity of the thought, he felt a little spark of life. *Good, good, keep it up, man. You're about to have a wank,* he told himself salaciously, *in the all-new, design-award-winning Finbar's Hotel. This is very postmodern altogether. That woman out there has flown halfway round the world for the Holy Grail of your little jarful. Think what the pope would say to that!*

This last taboo was almost too much for Padraic; he felt his confidence begin to drain away at the thought of the pontiff peering in the bathroom window.

Dirty, think honest-to-god dirty thoughts. Suddenly he couldn't remember any. What did he used to think about when he was seventeen? It seemed an aeon ago.

He knew he should have come armed. An hour ago he was standing at the Easons magazine counter, where the cashier had looked about twelve, and he'd lost his nerve and handed her an *Irish Independent* instead. Much good the *Irish Independent* would be to him in this hour of need. He'd flicked through it already and the most titillating thing in it was a picture of the president signing a memorial.

This was ridiculous. *You're not some Neanderthal; you were born in 1961.* Surely he didn't need some airbrushed airhead to slaver over? Surely he could rely on the power of imagination?

The door opened abruptly. Sarah, who had turned her armchair to face the window so as not to seem to be hovering in a predatory way, grinned over her shoulder. "That was quick!"

Then she cursed herself for speaking too soon because Padraic was shaking his head as if he had something stuck in his ear. "Actually," he muttered, "I'm just going to stretch my legs. Won't be a minute."

"Sure, sure, take your time."

His legs? Sarah sat there in the empty room and wondered what his legs had to do with anything. Blood flow to the pelvis? Or was it a euphemism for a panic attack? She peered into the bathroom; the jar was still on the sink, bone-dry.

Five minutes later, it occurred to her that he had run home to Carmel.

The phone rang eight times before her friend picked it up. "Sarah, my love! What country are you in?"

"This one."

"Is my worser half with you?"

"Well, he was. But he's gone out."

"Out where?"

Curled up on the duvet, Sarah shrugged off her heels. "I don't know. Listen, if he turns up at home—"

"Padraic wouldn't do that to you."

There was a little silence. In the background, she could hear the *Holby City* theme on the television, and one of the boys chanting something, over and over. "Listen, Carmel, how did he seem this morning?"

Her friend let out a short laugh. "How he always seems."

"No, but was he nervous? I mean, I'm nervous, and it's worse for him."

"Maybe he was a bit," said Carmel consideringly. "But, I mean, how hard can it be?"

Who started giggling first? "Today is just one long double entendre," said Sarah eventually.

"How long?"

"Long enough!"

And then they were serious again. "Did you bully him into it, though, Carmel, really?"

"Am I the kind of woman who bullies anyone?"

This wasn't the time for that discussion. "All I mean is, I know you want to help."

"We both do. Me and Padraic both."

"But you most of all, you've been through the whole thing with me, you know what it's been like, with the clinic . . . And I swear I wouldn't have asked if I had anyone else." Sarah was all at once on the brink of tears. She stopped and tried to open her throat.

"Of course." After a minute, Carmel went on more professionally. "How's your mucus?"

"Sticky as maple syrup."

"Good stuff. It's going to happen, you know."

"Is it?" Sarah knew she sounded like a child.

"It is."

All at once she couldn't believe what she was planning. To wake up pregnant one day and somehow find the nerve to go on with it, that was one thing, but to do it deliberately . . . *For cold-blooded and selfish reasons,* as the tabloids always put it. In fantastical hope, as Sarah thought of it. In fear and trembling.

"Are you sure you can't come over for a little visit?" asked Carmel.

"I really can't. I've a meeting in Brussels tomorrow morning, before I head back to the States."

"Ah well. Next time."

Padraic was leaning on the senior porter's desk, which was more like a lectern. He spoke in a murmur, as if at confession.

"Our library on the third floor has all the papers as well as a range of contemporary Irish literature, sir," muttered the slightly stooped porter, as if reading from a script.

"No, but magazines," said Padraic meaningfully.

"We stock *Private Eye, Magill, Time* . . ."

"Not that kind." Padraic's words sounded sticky. "Men's magazines."

The old man screwed up his eyes. "I think they might have one on cars . . ."

"Oh, for Christ's sake," he said under his breath.

Then, at his elbow, just the woman he could do without. "Are you all right there, Padraic?"

"Máire." He gave her a wild look. She was just trying to catch him out at this stage. Was she following him all over the hotel to examine the state of his trousers? Just as well he didn't have the bloody erection he'd spent the last fifteen minutes trying to achieve. She'd probably photograph it for her files.

"This gentleman—," began the porter in his wavering voice.

"I'm grand, actually." And Padraic walked off without another word.

What did it matter if they thought he was rude? Máire had clearly made up her mind that he was cheating on Carmel with his wife's best friend. When the fact was he would never, never, never. He wasn't that type of guy. He had his faults, Padraic admitted to himself as he punched at the lift button, but not that one. He was a very ordinary man who loved his family. There was nothing experimental about him; he didn't even wear coloured shirts.

Then what the fuck am I doing here?

He didn't have a key to room 101; he had to knock. Sarah let him in, talking all the while on a cordless phone. Her smile didn't quite cover her irritation. "Cream," she said into the phone. "Cream linen. But it didn't travel well." He gave her a thumbs-up and headed into the bathroom.

Now he was well and truly fucked. Tired out, without so much as a picture of Sharon Stone to rely on. Funny how it seemed so easy to produce the goods when they weren't wanted.

He considered the gallons of the stuff he'd wasted as an adolescent when he locked himself into the bathroom on a daily basis. He thought of all the condoms he'd bought since he and Carmel got married. And tonight, when all that was required was a couple of spoonfuls . . .

He sat on the toilet and rested his head on his fists. What on earth had induced him to agree to this mad scheme? It just wasn't him. He knew Irish society was meant to be modernizing at a rate of knots, but this was ridiculous. It was like something off one of those American soaps with their convoluted plots, where no one knows who their father is until they do a blood test.

Sarah was still on the phone; he could hear her muted voice. Who was she talking to? She was probably complaining about him, his lack of jizz, so to speak. Padraic stared round him for inspiration. A less sexy room had never been devised. Sanitary, soothing. The only hint of colour was Sarah's leopard-skin toilet bag.

Reckless now, he unzipped it and rifled through. *Pervert,* he told himself encouragingly. Looking through his wife's friend's private things . . . her spot concealer, her super-plus tampons. He felt something stirring in his trousers. He sat down again and reached in. He clung to this unlikely image of himself as a lecherous burglar, an invader of female privacies. A man who could carry a crowbar, who might disturb a woman who was having her bath, some independent single businesswoman with sultry lips, a woman like Sarah . . .

Oh my god. If she only knew what he was thinking, barely ten feet away—

Never mind that. *Hold on to the fantasy. The crowbar.* No, chuck the crowbar, he couldn't stoop to that. He would simply surprise . . . some beautiful, fearful woman and seize her in his bare hands and—

If Carmel knew he had rape fantasies she'd give him hell.

Never mind. Do what you have to do. Keep at it. Nearly there now. Evil, smutty, wicked thoughts. The gorgeous luscious open-mouthed businesswoman . . . bent over the sink . . . her eyes in the mirror . . .

By now he had forgotten all about the jar. His eye fell on it at the last possible minute.

Now wouldn't that have been ironic, Padraic told himself as he screwed the lid back on with shaking hands.

It didn't look like very much, it occurred to him. He should have brought a smaller jar. A test tube, even.

He gave himself a devilish grin in the mirror. Endorphins rushed through his veins. Now what he'd love was a little snooze, but no, he had a delivery to make.

Sarah was reading some spiral-bound document, but she leapt up when he opened the door, and the pages slid to the floor. "Wonderful!" she said, all fluttery, as he handed over the warm jar. Her cheeks were pink. She really was quite a good-looking woman.

"Hope it's enough," he joked.

"It's grand, loads!"

It struck him for the first time that she might need some help with getting it in. *Oh god, please let her not upend herself and ex-pect me to . . .* But he was too much of a gentleman to run away. He hovered. Sarah, acting like she did this every day, produced a syringe.

"Wow," said Padraic. "I hope they didn't search your bag at customs."

"No, but it did show up on the X-ray screen." She gave a breathless little laugh.

"Wow," he said again. Then, "It might have been easier to do it the old-fashioned way!"

It was a very cold look she gave him. Surely she couldn't think he meant it? A touchy subject, clearly. (Weren't they all, these days?) Padraic knew he should never make jokes when he was nervous. He felt heat rise up his throat.

"I'll get out of your way, then, will I? Treat myself to a whiskey. Maybe you'll come down and join me after?"

He couldn't stop talking. Sarah smiled and nodded and opened the door for him.

She tried lying on the bed with her bare legs in the air, but it was hard to keep them up there. *Hurry, hurry,* she told herself; the jar was cooling fast. How long was it they lived? Was it true that boy sperm moved faster but girl sperm lived longer? Or was it vice versa? Not that she gave a damn. She'd take whatever God sent her, if he was willing to use this form of special delivery. *Please just let this work.*

Finally, she ended up lying on the carpet with her feet up on the bed. She felt almost comfortable. It was crucial to feel happy at the moment of conception, someone at work had told her. Awkwardly, leaning up on one elbow, she unscrewed the lid of the jar and began to fill the syringe. It was certainly easier at the clinic, where all she had to do was shut her eyes, but it felt a lot better to be doing this herself without anyone peering or poking. Just her and a little warm jar full of magic from a nice Dublinman with a name. Nothing frozen, nothing anonymous.

There, now, she had got a good grip on the plunger. She would just lay her head back and take a few relaxing breaths . . .

The knock came so loud that her hand clenched.

"No thank you," she called in the direction of the door.

No answer. She took one huge breath and pressed the plunger.

Afterwards, she could never remember hearing the door opening. All she knew was that the assistant porter was standing there staring, in his ludicrous striped jacket, like something out of Feydeau. And she was on her feet, with her skirt caught up around her hips. "Get out," she bawled. She tugged at the cloth and heard a seam rip. There was wetness all down her legs.

The boy started to say something about turning down the sheets.

"Get out of my room!"

The door crashed shut behind him.

Afterwards, when she had mopped herself up, Sarah scrubbed at the carpet with a damp facecloth. The mark was milky, unmistakable against the square of red wool. They'd think she and Padraic had done it right here on the floor.

She wanted to go down the corridor and find that porter. She longed to spit at another human being for the first time in her life. "Look, boyo," she would scream in his ear, "if I can make myself pregnant, I'm sure I can turn down my own sheets."

But she hadn't, had she? All she'd done was stained the carpet.

The funny thing was, now he'd started, the dirty thoughts wouldn't stop coming. They raced merrily through his head. All the way down in the lift Padraic watched the other passenger in the mirrored wall. She was fifteen years too old for the red dress and black leather, but still, not bad at all. A hooker, or just somebody's bit on the side? This hotel was a stranger place than it looked from the outside; behind all that fresh paint you'd never know what was going on. He shook his head to clear it as the lift glided to a stop. He let the woman get out first.

The Irish Bar was stuffed with people, singing rebel songs Padraic hadn't heard in years; it seemed to be some sort of wake. After two whiskeys he felt superb. Relief and alcohol danced through his body together, while his hormones played "It Had to Be You."

Tonight had demanded his all, and his all was what he had given. With a bit of luck, one lonely frustrated woman's life would be transformed, and a little bit of his DNA would grow up next door to the Pacific Ocean. With a light tan and Rollerblades . . .

There was his cousin, consulting a clipboard and talking to the barman. He shouldn't have got so het up earlier; she was only taking an interest. He'd been in a bit of a state, he could admit that now. When he'd finished his third whiskey, Padraic gave a little wave, but Máire didn't seem to see. He squeezed his way over and waited for a break in the conversation, then put his hand on her arm.

"Hello again," she said.

"It's not what you think," he announced satirically.

"Right." She seemed to be speaking to her clipboard.

"No, really. I mean, yes, I'm here to meet a woman, obviously, but it's about a hundred and eighty degrees opposite to what you're obviously thinking."

Máire looked up, and her eyes were hard. "Listen, Padraic, it's none of my business."

"But the thing is, Carmel knows I'm here," he assured her, tugging at her sleeve. "Old school friend. Carmel set the whole thing up, in fact."

His cousin looked slightly revolted, and he was just about to explain, when he remembered that he had promised both Carmel and Sarah never to tell a soul about their little arrangement. So he had to let go of Máire's sleeve. She was out the door like a shot.

Knees against the bar, he idled over his next drink, planning how to describe the evening to his wife. *Oh, we got the business over with in the first ten minutes—nothing to it.* But he mustn't make it sound like too much fun, either. Carmel was being remarkably kind to her friend, when you came to think about it—lending out her husband like a sort of pedigree stud. He savoured the image.

Funny, he thought. That old porter's paging another Mr. Dermott. Then two things occured to Padraic: that it was him who was being paged, and that he was very nearly pissed. He'd only had a few, but then he'd forgotten to have dinner.

"The lady upstairs would like to know when you're coming back, sir," said the porter. A little too loudly and pointedly, Padraic thought.

He was up in room 101 in three minutes.

"I'm so sorry," Sarah stuttered. "I can't believe—"

He acted like a gentleman. He assured her it could happen to anyone. (Anyone, he mentally added, who made a habit of inseminating herself in hotel bedrooms.) He swore the stain would hoover out; "These people are professionals." (He could just imagine the chambermaid telling Máire that her cousin had spurted all over the carpet.) He grabbed the empty jar and headed back into the bathroom.

This time, Sarah said to herself, she'd stay calm. This time she'd lock the door. This time she'd get it right. And then tomorrow she'd be on her way back to Seattle, and . . . *Maybe. You never know. Carmel said it would happen.* This was still the right day. Her chances were pretty good.

Padraic popped his head out of the bathroom. Only now did she notice how dark red his face had gone. "I might be a little while."

"How many have you had?" She didn't mean it to sound quite so cutting, but she thought she had a right to know.

He leant on the doorjamb. All the softness went out of his voice. "What's that supposed to mean?"

She shrugged.

"I thought my shift was over, you know," he went on acidly. "As far as I knew you'd got what you wanted, you were finished with me, and I had the right to a drink."

"You've had more than one," she pointed out neutrally.

"And if you'll give me a minute," he shouted, "I can still fucking well get it up."

They avoided each other's eyes.

"Jesus," he added, "no wonder . . ."

He turned to go back into the bathroom, but Sarah was on her feet. There was nothing she hated more than unfinished sentences. "No wonder what?"

"No wonder you have to resort to this sort of carry-on."

Her eyes stood out in her face. "You mean because no man would have me? Is that what you think?"

"I never said that." Padraic was leaning his head against the doorjamb now. "It's just, you must admit, you come on a bit strong."

"That's because this is my last chance," she bawled at him.

He shifted on the spot. "Don't say that. Sure, a fine-looking woman—"

"Getting a man is easy," she spat.

He was taken aback. The pity in his eyes faded.

"It's having children with one that's turned out to be impossible," she said between her teeth.

"Why didn't you and Eamonn—"

"Because we were divorced by the time we were thirty. Then the guy I was with for six years after that didn't happen to like children. You're welcome to all the details." Sarah's voice was shaking like a rope. "I'm thirty-eight years old. I've been paying a clinic thousands of dollars a month for fertility drugs that make me sick and frozen sperm that doesn't work. What else do you suggest I do?"

He considered the carpet. "I was just . . . I suppose I was wondering why you left it so late."

"Oh, don't give me that. Just don't you dare." She felt breathless with rage. "How was I meant to know what I wanted at twenty-five? Men have no fucking idea. You'll still be able to make a woman pregnant when you're seventy!"

Padraic flinched at the thought.

After a minute, very quietly, he asked, "But sure . . . why me? Couldn't you just have gone out one night and picked up a stranger?"

Sarah sat on the edge of the bed and wept. Her elbows dug into her thighs.

"I didn't want the child of some pickup," she said at last, very slowly, the words emerging like pebbles. "Quite apart from what else I might pick up from him." She waited till her voice had steadied enough for her to go on. "I wanted the child of a nice man, and all the nice men were taken."

After a long minute, she felt the bed bounce as Padraic sat down beside her. "Not all, surely," he said after a minute. He sounded like a child who'd just been told the truth about Santa Claus.

Her smile came out a bit twisted. She turned her head. "Don't worry about it, Padraic," she drawled. "I get by just fine without the husband and the SUV and the house in the suburbs."

He didn't know how to take that. She watched him staring at his shoes.

"All I want is a child." Sarah said it softly. She was never so sure of anything in her life.

"OK," he said after a minute. "I'll have another bash." He stood up. "You haven't seen me at my best tonight," he added hoarsely.

She gave a little sniff of amusement and wiped her eyes. "I suppose not."

"You try getting an erection in a toilet without so much as a copy of *Playboy*. I'm not seventeen anymore, you know."

Sarah giggled and blew her nose. "Sorry." *Go on*, she told herself. *Make the offer.* "Shall we just call the whole thing off, then?"

She could tell he was tempted. Just for a minute. Until he thought of what Carmel would say.

"Not at all," said Padraic. He stood up. "A man's gotta do."

"Are you sure?"

"I'm going back in there," he declared, "and I'm not coming back out empty-handed. You just lie down and think of Ireland."

"No," she said, jumping up, "I'll go in the bathroom. You could do with a change of scenery."

She handed him out his jar, then locked the door. She looked herself in the eye, then turned on the cold tap and washed the salt off her face.

Padraic stood before the wardrobe mirror and stared down into his trousers. Not an enticing sight. Visibly tired, old before its time. He eyed his face and counted his wrinkles. Salmon couldn't eat after they mated, he remembered; they just shriveled away. What was there left for him in this life, now he had served his time, genetically speaking?

But tonight's job wasn't quite over yet.

He felt utterly exhausted. Nerves, alcohol, and a fight to round it all off. But he had to rise to the occasion now. *Noblesse oblige.* He thought of Carmel's last birthday. He'd been knackered from work, and half a bottle of champagne hadn't helped, but he knew she wanted to be ravished, he could almost smell it off her. So he had claimed to be full of beans, and though it took an enormous effort, it was all right in the end. He'd known it would work. It always worked in the end, him and Carmel.

Padraic lay down on the bed. He wanted to be home in her arms.

This room had no more resources than the bathroom, really. He flicked through the TV channels (with the sound down, so Sarah wouldn't think he was time wasting). Not a drop of titillation. After five minutes of *Dirty Dancing*, he realized he was finding Patrick Swayze far more appealing than the girl, and that raised such disturbance in the back of his head that he switched off the telly.

He lay down again and scanned the room. The prints were garish abstracts; nothing doing there. There was the phone, of course. If only he had memorized a number for one of those chat lines. He'd rung one once, in a hotel room much nastier than this one, somewhere in the North of England. All he remembered was that the woman on the line had a terribly royal-family accent, and spoke very, very slowly to bump up his bill.

If he rang downstairs and asked for the number of a chat line, he was sure to get Máire. She'd tell her mother. She'd probably tell *his* mother.

Padraic shut his eyes and tried out a couple of trusty old fantasies. Only they weren't working anymore. He wondered whether one traumatic evening had rendered him permanently impotent. He felt exhausted. Somehow the idea of having a voluntary sexual impulse seemed like a remnant of his youth. Maybe that was it, his lot.

All at once he knew what number to ring.

"Hello there," said Carmel, and her voice was so warm he thought he could slip right into it and sleep. "Are you coming home soon?"

"Any minute now. I just need a bit of help," he admitted.

"Are you still at it?"

"She spilt the first lot."

Carmel let out a roar of laughter. "I should have warned you," she said. "When we shared a flat, Sarah was always knocking over cups of tea."

"Are you comparing my precious seed to a beverage, woman?"

"The comparison is entirely in your favour." Her voice changed for a minute; her mouth moved away from the phone and he heard her say, "You go and brush your teeth, love. I'll be up as soon as I've finished talking to Daddy."

He wanted to tell her to say good night from him, but he wasn't meant to be thinking like a daddy now.

Carmel's voice was all his again now, going low like only she could do. For a respectable wife and mother she could sound like a shocking wee slut. "Are you ready for round two, big boy?" she asked.

"I don't think I can."

"Can't means won't," she said in her best schoolmistress voice. He laughed into the phone, very softly.

"All right now," she crooned. "Enough of this nonsense. Shut your eyes."

"I just want to come home."

"You are home."

"I am?"

"You're home in your bed with me. Nothing fancy."

"Not a seedy motel?"

"Not Finbar's Hotel, either. We could never afford it. You're home in bed with me and the kids are fast asleep and you're flat on your back, with your hands above your head."

"Surrendering, like?"

"Exactly."

Carmel, he thought a few minutes later with the part of his mind that was overseeing the rest, should consider a career move. She could make a mint on one of those chat lines. And to think of all this lewdness being saved up for a big eejit like him. He kept his eyes squeezed shut and pretended his hands were hers. She always knew what to do. She was working him into a lather. She was going to make it all right.

Sarah was leaning against the sink, praying. It had been so long, she hardly remembered what to say. She got the words of the Hail Mary all arseways, she knew that much. *Blessed is the fruit?* Mostly what she said was *please.*

The bathroom door opening made the loudest noise. Padraic's grin split his face like a pumpkin. She seized the jar. Half as much as last time, but still, there must be a few million ambitious little wrigglers in there. She rushed over and lay down on the carpet.

"Will you be all right now?" he asked.

"Yeah, yeah," she said, "you go on home."

He gathered up the pile of presents for his boys. When he was at the door, he turned to give a little finger wave. She had already filled the syringe.

"See you at Christmas, I suppose," he said. And then, "Fingers crossed."

They both crossed their fingers and held them in the air.

Sarah started laughing before the door shut behind him. She was still laughing when she pressed the plunger.

Expecting

I thought I saw him last Friday, stooping over the grape-fruits in my local supermarket. Without stopping to make sure, I put my half-full basket down beside the carrot shelf and walked out the door marked ENTRANCE ONLY.

It might not have been him, of course. One round silver head is pretty much like another. If I'd seen his face, if the strip of mirror over the fruit counter had been angled the right way, I'd have known for sure: soft as a plum, as my mother would have said, if she'd ever met him. But it was probably someone else, because he never shopped on a Friday, and why would he come all this way across town to a perfectly unremarkable new supermarket? Besides, I never told him where I lived.

We had only ever met on Saturdays, in the windswept shopping centre I had to go to before the supermarket opened down the road. That first time, I was toying with an angora jumper on the second floor of the department store when I caught his eye. I figure they're safe to smile at if they're over sixty. He moved away with something long and green over his arm; I shifted over and browsed through five kinds of silk dresses before realizing I was in the maternity section. Not that it mattered much, of course, since anyone can wear any old shape nowadays.

The elderly gentleman held the heavy swing door open for me to go through first. "Best to take things easy," he commented, and I smiled, trying to think of something original to do with pasta for dinner. As we emerged into the shopping centre he asked a question that was half drowned out by the clamour of the crowd. I said "Mmm," rather robotic as usual among strangers. Thinking back, later that afternoon, I did remember hearing the word *expecting*, but I presumed he meant rain.

I bumped into him again in the charity furniture shop ten minutes later. Gallant, he insisted on lifting a table for me to look at the price. I only clicked when he said, "The dress is for my daughter; she's due in July. And yourself?"

I shook my head.

He must have thought I was rebuking his curiosity; his face went pink from the nose out. "Pardon me."

"No no, it's all right," I flustered.

"Early days yet, then," he said confidentially.

It suddenly seemed like far too much trouble to explain; we could be standing here all day. Besides, this garrulous stranger would think me a fool, or worse, a wistful spinster type given to browsing through maternity dresses. So I said nothing, simply grinned like a bashful mum-to-be, as the magazines would say.

It's not the first mistake, but the first cowardice, that gets us into trouble. Why was it so hard to say that I hadn't heard his original question, as we came out of the department store? If only I'd said, "I'm afraid I'm not expecting anything!" and made an awkward joke of the old-world euphemism.

And of course when the following Saturday, cup in hand, he

edged over to my table in the shopping centre's single faded café, it was impossible to go back to the beginning. He told me all about his daughter's special high-calcium diet. I saw now that clearing up that first misunderstanding would have been child's play compared to this: How could I admit to having lied? I tucked my knees under the table, nodding over the pros and cons of disposable nappies.

He was lonely, that much was clear. I was a Saturday shopper because it was the only day I had free, whereas since his retirement he had developed a taste for the weekend bustle at his local shopping centre. But not a weirdo, I thought, watching him swallow his tea. All he wanted was to chat about this cyclone of excitement that had hit the year his only daughter got pregnant at thirty-three. "Me too," I said without thinking. Thirty-three, really? He thought that was a wonderful coincidence. And from amniocentesis we slipped on to living wills and the judicial system, his small mobile face shifting with every turn of conversation.

For a few weeks the office was a bag of cats, and I forgot all about him. Then one Saturday, rushing by with a baguette under my arm, I saw him staring bleakly into the window of what used to be the Christmas Shop. For the first time, it was I who said hello. When, after pleasantries about crocus pots, he began telling me about his daughter, and how the hospital said it was nothing she'd done or not done, she hadn't overstrained or failed to eat, just one of these things that happen in most women's lives, I wished I had followed my first impulse and walked right by. I didn't want to spare the time to sit beside him, making fork marks in an almond slice.

He fell silent at one point, and as some kind of strange compensation I began to rhapsodize about my own phantom pregnancy. I'd never felt better; it was true what they said about the sense of blooming. Instead of wincing, his face lit up. He said he would bring me a cutting from last Sunday's paper about prenatal musical appreciation. I promised him I was drinking lots of milk.

Walking home with a box of groceries on my hip, I began to count weeks. If I had met him just after payday, which was the fifth of the month . . . I realized with a spasm of nausea that I should be beginning to show.

At this point the ludicrousness of the whole charade hit home. Since it was clearly impossible to explain to this nice old man that I had been playing such a bizarre, unintentional, and (in light of his daughter's miscarriage) tasteless joke, I would just have to make sure I never saw him again.

But I didn't manage to make it to the huge supermarket in the town centre after work any day that week. Come Saturday I crawled out of bed late and pulled on baggy trousers. His steel-wool head was before me in the queue at the flower stall; when he looked around, I waved. Yes, his daughter was back at work, these daffs were for her, and wasn't a bit of sunshine wonderful? Only when he had walked away did I realize that I had my hand on the small of my back, my belly slumped over my loose waistband.

The next Saturday I did my hand washing and baked scones with the end of the cheddar, then sat knotted up in an armchair and read some papers I'd brought home from work. My mother dropped by; when I offered her some tea, there wasn't any milk or sugar, so I had to justify the empty shelves by claiming not to have felt well enough to go out.

Afterwards, I lay on the sofa with the blanket she'd put over me, watching the sky drain. I was heavy with a lie I couldn't begin to explain. If I'd made a joke of it to my mother, she'd probably have called him a nosy parker.

My ribs were stiff; I shifted to face the rough woolen back of the sofa. If it were true, would I be throwing up in the mornings?

Would I be feeling angry, or doubtful, or (that old pun) fulfilled? I grinned at myself and went to put on my makeup for a night out dancing.

The following Friday I managed to sneak away from work early enough to shop in town. I had packed my briefcase full of papers, then shoved them back in the in-tray.

Saturday I spent hoeing the waking flower beds outside my basement flat. Some friends arrived with *Alien* and popcorn. One of them noticed me holding my stomach after a particularly tense scene and raised a laugh by warning me not to throw up on the sofa.

Truth was, I'd been trying to remember at what point it would start kicking. For a few seconds I'd believed in it.

It was time to call a halt. The next Saturday I trailed up and down the shopping centre for an hour and a half in the spring chill. Every time I went into the library or the pet shop, I was sure he had just left. When the tap on the shoulder did come, as I was reading the list of prices in the window of the hair salon, I jerked so fast he had to apologize. But looking shocked and pinched did suit my story, I supposed.

As we neared the top of the café queue, his bare tray shuffling along behind mine, I rehearsed my opening line: "I'm afraid I lost the baby." It sounded absentminded and cruel. I tried it again, moving my lips silently. The beverages lady cocked her ear, thinking she'd missed my order; I cleared my throat and asked for a strong coffee. It was all my fault for having let a tiny lie swell into this monstrosity.

Before I could begin, he placed his shopping bag on the chair between us. "I'm glad I caught you today," he said pleasurably. "I brought it along last week, but I didn't run into you. I was going to return it, but then I thought, who do I know who'd make good use of it?"

Under his bashful eyes, I drew out the folds of green silk. "Wouldn't your daughter wear it anyway?" I asked.

He shook his head hastily.

"You shouldn't have," I said. "It's beautiful." I slumped in the plastic seat, my stomach bulging.

He folded the dress back in its tissue paper and slipped it into the bag.

Though I didn't even know his surname, I felt like I was saying good-bye to a lifelong friend, one who had no idea that this was good-bye. I insisted he have a third of my lemon tart. We talked of Montessori schools and wipeable bibs, of our best and worst childhood memories, of how much had stayed the same between his generation and mine but would be different for my baby. We decided it was just as well I was due in August as the weather might be mild enough to nurse in the garden. When I looked at my watch it was half two, the coffee cold in the pot.

As I stood up, I had a hysterical impulse to say that if it proved to be a boy I'd name it after him. Instead, I mentioned that I was going off on an early summer holiday, but yes, of course I'd be home for the birth.

The new regime was a manageable nuisance. On Saturdays now I went straight from karate class to a shopping centre twice as far away in the other direction. An old friend of mine, meeting me laded with bags on the bus, mocked me for being so upwardly mobile, to go that far in pursuit of walnut-and-ricotta ravioli. One Saturday in May my mother asked me to come along to the old shopping centre, to help her with a sack of peat moss, and I had to invent a sudden blinding headache.

The dress I wore as often as the weather allowed; it seemed the least I could do. The leaf-green silk billowed round my hips as I carried my box of groceries close to the chest. There was room under there for quintuplets, or a gust of summer air. When August came and went and nothing happened, I felt lighter, flatter, relieved.

That was five years ago, but always I keep one eye out for him, even on the streets of other cities where my new job takes me. I have my story all ready: how I shop on Sundays now when my mother can take the children, two boys and a small girl, yes, quite a handful. He's sure to compliment me on having kept my figure. And his daughter, did she try again?

I felt prepared, but last Friday when I thought I saw him among the grapefruit I backed out in panic. What do you say to a ghost, a visitor from another life?

It occurs to me all of a sudden that he may be dead. Men often don't live very long after they retire. I never thought to ask how old he was.

I find it intolerable not to know what has become of him. Is this how he felt, wondering about me? On Saturday when I woke in my cool white bed, I had to fight off the temptation to drive down to the shopping centre and park there, watching through the windscreen for him to walk by.

The Man Who Wrote
on Beaches

As a child he'd never known what to put. He always started out along the expanse of saturated sand with a yip of excitement, but after scraping the first great arc with the edge of his sneaker, he'd stand with his leg extended like a dog trying to piss. Everything took so long on sand, you might as well be using Morse code. You'd better be sure you still meant what you were writing by the time it was done. Once he'd put HELLO, but his brothers laughed and scuffed out the O with their toes.

Then another time on another beach, some New Year's Day when he was maybe fourteen and alone, he'd written COCKSUCKERS in letters as long as himself. It looked so terrible, printed so starkly for the clouds and every passing stranger to read, and he'd thought the first wave would wipe it out, but in his nervousness he'd dug too deep with the crescent of mussel shell, so the small frills of water only smoothed his words, glossed over a mistake he'd made on the K. The letters looked graven, as if on a headstone, the obscenity emerging from the beach itself. So after such a long while of standing with his back to the wind, he'd dragged a line through the whole word with the toe of his pointed shoe, lurching along on the other foot, but still it was legible or could be guessed at anyhow, since no other word looked like that one.

The day he was forty-three, he accepted Jesus Christ as his Lord and Personal Saviour. It was quite a shock to his system.

A few weeks before, he had been driving through downtown Tacoma on a sticky afternoon much like any other. Traffic was slow as molasses and he found himself staring at a bus shelter with a poster on it that said in large pink letters, JESUS IS THE WAY.

He might well have seen it before, on other days when he'd been preoccupied with what to make for dinner or whether Margaret had remembered to call the IRS from the office about those tax forms, but the fact was that only on that particular day was there a chink open in his mind as he glanced at that bus shelter, a crack wide enough for those words to drop in. And for a moment he forgot a lifetime's worth of wisecracks about the Born Agains; for a moment he thought, *What if it was true? What if just maybe?*

Wouldn't that explain a lot of things, like what a mess this country had gotten itself into? Wouldn't that make some sense of how his life had turned out after all the promising things his report cards had said, after all his dumb dreams of changing the world?

Not that he was complaining. He'd been to Corsica and Bali and Scotland and the Everglades; he had a home with a view of Puget Sound and a good job and a great collection of German steins and a lot of laughs. Above all, he had Margaret, who was twice what he deserved. But it struck him sometimes that in a couple more decades he would be dead without ever having figured things out. And think of it: All these years he'd been using the word *Jesus* as a colourful form of ouch—if he dropped a wrench on his foot, say—when for all he knew the Born Agains were right, and Jesus just might be the way.

He was still half joking, or at least he thought he was.

Waiting for the lights to change, he tried it out loud. "Jesus?" so it sounded like he was calling softly over the car door to someone in the street he thought he remembered from high school who probably wouldn't know him anymore.

But all at once he was sick to his stomach, felt so bad in fact that when the light changed he pulled right instead of left and parked in front of a fire hydrant. He laid his wet forehead on his hands where they gripped the steering wheel and said, maybe out loud or maybe in his head, he didn't know, "I'm nothing, I'm scum, Jesus, Jesus, Jesus."

When he finally got home he watched some drag racing and waited for it to wear off, like a hangover, or heartburn. Margaret came home with antipasti from the deli; she felt his back where his T-shirt was stuck to it. He blamed the heat.

But by the weekend he still felt the same way. So come Sunday morning he walked down the road till he came to the first building with the word *Jesus* on it.

It was the Church of Jesus Our Lord. He thought he'd bolt at the end of the service, but strangers gathered round to welcome him. It turned out it wasn't them who'd paid for the sign at the bus shelter downtown, that was the Church of Christ Crucified, but still, "No objections," said the pastor. "It was Our Lord who led your feet to our door."

He still felt sick, standing there. These people weren't his sort of people, or so he would have said a week before. Their phrases were foreign to him; there was talk of missions and calls and walks with God. When they used words like *voice,* or *light,* he was never sure if they were to be taken literally. Their clothes were funny and the pastor stood too close to him. He knew he might turn these people into a big joke at the next office party. He felt like James Dean and wished he hadn't worn his leather jacket. He felt like a sinner. And when an old lady who'd introduced herself as Mrs.

Keilor said, "See you next week," part of him was so relieved he thought he might go down on his knees and cry.

Which was exactly what he did a few weeks later, on his forty-third birthday. Pastor Tull said it took a lot of folks that way.

For the first few weeks he hadn't said a word to Margaret about where he was going; he let her think he was stretching his legs. And when he began to mention the church it was all very cool; he tried to sound like an anthropologist on the Nature Channel.

"Do you actually believe any of that stuff?" Margaret asked lightly in the middle of Sunday dinner, and he shrugged and took another slice of salmon.

But on his birthday he walked home and told her he'd accepted Jesus Christ as his Lord and Personal Saviour. He said it all in a rush before he lost his nerve; he could hear how odd the words sounded as they left his mouth, like a very dry sort of joke.

Margaret let out a single whoop of laughter. He didn't take offense; it was a sound she always made when an appliance broke down or she slept through the alarm and missed her car pool. After a minute she came over to give him a hug with stiff arms and say, "Whatever makes you happy." As if it was a line she'd found in a magazine.

A couple of months on, he started bringing her to the odd church social. She seemed to come willingly enough, just as years ago she used to accompany him to occasional hockey games, because that was his thing. She recognized a guy from her accounts department, and they talked about the crazy new ventilation system. She admired Pastor Tull's moustache.

Mrs. Keilor was in charge of the salad table. She whispered a question about whether his wife was saved, too. "Not yet," he said, as if he had great hopes. He was afraid somebody would ask Margaret the same question; he kept one ear out for her sharp laugh.

Margaret had no time for the abstract; that was something he always used to love about her. If she couldn't touch it, smell it, taste it, then it didn't matter. Her favourite exclamation was "Unreal." Whenever he started talking hypotheticals, she would reach for her sewing box, so the time wouldn't be completely wasted. Once she got around three sides of a cushion cover while he was wondering aloud about the future of democracy.

He didn't talk about his ideas, these days. He kept his new books on his side of the bed; he left his new cassettes in the car so he could play them on the way to work. He only watched the Bible Channel on the evenings when Margaret was out at the Y. And she quietly worked around this latest and most obscure of his hobbies.

He waited for her to ask, but she didn't. He would have welcomed her questions; he still had a bunch of his own. But Margaret was content not to understand. He couldn't figure that out. How she could bear not to know what was going on in his head. In his heart. In what he was learning, with some embarrassment, to call his soul.

He was dreaming about Jesus these days; that was something he wouldn't have told Margaret even if she'd asked. In the dreams he was generally walking up a mountain behind Jesus, who only looked about twenty-two, thin but surprisingly solid. You could lean your head on his bony shoulder. Jesus could speak without moving his lips.

He never had difficulty getting up these mornings; he just asked Jesus to get him out of bed and next thing his feet were on the rug. And work got done just like that. The things he had expected to be hardest were almost easy. He had thrown away his Zippo the day after his birthday and hadn't had a single drag since. Every time he got the craving he said, "Jesus, Jesus, Jesus," in his head till it went away. The same with beer. After Josh Miles at the church, who used to be an alcoholic, took him aside for a word, he saw he was better off without the stuff. Now he didn't miss it, didn't need it. He still dusted his stein collection, but he was thinking of donating it to a charity raffle. After a couple of weeks, Margaret got the hint and stopped asking would he like a cold one from the refrigerator. She teased him a little about what a clean-living guy he'd become—but not in front of friends.

Another thing, he wasn't sure their friends were his friends anymore. They were the same people; it was him who'd changed. For the first year ever he put down every cent he'd made on his tax return. He could only talk about things like that to his church friends, those people in cheap shoes he'd have bust a gut laughing at a couple of months back.

What he couldn't tell them, though, was that Margaret wasn't his wife.

At a church picnic he watched her blowing bubbles with a four-year-old. Mrs. Oberdorf had her eye on him. "You and your wife been blessed with any children?" she asked in her cracked voice.

"Not yet."

She nodded, her mouth twisted with sympathy.

He hoped she'd think it wasn't their fault. He hoped she wouldn't use the word *husband* in front of Margaret.

One evening when she was pinning up new drapes he said it. "We should get married one of these days." But it didn't sound romantic enough. It sounded like clearing out the garage.

Margaret took the pins out of her mouth. "You think so?" She had this way of letting words hover like smoke.

"I know we used to say we didn't need it, but recently I've been reconsidering."

She pinned up another fold of fabric.

"It might feel good. It might be the thing to do," he added, as if he were kidding around. He hoped she wouldn't hear the guilt behind his voice.

"OK. What the hell," said Margaret. He winced, but not so she'd notice. "We've both done it before and it didn't kill us."

Then she laughed until he laughed, too, and she came over and kissed him on the ear.

But as he was signing his name in the register—his ballpoint pressing the paper a little too hard—he knew that this time wasn't going to be like those other times. Neither he nor his first wife in DC nor Margaret nor her first husband in LA had had the slightest idea what they were really doing. This time would be the real thing, because now he knew what a promise was. Now he knew what the words meant.

To show she wasn't taking the whole thing too seriously, Margaret was wearing red. He didn't care; it looked good on her. "You can bring your God buddies if you like," she'd told him, but he said that was all right, he'd rather keep it small, just the two of them and a pastor (not Pastor Tull, just some Unitarian) and a few friends who drove down from Seattle and Vancouver.

After the ceremony he was high like he hadn't been since that time he tried cocaine at the prom. He was a bank robber who'd made it to Acapulco.

The next Sunday after church he said the word. "My wife and I are taking a vacation," he mentioned to Mrs. Keilor, and relief stabbed him through the ribs.

For their honeymoon—about ten years too late, according to his mother in San Francisco, but she sent them a check anyhow— he and Margaret were going to drive right down the West Coast. That first night in a motel in Mount Saint Helens he lay under the weight of his wife and moved and shut his eyes. It felt like he was running down the right road at last. But later when he was letting the condom slither off him, he wanted to cry.

They hiked up a volcano the next day, cinders crunching like cornflakes under their feet. Later they squatted over tide pools and saw anemones blossom like green doughnuts and purple sea urchins as big as their hands. Margaret tilted her face up to the sun while he took pictures and figured out the distances between towns.

In Eugene, Oregon, he woke up in the middle of the night and had to shake her awake. "Honey," he said urgently. Then, apologetically, "Honey, I just realized, we're meant to have children."

The words shocked his ears.

At first Margaret didn't answer, and he thought she was still asleep, till he saw the line of her jaw. Then she said, "For god's sake."

Exactly, he was tempted to say, but didn't.

In the morning he woke up to find her packing.

He stared at her knotted hands, ramming two pairs of his socks into a corner. "Who was it," Margaret asked, "just remind me who was it who talked me out of it all those other times?"

"You were never sure —," he began.

"That's right, I wasn't sure, but you sure were." A little bead of spit on her lip caught the sunlight. She plucked up another pair of socks but didn't put them in the bag. "Who was it always told me it would be madness to go off the Pill? Who was it said we'd lose all our freedom, tie ourselves down?"

His throat felt like it was full of wadding. He cleared it. "Guess everybody gets tied down one way or another."

Margaret's hands were jammed into the pockets of her silky dressing gown; her nails were stretching the seams. "Who was it kept saying he wasn't ready?"

"I don't know," he said, nearly whispering. "I don't know who that guy was." There was a silence so complete he could hear the chambermaid vacuuming at the other end of the motel. "But I'm different now."

"You can say that again." She stared at him; her eyes were hard as hazelnuts. "You're on another planet."

"I'm finally ready," he pleaded.

"Oh yeah?" Her voice was bigger than the room. "Well I'm forty-two, so you and your friend Jesus can go to hell."

It took them two days to drive home. Awhile before they stopped for a burger on the first day he thought Margaret was crying, but she was looking out the window so he couldn't be sure. At the motel he called his mother and told her there'd been an emergency at work and he'd been called back. She'd always been able to tell when he was lying, but she didn't say so.

When they pulled into their driveway at the end of the second day, Margaret laid her hand on his thigh and said, "OK."

He wasn't sure what it meant. Pax? Or, this marriage is over?

"OK," she said, "let's give it a shot."

She got pregnant twice before the end of the year, which he took as a good sign. The first one made it to two months, the second to five. That one was a boy. He made the nurse give him the little body, for burial. Quite a few people from the Church of Jesus Our Lord turned up, though Margaret didn't come back with them for the chicken supper afterwards, which everybody said was understandable.

The strange thing was that he had known the boy wouldn't make it to term. At the funeral it was like there was cotton wool round his heart, keeping the pain at bay. He and Margaret were going to have a girl; he just knew it.

He didn't mind waiting a little while longer so Margaret could build her strength up before trying again. It felt strange to be buying rubbers—in a drugstore in the next town, so no one from the church would see him—but he thought Jesus probably wouldn't have a word to say about it, under the circumstances.

On Christmas Eve he asked Margaret to come to church with him, just for once. On the way home she said, "One last shot, OK?" as if she were talking about pinball.

That night as he came his legs shook like bowstrings. His mind swam inside her. He could almost see the egg, glowing at the end of the dark tube; he registered the shock when the single chosen sperm, blindly butting, felt the membrane give way and seal him in.

The next day he started making a list of girls' names. He kept the list in the glove compartment so as not to annoy Margaret, who didn't believe in counting chickens.

Nothing happened till March, when Margaret started throwing up her Cheerios and smiling at strangers. "Third time lucky," he told her on the way home from the ultrasound. His head was so full of a single image—the tiny curled chipmunk that was going to be their daughter—that he could hardly see the road. The nurse said you couldn't be sure so early, but yes, it did look kind of like a girl.

"Laura?" he suggested, idling at a traffic light. "Leona? Lucy?"

"We'll see," said Margaret, smiling. And then, "The light's changed."

As the time went by, he bloomed. It was no hardship, he found, to be patient with a pushy new guy at work. When Margaret's strange uncle who picked his nose came to town, they put him up on the sofa bed for a whole week. Prayer was easy; he'd never had so much to say.

Margaret, on the other hand, was getting more wired by the month. She wouldn't let her forty-third birthday be celebrated in any way, not even dinner out, not so much as a bunch of flowers or a card. The bigger she grew, the more substantial their future seemed to him, and the less she seemed able to believe in it. He wondered if she was frightened about the birth; it did seem to him a terrible prospect, and he cracked a joke about how the human race would soon die out if women were as cowardly as men.

Margaret didn't laugh.

"You'll have to trust God, hon," he said, a little nervously, as he knew the word made her twitch, but it was the only one he could think of.

She laughed then, and said, "I've never even met him."

He had a feeling everything would be better once they were a family. With Laura coming to church with him every week, first in one of those slings on his chest, and then in her little black patent shoes, surely Margaret wouldn't want to be left behind. It made sense that once she saw how good Jesus had been to them, she'd understand all the rest of it.

Meanwhile, she didn't understand the slightest thing he said. She was always taking offense. She thought he was looking for sex when he was just as happy stroking her belly. She said the baby kept kicking her in the ribs. One day he was playing chase-the-foot when Margaret shoved him so hard he fell off the bed.

When he got to his feet, she was laughing in that appalled way of hers. "Oh, I'm such a bitch these days," she said between snorts. "I'm so sorry, honey, I'm so sorry. I'm scared, you know?"

"Of the birth?"

"No, moron," said Margaret, still laughing. "Scared it won't happen."

He could tell she was an inch away from tears so he lay down beside her.

San Francisco should be leveled to the ground, he thought, when his mother called to tell him about her knee. It was only a little fall, but she'd rolled about twenty feet down the sidewalk till she landed against a fire hydrant.

He knew he should be there to take her home from the hospital. If there was ever a time to be a good son, this was it. But he rested his ear on Margaret's drum of a belly and couldn't lift it away.

"Get out of here," she said, pretty gently. "Those bastards owe you two weeks of vacation."

"Not now."

"Yes, now. Get out of my hair for a while. It'll be a good three months before this baby lifts a finger."

So here he was, back on the coast. By the time he passed the Oregon state line he was breathing easier, and the farther he drove, the more peaceful he felt. He took his time; he saw all the places he and Margaret had missed on their truncated honeymoon. He could feel the horizon curving around him like a hand.

It was then he started writing again. Just on beaches, at first. There was a little cove beside a lighthouse, washed clean as a slate by the morning tide. There was one small girl picking up shells on the waterline, and her family sunbathing farther up the beach. He stood staring out to sea, and all at once he knew what to write. JESUS IS THE WAY, he put, in letters so big and clear they could probably be seen from a low plane. All the time he was marking them with the toe of his shoe, he was thinking of the surprise people would get when they wandered down the beach that afternoon. That's how you did it: by surprise. Minds were like mussels: You shouldn't try to force them open; it was better to catch them at an idle moment and slip inside.

He was just finishing the Y when he noticed the little girl's mother. She was standing at a distance, reading the words upside down. When his eyes met hers, she grabbed the child's hand and hurried back up the beach.

It gave him an odd feeling, as if she thought he was some kind of pervert or something. But you couldn't expect people to understand if they hadn't gone down their road to Damascus yet. That's all he wanted: to give people a glimpse of it, to throw strangers a split second of the joy that was filling him up these days so he hardly needed to eat except for a bag of grapes in the car.

Whenever he got a surge of happiness, he wanted to ring Margaret, but she'd said the sound of the phone was getting on her nerves these days, and he knew she needed a break from him, so he sent her postcards instead. He told her things he'd never thought to mention before. "Did you know you are the most beautiful woman in the world?" he wrote on a picture of a glacial lake, and "I love you more every day," on a shot of a leaping salmon.

Words were pouring out of him. He was a bit shocked with himself, the day he wrote on a wall outside Portland. He hadn't done a thing like that since he was a kid. But this wall already said DONT MES WITH THE MOFO BOYZ, LOLA SUCKS DICK, and ME N U 4EVER '03, so he felt he could only improve it by adding JESUS SAVES with a little can of white spray paint he got at the corner hardware store.

Then, when he was walking through a grove of old-growth redwoods the next afternoon, his heart started to knock like a rattle. The forest was bigger than the biggest cathedral, but humans had had no share in the building. He felt like an insect. The trees were wider than he was tall, and taller than anything; all he could hear was a lone woodpecker. At one point where a huge tree had fallen across the path, the rangers had cut a section away to let walkers through. On the weathered wood, ridged by the chain saw, someone had cut ANGIE LOVES JEFF. He couldn't resist; he took out his Swiss army knife and carved the words JESUS LOVES US ALL.

These days Laura was so clear in his mind that he could nearly see her, running along beside him. When he rented a gas lantern to go down an old lava tube, clambering down from the glare at the tunnel mouth into the cooling darkness, he promised himself that he'd bring her here someday. Half a mile in, where the floor was slick with ice and the roof of the cave reached its highest point, he'd hold the heavy lantern up to show her the ridges and grooves the lava had left when it flowed away, the tiny kiss shapes of its final drops. Then he'd turn off the lantern for a minute and she'd yelp with fright, but she'd grip his fingers and know that everything was going to be all right.

The next day he saw the best sunset he'd ever seen in his life. There was a phone booth by the side of the road, so he pulled in and rooted around in the glove compartment for his bag of quarters. Margaret would be out at her organic gardening class; he could just leave a message.

But she was home. At first he didn't recognize her voice, it was so muffled. She must have been drinking. When he said, "Margaret? Honey?" there was a click.

The connection must have broken. So he fed in more quarters and tried again.

When she picked up the phone again, the first thing she said was "I lost it."

"What?" he said stupidly.

"You heard me."

"You lost it?"

"It wasn't my fault."

He hardly knew what he was saying. "Was it a girl?"

There was such a long pause he thought the line was broken. Then Margaret said, "It doesn't matter."

The phone seemed stuck to his ear; sweat was running down his throat. "Margaret, honey," he said, as if that were a sentence.

"It's over."

It seemed a matter of urgency to say the right thing now. There was a sudden beeping, and he fed in his last quarters. "Listen," he said, too loud, as if his voice had to cover the distance by itself. "Listen, we'll try again in a little while."

"Like hell we will," she roared.

His legs were shaking; he leaned back against the glass.

"To think I let you put me through this, you and your fucking Jesus!" Margaret's voice crackled down the line. "At forty-three, to think I was such a fool."

There was a silence that seemed impermeable.

"You know, I was happy enough before we went and got married." Her sobs were as loud as the words they punctuated. "I had a full life. I was perfectly happy enough with no ring and no children. Weren't you? Weren't you happy enough?"

He was still trying to think of an answer when the line went dead.

The sun was a smear of red at the base of a dark sky. He went down and sat on the beach until his legs stopped shaking.

The last of the light caught blades of shell in the sand. He dug one up with the point of his shoe. He couldn't think of anything to write, so he pushed it back, pressing down till he felt the hard damp sand give way and bury it.

He knew he should call the hospital to leave a message for his mother that he wasn't coming, but all he had in his pockets was small change. So he turned the car around and started the long drive home.

Oops

James was overnighting with his oldest friends before a flight to the Yucatán. He'd managed to avoid ever sleeping in Eoin and Neasa's flat before. It was a dingy little fourth-floor on the wrong quay of the Liffey. Back in his twenties, some years before the Dublin boom began, James himself had been farsighted enough to snap up an elegant little cottage in Ballsbridge, which was now worth nine-and-a-half times what he'd paid for it—a thought that always gave him a frisson of satisfaction. But unfortunately on the day before his trip to photograph the Yucatán for *Luxury* magazine, the workmen were in to install a sauna in his basement, and the dust played havoc with his sinuses, so he had no choice but to accept his friends' offer.

As always, James averted his eyes from the flat itself—cluttered with equipment his friends were storing for the rest of their sax quintet—and he remarked that they'd got an *outrageously* good view of the river. After dinner he insisting on taking them to a new club where you didn't actually have to dance if, like Neasa and Eoin, you loathed what passed for music these days; you could just lie around on yellow velvet couches on the balcony and look down on it all.

Back in the flat, their sofa bed felt to James like a grill, only slightly padded with tinfoil. In the middle of the chilly January night, he staggered along the tiny corridor to the loo. Fumbling around on the shelf for paracetamol to ward off his hangover, his fingers found a curved white oblong of plastic; a futuristic glasses case, maybe, or a makeup holder? Curious, James pressed the little button on top. Suddenly a tiny blue light came on. "Oops," he said under his breath, and stepped back, knocking several dusty bottles of essential oils into the bath with a dreadful clatter. He pressed the button again, but the light wouldn't go off.

He thought no more about it till a fortnight later when he got back to Dublin Airport with a Yucatánian glow to his cheekbones. Picking up some melatonin to ward off jet lag in the pharmacy, he noticed a cardboard woman in a red dress, holding the same strange little device in her hand. A speech bubble said TIMERA™: BECAUSE I NEED TO KNOW.

James goggled at the small print. She needed to know what? TIMERA™ IS THE NEW AND UNIQUE FAMILY PLANNING DEVICE THAT WORKS IN HARMONY WITH NATURE'S CYCLES TO GIVE YOU CONTROL OVER YOUR BODY AND YOUR LIFE. What a laugh, thought James, a contraceptive computer! He quite understood that Neasa and Eoin had never wanted to swap their shiny saxophones for smelly babies; it was only natural.

But then he remembered the little blue light that had come on when he'd pressed the button. Oh Jesus, he thought then.

As the taxi inched its way through the gridlocked city, James shut his eyes and thought furiously. He wished he'd paid more attention to that lesson on the rhythm method at the community school that he, Neasa, and Eoin had all left nearly twenty years ago. He regretted his lack of information about women's innards in general. Maybe what his wretched fumbling with the button had done was to reset the thing so the days the machine would now call safe would, in fact, be highly dangerous. Oh Christ, why hadn't the woman just stayed on the Pill like everyone else?

James had his Nokia out and their number half dialed before he thought of what he might say. *Hi, I'm passing through Swords; I just thought you should know that two weeks ago I pressed your little button* . . . Hot mortification swept up his face. He was being paranoid, ridiculous. He put his phone back on his belt and put the matter from his mind.

Till a soft May evening in his little house when he was feeding his old friends crispy duck legs in chile-lime broth, and Eoin burped faintly and said, "What'cha think, Neasa? Is it time for the news?"

James assumed they wanted to switch on *Newsnight,* but no.

"I'm pregnant," Neasa told him, with a tight little grin.

He thought he might throw up there and then, on his grandmother's linen tablecloth. But his mind was working at top speed, churning out conclusions: (*A*) It was all his fault. (*B*) The constant anti-abortion propaganda in their teens must have worked, because clearly Neasa and Eoin had decided to go through with having this baby. (*C*) He must never, never, never tell them what he'd done.

"Wow!" he shrieked, his face a mask of delight.

He knew this appalling accident would transform his friends' lives; what he never expected was how much it was going to change his own.

He dropped heavy hints until they asked him to be Angela's godfather, and his christening present was 1,000 euros in a savings account, to start her college fund. (He'd wanted to make it 5,000 euros but knew that would look suspicious.) Then he became the regular Tuesday babysitter, plus any evening Eoin and

Neasa were off at a jazz gig. Because, in fact, they didn't give up their music, not at all; that baby could fall asleep only to the sounds of the sax.

When at, say, five years old, Angie stayed the night in her uncle James's cream-linen spare room in Ballsbridge, he always fed her organic vegetables and put Gregorian chant on the mini-disc player. Whenever he went abroad on a shoot—which wasn't as often, now, because of what he wryly called his "family respon-sibilities"—he brought home exquisite and educational toys. He would leave his darkroom at a moment's notice to drive her halfway across Ireland to reconstructed folk villages and drama festivals. On Angie's tenth birthday, James started giving her regu-lar fistfuls of banknotes, and once when she was furious with him after he called her T-shirt sluttish, she told her parents about the money and got him into serious, though temporary, trouble.

His other friends thought he was mad. He'd never told any of them about what he thought of as his secret parenthood: the fact that, by one careless mistake, he had made this child happen.

At thirteen, the girl announced her name was now Ang, to rhyme with *bang*. For the next four years she was foul.

"Sometimes I don't like her at all," Neasa said softly to James, looking out the window of his house to where her daughter sat be-tween the fountain and the Japanese maple, talking on her mobile, her back as convex as a shield.

His friend's confession filled him with panic. He had thought it was working out all right. He had assumed that every child turned into a wanted child, even if she'd been unwanted to begin with, even if her conception had been a bloody awful blunder, never meant to happen. But then, how could he say that Ang had never been meant to happen?—since he loved her, himself, with a guilty fervour of ownership that was unaffected by any of her shift-ing moods, unaffected by all the nasty things she'd said to him over the years, from her first howl of "You're poo" to their latest spat, when she'd called him a "sad old suburban queen."

The summer she left school, she emerged from adolescence, shakily, like a convalescent. One day James looked at her across the table of a noodle bar and realized that she was an utterly charming young woman, sitting here, telling this middle-aged man her plans to work her way across Australia, her eyes shining at him as if he mattered to her, as if he always would. How did this happen?

At Ang's good-bye party, James gave her a discreetly wrapped bumper pack of extra-strength condoms; she blushed, but said yes, of course, she promised she'd be careful.

Four martinis later, James sat heavily on the arm of Neasa's chair and murmured in her ear, "I know you never wanted to have her, but isn't she fabulous?"

Neasa stared at him.

"Sorry, what I meant was—," he backtracked. And then he couldn't help himself: the eighteen-year-old story was spilling out in a passionate hiss—the little plastic machine, the terrible blue light.

Neasa was smiling strangely. "You daft egg," she said at last, "you poor eejit! It was for ovulation, not contraception."

He could feel his eyes cross.

"We wanted a baby. We'd been trying for a year and a half." She laughed a little hoarsely.

"So what you're telling me," he said blankly, "is that I made no difference."

"None at all!" She grinned at him

And James, who should have felt relieved, went home early from the party with a stitch between his ribs as if there was something he'd lost.

Through the Night

What sent Una over the edge was people asking "Does she sleep through the night?" For some reason it was often the first thing strangers said after "What a lovely baby." Una was all right with the lovely baby line, she could smile and nod, her eyes only slightly shiny, and she could even cope with remarks like "It must be so much fun!" If she just kept nodding and smiling, she found, people assumed that having a two-month-old baby was just like in the diaper ads, or the way they dimly and fondly remembered it. "Treasure every moment," the bank manager commanded her, rubbing his beard. All this Una could take. But when someone approached her in the supermarket or queuing at an ATM and tickled whatever bit of Moya was sticking out of the sling and said the fatal words, "Is she sleeping through the night yet?" . . .

Before the birth, before Moya—B.M., as Silas called it—Una had not been a crier. In fact, she'd been known for her ability to sit dry-cheeked through *Titanic* or *It's a Wonderful Life,* while Silas was gulping by her side. Before her periods she'd turn slightly snappish, and when her father died, back in Ireland, she'd gone very quiet for a month or so. But crying wasn't something she did. Even pregnant, she'd maintained her steadiness.

These days—A.M., After Moya—Una didn't recognize herself. It was as if there'd been some transformation at the cellular level; a weakening of all the walls. She cried sitting on the toilet— "Just coming, Moya, just a minute; I promise, Mum needs just a minute more"—she cried when she couldn't get her snowboots laced up one-handed and had to shout for Silas; she cried when he was at the office and it took her four hours to make and eat a peanut butter sandwich. She always let herself cry in the shower because her face was wet anyway so it didn't count. She dissolved every time she had to answer the phone, if not with the first hello then as soon as Moya's name came up; she cried so much when trying to book an electrician to fix the furnace thermostat that she had to put the phone down.

Whenever Una slept—for of course she did get to sleep, at certain periods in each twenty-four-hour cycle when Silas took Moya downstairs between feeds (it was just that these tainted, uneasy mouthfuls of unconsciousness bore no relation to the blissful, unthinking seven-hour nights she'd known B.M.)—whenever she slept, she didn't have time to dream, and only the cheap digital watch she kept on her wrist at all times convinced her that she'd added, say, another forty-three minutes of sleep to her total. She wept in the night when she slumped over to nurse Moya again and looked down the street where not a single other light was on. She wept hardest in the early morning when she was meant to be catching up on her sleep, when the baby was downstairs with Silas but Una could still hear her shrieks through three wooden doors, could hear them so faintly but persistently that she thought she might be having an aural hallucination.

Delusions of all kinds afflicted her. Again and again in the night she'd hear Moya's whimperings from the cot attached to the bed, and lean over, pick up the baby, put her to her breast . . . but why were the cries continuing, getting more frantic? She'd wake properly then and realize that Moya was still lashing about in the cot, so who was this other baby at her breast? Only the balled-up duvet, which fell apart in her sweaty, shuddering hands. And there was Silas, smooth-faced in sleep at her side, like some absolute stranger.

But even to use the terms *night* and *day* was misleading. Day and night were human inventions, Una realized, and Moya—a startled visitor from another planet—had never heard of them. There no longer was any night for Una, in the old sense, the switch-off, shed-your-troubles, knit-up-the-raveled-sleeve-of-care sense. Hers was a work shift that never really ended even when she was meant to be relaxing, one long day that spun on sickeningly through dark and light, sound and silence. She didn't hate other people, not even Silas; she lacked the energy, or perhaps it was that she felt entirely cut off from them, marked out by her fated, perpetual punishment.

Una had always got on well with her mother, despite their differences. So when Rose flew in from Cork for a weeklong stay, Una put the baby down on the rug, for once, and fell into her arms.

"Barry's Tea," said her mother, unpacking her bag, "and Bewley's Dark Roast, and a couple of boxes of Black Magic, aren't they your favourite?"

"That's lovely, Mum," said Una regretfully, "but I'm off caffeine, in case it keeps Moya awake."

"How many times does she have you up at night now?"

Una gave a little shrug. "Five or six."

"How long each time?"

"Forty minutes, an hour."

"Ah, you poor child! No wonder you look so awful."

Which, of course, made Una cry.

That first night, Rose took her pill and popped in her earplugs, as always when she was in a strange place. Before she swallowed it, she did register a pang of guilt, but it would hardly do any good for her to be lying awake listening all night, would it?

Rose's idea of being a good grandmother was taking the baby for long walks, but the hard-packed, jagged snow of an Ontario January made it impossible to get the buggy round the block. "Besides, it's too cold to take her out," said Una, putting the wailing baby back against her chest, tightening the sling and swaying from side to side.

Her daughter wore a glazed look, Rose thought, like someone with Alzheimer's. "It'll be lovely when the weather warms up," she said blandly, before remembering that spring here didn't come till May.

Silas dropped them off at a café downtown on his way to work. Two sips into her decaf latte Una unbuttoned her shirt to feed Moya. This startled Rose, but she didn't let it show; times change, and sure, why not? She looked around to see if there was a smoking section, but apparently not; she decided it wasn't worth standing outside in the driving snow.

Una discussed her mental state as if it was a not-particularly-interesting ongoing war in a country she couldn't spell. "Not *depression*, I wouldn't call it that, Mum; I've only got three of the eight symptoms in the books."

That was something else Rose found strange: It was all books nowadays; young mothers didn't so much as wipe a bottom without consulting the authorities ("Front to back for girl babies," Una had corrected her this morning).

"Some women I've talked to at La Leche meetings, they say the baby blues are so normal"—Una broke off to yawn—"It's probably hormones, or the shock of giving birth. Like, I remember, the day we came home from the hospital, I was convinced Moya would never be safe in the outside world; I had this craving to put her back in."

Rose had a simpler explanation. "Wouldn't anyone lose their marbles from this kind of sleep deprivation? Sure that's how they torture prisoners!"

Una smiled faintly.

"If I could just buy you one good night's sleep! I really don't—I've been casting my mind back thirty years," Rose said, her forehead wrinkled, "but I really can't remember having such a hard time with you or Donal." Of course, their father had given them a bottle at three in the morning, that helped, and because they were in their own room she hadn't been roused by every little peep out of them. "You were both awfully good . . ."

She'd forgotten: That was one of the forbidden terms. "They're not good or bad, Mum," Una repeated. "They're just babies with needs."

Rose decided to be frank. "But it's ridiculous for Moya to be carrying on like this, at the two-month mark. She's preying on your feelings, I'm afraid; you cuddle her so constantly in that sling thing, she's spoiled rotten—" *Damn,* that was another of the words.

"There's no such thing as *spoiling* a two-month-old," her daughter said tightly. "The current scientific consensus—"

"Oh, I'm not saying there's any badness in her," Rose interrupted. "I just mean she's got into dangerous habits."

Una's stare was cold. "Babies worn in slings for three hours a day cry less and thrive better, it says so in all the books."

Moya let out a high-pitched wail; Una switched her to the other breast. Rose bit her lip and suggested they have a couple of those lovely looking muffins. By the time she came back with the plate, Una's cheeks were striped with tears again.

Rose found, over the next few days, that every conversation with her daughter ran straight into a wall. The present generation seemed hedged in by rules, miserably committed to something known as "attachment parenting." (In her day, Rose would have liked to say, they'd just got on with it, watched a lot of telly, and had a laugh when they could.) Everything she suggested had already been judged impossible. No, Una couldn't pump milk for Silas to give the baby at night, because she felt she only barely had enough as it was, and if she skipped a feed she might jeopardize her supply. Sorry, Una wasn't willing to leave Moya with a babysitter so she could have a proper slap-up lunch out with her mother. No, she didn't see how it would help to try to make the baby sleep in her own room.

As for the little bits of folk wisdom Rose couldn't help offering when she saw her sunken-eyed daughter leap up again—"Give her a bottle of water instead, surely she can't still be hungry," or "Why wouldn't you let her grizzle for five minutes, see if she'll drop off back to sleep"—these were received as if she'd proposed sticking the infant's foot in a broken beer bottle. The briefest suggestion of giving Moya some kind of sedative to let Una catch up on some sleep sent Una off on a five-minute rant about adults poisoning babies for their own convenience.

"Sweetheart," Rose burst out finally, "I don't mean to play the interfering granny, I really don't, you're doing a marvelous job"— Moya made a choking sound and brought up white curds on Una's sleeve—"I just can't stand seeing you in this state. Don't you think you're being a bit hard on yourself, playing the martyr?"

Una's eyes were huge. With fury? Or just exhaustion?

"Babies are tougher than they look. I didn't run to pick you up every time you opened your mouth, and you grew up all right, didn't you?" There was a pause. *Didn't you,* she wanted to ask again.

Nobody quite understood, Una thought, and her mother least of all. Hadn't she chosen to have Moya, planned it, wanted it for years? So she just had to do it the best way she could, even if she felt tangled in a nightmare that wouldn't let her wake up. From the sound of it, her mother's generation had ignored all their instincts when it came to looking after tiny, vulnerable human beings. They'd smoked and drank through pregnancy and labour, bottle-fed their babies and left them dangling from doors for hours, dosed them with alcoholic gripe water, jammed plastic pacifiers in their mouths, left them in barred cots to cry it out . . . Of course they needed to believe that they'd done what was right, instead of just what was handy. But who could say how much of the fucked-up state of so many of Una's friends might not be due to buried memories of wailing away alone on those long-gone nights?

"Darling, it's just that you're in such a bad way," Rose was saying. "Tonight, why don't I stay up with the baby for an hour or two?"

But could I trust you to bring her in when she's hungry? Una wanted to say. Instead she forced a smile and said it was OK, she was feeling not too bad this evening.

It was quite pleasant to have company while Silas was out, she supposed, but on the other hand, guests always needed looking after. And Rose, with her dry-clean-only cashmere, after-dinner cognac, and shivering smoke breaks on the porch, seemed such an irrelevance. Shouldn't Moya have brought them closer together instead of the opposite? To avoid discussing the contentious subject of the baby, Una would raise some topic of the day—airline security or pensions or the Atkins diet—but of course all she cared or knew about at the moment was the baby, so all she could contribute was the odd robotic syllable.

Rose, for her part, seemed to be learning to resist the temptation to give advice—which left her with nothing but platitudes. "Hang on in there," she'd say, squeezing her daughter's shoulder. "It'll be different when she's more active; she'll suddenly get the hang of day and night, wait till you see. One of these mornings you'll wake up after a good night's sleep, you'll hardly believe it!"

Una nodded, as if talking to a mad person at a bus stop.

The morning she was to fly back to Dublin, Rose woke early, for her, and pulled out her earplugs. She lay listening to the beautiful silence till she heard Silas pulling the front door closed behind him. She put her dressing gown on and peeped round the other bedroom door. There lay the baby, in the cot attached to her parents' bed, and there was Una, flat on her back, her arms uncurled, as if drifting down a stream. Her face was peaceful, almost young again.

Rose must have stood on a creaky floorboard as she backed out, because suddenly Una was bolt upright, eyes wild. She snatched up the baby, who began to shriek.

"Good morning," said Rose, like some nervous chambermaid. She rather wished she'd stayed in bed.

"Jesus. Jesus Christ," Una said into Moya's fuzzy scalp. "It's light out."

"It certainly is. Twenty past seven."

"I thought she'd died in the night." Una's face was contorted with tears again.

Rose suppressed a sigh. "She's grand. She's had a lovely long sleep, that's all."

"I don't believe it. Could she have been crying and I just didn't hear her?"

"There wasn't a peep out of her," said Rose firmly, not men-
tioning the earplugs.

Una managed a weak laugh.

"Didn't I promise you things would get better?"

"You did."

"Now, don't be expecting her to pull off a trick like this every
night—"

"I won't," Una assured her mother. "I don't care if she doesn't
do it again for months. Now I know it's possible—" Faith glittered
in her eyes.

"So how do you feel?"

"Fabulous."

"I'll bring you up a cup of coffee," said Rose.

"Decaf," said Una, with a smile, sinking back into the pillows
with Moya.

That hadn't gone quite the way she'd planned, Rose thought
as she went down the stairs. She'd meant to move from told-you-
so to a cheerful confession that she'd given the baby half a tea-
spoon of her cognac last night. *See,* she'd intended to say, *it did
you good, and it didn't do her a bit of harm!* But something in
Una's eyes had made her reconsider this morning, and perhaps
discretion was the better part of motherhood, after all.

Do They Know It's Christmas?

Trevor could barely see the traffic light through sheets of rain.

"Quick, before it turns red," muttered Louise.

"It's amber."

"Amber means go if you can. Go on!"

It was red now; he hit the brake and felt it judder. The wipers kept up their whine.

A small sigh. "Sorry I snapped," she said.

"That's OK." Leaving Limerick, they'd been snarled up in Christmas-shopping traffic for the best part of an hour.

"I should have rung Mrs. Quirk to ask her to look in on the babies," Louise muttered.

"Mallarmé hates her," Trevor pointed out.

"I know, but it's better than leaving them alone on such a hideous evening. I'd try her now, but the phone's acting up again. Hey, we could ask your folks for another one for Christmas."

The mobile phone had been unreliable ever since Proust had ripped the charger out of the wall. "Proust's always so curious

about things," said Trevor. "Do you think he's the most intelligent
of the three?"

Louise turned on him. "That's not a fair question."

"I know, I know, I don't mean it . . . divisively."

"They're all really bright in their own ways. Light's changing," she pointed out.

His tires squealed through the puddles. "You think they're all
perfect," he accused her fondly.

"No I don't. Well, nearly," she conceded. Nose pressed to the
blurred window, her tone sank again. "I wish we were home."

"Twenty minutes."

"Fifteen, if you shift your arse. Gide gets so fractious when it
pisses down like this."

"We're living in the wrong climate," he observed, not for the
first time. "Not to mention a cultural wasteland."

"Yeah, well next time Barcelona University has simultaneous
openings in classics and sociology we must remember to apply."

"Ho ho ho," he chuckled like some grim Santa.

Trevor's favourite moment was always when he put his key in
the lock. Eruption, joyous noise, crashes against the other side of
the door. Tonight he tried to take his raincoat off, but Gide felled
him.

"Sweeties, gorgeous-gorgeousnesses," Louise was crooning,
Proust swinging high in her arms. "We're home, yes we are, yes
we are."

"Let Daddy get up. No licky face, no licky," Trevor was telling
Gide gruffly.

"How's he meant to know not to lick it when you offer it to
him like a big jam doughnut?" Louise bent down to kiss her husband under one eye. "Mallarmé doesn't lick faces, does she, lovely
girl. Who's a lovely quiet girl?"

"Did you miss us, Mallarmé?" Trevor asked, sleeking her yellow fur. "Were you bored silly? Just another three days till the holidays and then walkies anytime."

Proust writhed in ecstasy in Louise's arms, and Gide began another round of barking.

"Trevor!"

"I said the *W*-word, didn't I?" Trevor rebuked himself.

As he was putting away the bagfuls of Christmas shopping, he said, "We've bought no presents for them yet."

"Oh, I know. Do you think—one big one each, or several smalls?"

"Smalls, definitely. They love tearing off the paper."

"They always like some new squeakies. But remember last year," said Louise, "when we gave Gide that rubber apple that was too small and I had to do the Heimlich manoeuvre?"

"That was the most terrifying moment of my life," said Trevor. "Hey, I asked the dean of arts what he's getting his poodle and he said nothing."

"You mean he didn't answer?"

"No, I mean he said, *'Nothing.'* He said, and I quote, *'She doesn't know it's Christmas!'*"

Later on, Trevor was making his weekly call to his parents in Belfast. "Not much new, Mum. Except that Proust just gave us the fright of our lives by turning the telly on! With the remote."

"Is she the fat one?" asked his mother.

Trevor felt that familiar wave of irritation. "Proust is a he; he's tiny," he reminded her. "The one you mean is Gide, but actually he's been on diet food for three weeks and if you look at him head-on he's really not—" A rubber Bart Simpson, wet with drool, squeaked at Trevor's feet. "Not now, Gide, Daddy's on the phone." Proust was scrabbling against Trevor's leg; they really would have to steel themselves to clip his claws this evening.

His mother was making some remark about the *pack*.

"There's only three of them," he objected. "Greta's got three kids, and you never confuse the boys with the girls!"

She let out a short laugh. "Oh, Trev, it's hardly the same."

He'd given up on breaking his family of the habit of calling him Trev. He chewed his lip, as he picked up the wet toy to bounce it against the far wall. Proust raced after it, but Gide shoved him out of the way. "Be nice," Trevor warned them. "Share your squeaky." Then, with false warmth, "Tell you what, Mum, maybe they'll give you a framed photo for Christmas, with their names on."

A couple of minutes later he walked into the kitchen, where Louise was frying chicken breasts. "Save me a crispy bit," he said, to postpone what he had to say.

"Mallarmé likes the crispy bits. You're getting polenta. So how's life in Belfast?"

He let out his breath with the sound of a fast puncture. "We were talking about Christmas. I was telling Mum not to worry about bedding for the babies, we'll all sleep together on our blow-up mattress."

"Uh-huh."

"And she said actually this year, with Greta and Mick and all the kids being over from Sydney, she and Dad were wondering if we could maybe . . . do something with the dogs."

"Do something?" repeated Louise. "What does she mean? Do what?"

Trevor cleared his throat. "Not bring them."

Her eyes were little dark buttons.

The last three days of term crawled by; the stack of exam papers deflated. To celebrate the holidays, Louise and Trevor went for a long hike across the Cliffs of Moher. Gide barked fiercely at mountain goats. "Do you think Proust's coat is looking dull?" she asked.

"Hmm?" Trevor stared down into his half-zipped jacket, where Proust was curled up. "Maybe a wee bit."

"The vet says you can put vegetable oil in their food to increase shine. We'll have to take Mallarmé to that grooming place this week; she's all burrs," added Louise, watching the dog lope silently away towards a group of Japanese tourists.

"Yeah, she must have a bit of collie in her, she gets so snaggled. Mallarmé!" Trevor tried again, more loudly. "Mallarmé, no! Come back!"

"She won't bite, will she?" said Louise, breathless as she ran.

"She bit Mrs. Quirk last week."

"Only because she messed with Mallarmé's ears."

"Don't touch her ears," Trevor bawled at the tour group.

Afterwards, when Mallarmé was back on her leash, Louise burrowed around in the bag for dog biscuits and Mars bars. "You're brooding about Christmas, aren't you?"

"A bit," admitted Trevor.

"That was a really good phone message you left your parents."

"You think so?"

"Nicely balanced, you know, between warmth and firmness."

"You sound like that trainer." They'd gone on a night course called Good Dog! but dropped out after three weeks.

Louise giggled reminiscently. "Well, handling parents isn't so very different, I suppose."

"Except you know where you are with dogs," said Trevor. "They never claim to love you and then stab you in the back."

"Trevor!" she protested. "Leave it, Gide," she said, suddenly turning. "Drop it, dirty. Gide! Give. Give to Mammy."

He watched her wrestle a Ballygowan bottle out of the dog's jaws. "How can my parents have the gall to say leave them at home, when it's hundreds of miles away and we'll be gone for forty-eight hours!"

"I suppose we could hire a sitter," she volunteered.

"But they'd hate to be away from us at Christmas. I mean," he said, conscious of having strayed into irrationality, "they may not know exactly what it is—in the theological sense—but they can sense it's a special occasion."

"You know," murmured Louise, "there may be class issues involved here."

"Such as?"

"Well, your parents have a fundamentally suspicious attitude towards our lifestyle. Being academics, going to the opera . . . and I suspect they see our dogs as an expensive whim."

Trevor groaned. "It's not like we spent thousands of pounds buying pedigree puppies! We rescued them from the pound."

"Mmm," said Louise, "but remember how they made fun of the plaid coats and shoes? And there was this one time—I didn't tell you because I knew you'd be annoyed—but your dad asked me how much we spent a year on their food and vet bills."

He winced.

"It's understandable; he did grow up on a farm where dogs were just exploited workers," she added. "And your mother's from a tiny terrace where there was barely enough food for the kids."

"That's it," said Trevor, so sharply that Proust started to whimper and worry the zip of his jacket. "It's all about kids. They're trying to punish us for not having any! What my mother's saying at a sort of unconscious level is 'I won't let your pseudo-children under my roof. Lock them up and throw away the key.' "

"Oh, hang on, hon—"

"She is! She's saying, 'Have some real children like your sister, Greta, and then maybe I'll love you!' "

"Come on, Trevor, she does love you; they both do."

"Then what about the proverbial love my dog?"

Louise was scanning the skyline distractedly. "Did you see which way Gide went?"

Trevor jumped to his feet. *"Gide!"*

They both caught sight of him simultaneously, a hundred feet away, as he raced along the edge of the cliff.

That evening, during dinner, Proust left a long red scrape across Louise's collarbone. "Put him down on the floor," Trevor urged her. "Remember, the trainer said to punish him by withdrawing our attention. *Proust, sit!*"

"He's only acting out, poor baba," said Louise, setting him down. "They all are; they always pick up our vibes when we're upset."

"Make a nasty sound . . . ," Trevor dropped a fork on the tiles. Proust stared back at him, unmoved. "Then turn our backs."

They twisted away from him in their chairs. Trevor looked at his half-eaten risotto and felt his appetite drain away. He stood up and adjusted the framed photo of the dogs carrying the flower baskets on Louise and Trevor's wedding day. "How's he reacting?"

"Hang on," breathed Louise, peeking over her shoulder.

"Don't make eye contact," Trevor warned her.

"He's gone."

They found Proust in the living room, watching the blank screen.

"Do you think we've hurt his feelings?" asked Louise.

"Dunno. It's a fine line between gentle discipline and crushing his spirit. Proust?" Trevor crouched to stroke the tiny dog behind the ears. "I don't think he likes the Chopin."

"OK, I'll switch to Mozart."

"Proust? Want to turn the telly on again?"

They didn't check their messages till they were going to bed. There was only one, from Belfast. "Trevor, this is your mother," it began, as always. "Your dad and I have been thinking about it like you asked, and we've decided we really can't have your dogs this Christmas. Sorry about that, but. There's your dad's allergy, and Lucy and Caitríona are still awful small, and the general chaos and peeing on the rugs. Not to mention the incident last year, I didn't want to have to bring it up, but—"

The voice changed to a gruffer one. "Let me talk to him. Trevor, those creatures are a menace, especially the quiet one. After it bit your mother, I have to tell you, I thought it should have been put down. So let's have no more nonsense—stick them in kennels and let's all of us have a nice peaceful Christmas together, who knows when we'll get the chance again."

At two in the morning Trevor was wide awake in the dark. "Have they ever even seen a kennel? I still feel guilty about that time we went to Athens and left the babies in that, that *concentration camp*," he said, spitting out the words. "And Dad's always had a runny nose; he's only called it an allergy since he started watching *ER*. Animals get blamed for everything. Remember that part-timer in Spanish who claimed she'd gone to a party where there was a cat and she was wheezing for six months afterwards?"

"Calm down, sweetie." Louise was stroking his arm.

"And as for the so-called incident with Mum—"

"It wasn't a real bite."

"It was a quick reflex snap, that's all. I *told* her not to touch Mallarmé's ears."

"Anyway, no skin was broken."

"It's as if they said, 'Don't bring your Negro friends to our house,'" Trevor ranted. "It's a human rights issue. Well, a rights issue."

A silence. Then Louise rolled heavily away from him. "I give up," she said in a small voice. "It's not worth the grief."

"What do you mean?"

"You should go on your own, see your sister and all. And then when you come home on the twenty-seventh, we'll have our own Christmas dinner."

"Oh, but Louise!" He started to sit up. Did she want him to accept gratefully or to say he wouldn't dream of it? "You're wonderful. But you shouldn't have to make the sacrifice."

"Believe me," she said into the pillow, "I couldn't swallow a bite of turkey in that atmosphere."

Christmas Eve in Belfast, and Trevor had escaped into what they used to call the good room to ring Louise. He listened to *Santa's Pop Faves* blaring through the wall from the living room, mingled with the voices of his squabbling nieces, and longed to be back in the house outside Limerick, where Christmas crackers full of doggie treats would be hanging from the tree, and Louise and the babies would probably be curled up watching *Lady and the Tramp*.

Before he'd finished dialing, his father's bald head came round the door. "You on the phone, Trev?"

"It's OK," he said, putting it down.

"Carry on, don't mind me," he said, dropping heavily into an armchair.

"Louise is out, actually," Trevor lied, "probably on a walk." Then he felt awkward for having implicitly brought up the dogs; it wasn't as if he wasn't trying his best to make this a cordial visit.

His father blew his nose like an elephant trumpeting.

"How's your allergy?" asked Trevor neutrally.

"Nah, I'm just getting over a cold."

His mother came in and set down a large bowl of toffees. "I've just been mopping up the stairs; poor Lucy got sick."

"Why don't you take the weight off your feet, love?"

"Just for a sec, then. All right, Trev?" she said as she sat down beside him.

"Aye, Mum."

"The kids are wee dotes, with their Aussie accents, aren't they? Oh"—turning to her husband—"you'll have to have a look in the U-bend for me; wee Jasmine dropped my wedding ring down the sink."

His father let out a small sound of exasperation.

"Oh well, accidents do happen," she said.

The words burst out of Trevor. "That wasn't what you said last year about Proust chewing through the Christmas lights!" There was an awful silence. He tried to regain control. "I just think, Mum, there's rather a double standard operational here. I don't think you're aware how unconsciously biased you are towards Greta."

His father's eyes narrowed. "You high-and-mighty tosser."

"I beg your pardon?"

"You heard me, Professor Pillock, that's if your ears are *operational!*"

His mother flapped her hands. "Ah, stop it now—Trev's just missing his doggies."

Trevor nearly punched her.

His father grunted. "The boy's besotted!"

"Boy?" he repeated. "I'm forty-three years old."

"Then act it. Jesus Christ, if I have to hear one more word about those wretched animals—"

"I don't believe this!" Trevor was practically screaming. "I have to leave my entire family behind, while Greta and Mike jet in with three of the brattiest girls on the face of the planet—"

"Trev!" His mother's voice was a gunshot. "That's enough."

"At least the girls don't climb on your arm and start humping it," his father observed.

Trevor thought he might cry. "This is unfair, it's oppressive, it's humiliating—"

"Sure it's Christmas," said his mother.

He collected his bag and left. The drive was more than seven hours, but at least he was going the right direction this time. It was two o'clock on Christmas morning when he drew up outside the house. There was one light on, in the bedroom. Trevor let himself in quietly. In the hall he almost stumbled over the small table that they always left out for Santa. Suddenly starving, Trevor ate the mince pie in one bite and rinsed it down with the brandy. Upstairs, a door opened and the dogs hurled themselves down the steps. Trevor squinted into the light and grinned up at his wife. "I'm home," he said.

DOMESTICITY

Lavender's Blue

Leroy and Shorelle had always wanted a slate blue house. It had come up on their first date, in fact, driving to the lake: Shorelle said, "When I get a house I'm going to paint it that exact colour," indicating with one long manicured nail a three-storey redbrick Colonial with porch and gingerbread the shade of a rain-threatening sky.

"Me too," said Leroy, unnerved by the coincidence.

"Really? Are you just saying that?"

"No way! That's the colour I've always wanted."

She gave him a smile so slow, so intricately blooming, that he very nearly drove into the curb.

For the first three years they lived in Shorelle's apartment above a discount shoe outlet, then when the baby was coming they managed with the help of Leroy's stepfather to scrape together a ten percent down payment on a nice little two-bed in a neighbourhood that was neither too graffitied nor too suburban, neither too noisy nor too white. On the porch, the Realtor told them they wouldn't find the house they were looking for at a better price. "Is that because of the colour?" Leroy asked.

The Realtor screwed up her forehead. "What's wrong with the colour? It's a nice sort of faded adobe pink."

He let out a brief laugh. "I'd call it Puke Peach."

Shorelle rolled her eyes at him.

"Well, after closing day you can paint it whatever you like," the Realtor said a little crisply.

But life intervened, of course. Moving in and getting the place fixed up—curtains, wallpaper, bookshelves, magnets to keep the kitchen cupboards shut—took all their energy, and then Africa came along. (Leroy wasn't a hundred percent fond of that name, but Shorelle believed she should have the casting vote. "Twenty-six hours of labour, five stitches," she reminded him stonily.)

There was something the public health nurse said that stuck in Leroy's head: that the days would be long but the years would be short. That was so true; every day with a small mewling baby seemed like a mountain to climb, but *blink!* and here was Africa at her first birthday party, triumphant fists full of chocolate cake. And the house was still the colour of puke.

Leroy would have liked to paint it himself, but the sad fact was he had no head for heights, and now he was a father he was noticing in himself this strange, almost cheerful refusal to do dumb things: His life wasn't his own to risk. He never even rode pillion on his friend CJ's Honda Magna anymore. So he asked around for a painter who wouldn't rip him off. He ended up hiring a quiet white guy called Rod who lived a couple of blocks away.

"You picked your colour yet?" Rod narrowed his eyes at the roofline.

"Not quite, but it'll be some kind of slate blue."

Rod seemed to have been born with a neutral expression. He

handed Leroy a brochure. "That's the only brand I use," he said, "but they can colour-match whatever you want."

"Great."

That evening Leroy and Shorelle sat on the porch with Africa stumbling back and forth between them. They flicked through sheaves of paint chips. "Well, not Niagara," said Shorelle with some scorn, "and not Old China, either. Where do they come up with these names?"

Leroy snickered in agreement. "Who'd paint their house Muddy Creek?"

"Or Yacht Fantasy!" She pulled a strip of glaring royal blue from Africa's mouth and showed it to him. "Timothy says his clients come in with scraps of cloth, lipsticks, dead leaves, even, going '*This* is it.' Half the time he's got to talk them out of it."

"Why's he got to?" Timothy, owner of a small interior design company, was Shorelle's best friend from school, whom Leroy had always pretended to like. Before the baby, on nights when Leroy was working late, she used to go over there to watch black-and-white movies and eat Timothy's homemade gelato.

"Because they've got no clue what they're doing!"

"Well, I don't think we need to hire anyone to pick a paint for our house; it's not that big a deal," said Leroy flippantly. He held up three blues against each other; they seemed to melt in and out. "Is there one actually called Slate Blue?"

"Oh no, that would be too easy. Wait up—here's a Blue Slate, but it's not blue at all," Shorelle complained, "it's plain grey."

"This one's kinda nice—Porch Lullaby."

"Yeah, it's nice, but it's not slate blue."

"No."

"I thought we agreed—"

"We do," he assured her. "I just can't tell which is what we agreed on."

She laughed at his grammar, and Africa joined in, looking from face to face.

Finally, when they'd gone indoors, Shorelle found another brochure called Historic Tints. "Look, Leroy, I think we've got it—Evening Sky."

"What's historic about these ones?"

"Oh, that just means more expensive."

He groaned.

Over breakfast, they glanced at the Evening Sky chip and it still looked good, so Leroy dropped it off in Rod's mailbox on his way to work.

For three days it rained, and then they were at Shorelle's parents' for the weekend. By the time they got back on Sunday evening, roughly the top third of the house had been painted. Leroy turned off the car and stared up.

"Wow!" said Shorelle.

"Wow is right," he said in horror.

"Rod's a fast worker. Look, Africa"—as she heaved the drowsy child out of the car seat—"look at the lovely colour our house's going to be."

"That," said Leroy, "is not slate blue."

"Oh, Leroy."

"It's not what we chose."

"It must be. It just looks different against the peach."

"It's purple!"

"It's catching the last of the sunset, that's all."

The argument continued right through Africa's bath and bedtime. "You think it should be darker, then?"

"Not exactly darker," said Leroy.

"Lighter?"

"Just less gaudy. Bluer."

"What, like royal blue?"

"No! I'm just saying, right now it stands out like a neon sign."

"That's because everybody else on this street paints their houses boring neutrals," objected Shorelle.

Leroy stalked out on the porch to gather more evidence, but it was too dark to tell what he was looking at.

"It's a lurid shade of lavender," he told her in bed, in the whisper they always used after Africa had gone to sleep. "If you look at it with no preconceptions—if you didn't know it was meant to be blue—I'm telling you, purple's what you'd see. People are going to say, 'Oh yeah, you're the guys who live in that lavender house.'"

"Well, so?"

He stared at her in the dark. "You're fine with that?"

"Lavender's blue, anyway, like the song says."

He felt frustration tingling in the roots of his hair. "That's a nursery rhyme, Shorelle; they're not supposed to make sense. *Lavender's blue, diddle diddle, lavender's green* . . . I guess you're going to tell me it's green now?"

"That's the stalk and stuff," she informed him. "The leaves are green; the flowers are blue."

"They're frigging purple!"

First thing in the morning Leroy was out there again, staring at the freshly painted woodwork. He knew he was going to be late for work, but he hung around till Rod showed up in his van. "Hey!"

A nod for answer.

"I think we've maybe got a problem," said Leroy, clearing his throat. "Is that really the colour I gave you?"

Rod produced the dog-eared chip from his back pocket, set up his ladder, climbed up, and held the chip against the paintwork. Leroy could barely see it, which, he supposed, meant it was the same shade. "OK," he said unhappily.

"They colour-matched it."

"Yeah, I'm not calling you a liar. I just—I guess I didn't know it would come out so bright."

Rod climbed down.

"It's awful, isn't it?"

The painter didn't demur.

"Maybe it's because there's so much of it," Leroy hazarded. "And outside, in the sun. Or maybe because it's gloss, that must make it shinier. Or do I mean darker? More intense, I don't know."

Rod stood with arms folded, looking up at the woodwork.

Leroy shaded his eyes. "Shorelle likes it, can you believe that? I told her, it'd be great in a scarf or something, but not on a house."

"Women have different eyeballs," said Rod at last.

Leroy stared at him.

"I mean, literally. It's the layout of the light-receptor cells. So your wife and you are probably seeing different colours."

"Really, is that true?"

"Also, blues can be tricky." Rod seemed to be relaxing into conversation.

"You said it! Seems like they turn green or grey or purple depending what you put them up against." Leroy could hear a whining tone in his voice, so he deepened it. "And the names don't help. Evening Sky, it's nothing like an evening sky." Rod didn't answer, but Leroy became aware how foolish it was to pay any attention to the names some schmuck of a copywriter made up. "What do you think, Rod?"

A massive shrug. "You're the customer."

"I know, but you work with this stuff."

"You can have your house any colour you like. Take your time." He looked at his shoes. "It's up to you." Another pause. "It's you folks who've got to live with it."

What was he hinting? That this colour would be impossible to live with? Leroy tried to reckon up how much they'd already spent on Rod's labour and all those pots of historic lavender paint. "No, but what would you do?"

"Me personally?" Rod scratched his eyebrow with one stained finger.

"Sure."

"I kinda liked the peach."

"No way!" Leroy stared at the old flaking woodwork.

"But if you're looking to increase the resale, go for cream. It's classic."

Later, Leroy told Shorelle, "Rod's agreed to get on with sanding and priming the porch floor, so we've got a couple days to make up our minds about the colour."

"I thought we already had," said Shorelle, shredding a bit of beef with her fork to put on Africa's tray.

"Honey, don't be like that."

"I'm not being like anything. We looked at lots of brochures, we discussed it, we agreed—"

"We were in a rush! The light was bad. And those were the wrong colours. Here, look, I picked up some more paint chips at Home World today—"

"What were you doing way over there?"

"I drove by after from work."

"So that's why you were late picking her up from day care. They called—they left a message."

Leroy decided to ignore that. He would take a fresh tack. "Remember our first date? That house we drove past, the perfect slate blue?"

Half a smile.

"Let's go take a look at it again, compare it to these chips."

"Right now? I don't know. Africa's bath—"

"Oh, she looks clean enough, she can skip it for once."

The sky was pink and pearl, and the breeze coming in the sunroof was delicious. Leroy kept one hand on Shorelle's leg as he drove, and in the back Africa was making her birdlike sounds into her plastic cell phone.

"We've been up and down this street four times," Shorelle pointed out.

"OK, Ms. Clever, where do you think it was?"

She pursed her lips. "One of those side streets past the church?"

He shook his head. "Why would we have gone down a side street?"

"I don't know; you were driving."

"Well, exactly. I was taking you straight to the lake, I was all excited about our first date and maybe making out in the dunes, I'd hardly have started combing the side streets."

Shorelle scanned the houses. "Well, it's not here. Maybe they repainted it."

"Why would they have done that? It was perfect as was."

"Turn here," she told him, and he did, so suddenly that Africa's cell phone flew across the car.

"It can't be down here," he said over the child's screams. "It was a real big house, three storeys at least. Don't you remember?"

Shorelle was twisted round in her seat belt trying to retrieve the toy. "It was years ago," she said through her teeth.

When they got home there was still enough light in the sky for the gaudy shine of the top half of the house to make him wince. He was ashamed to think of people driving by, making remarks about it.

While they were brushing their teeth, he passed on Rod's theory about the sex of eyeballs. "Oh please," said Shorelle, spitting foam. "That's just bullshit male bonding."

"No, you're missing the point, he didn't say we see *better*—"

"Well, if it comes to that, far more guys are colour-blind than women are."

At four in the morning Shorelle took hold of his shoulder. "OK, I give in," she said, gravelly.

"What?"

"If you stop heaving about and let me get some sleep, OK, you can change the colour."

Halfway through his morning bagel, Leroy grinned at Shorelle. "So you agree it's a bit too purple?"

"No, I think it's beautiful, actually."

"But honey—"

"You win, OK, Leroy? Do it—tell Rod to throw away all that paint and start again, never mind the cost. Whatever makes you happy," she said, checking her watch.

He pored over the latest brochures. What if the colour he chose came out even worse than the first? Delphinium was pallid; Foggy Dusk looked like dirty water; Deep Shale was depressing. Denim Jeans had the potential to be glaring; Lake Prospect was plain navy. Leisure Time—what the hell kind of name for a colour was that? "Maybe we should err on the safe side and go for Rocky Creek," he suggested, sliding over the catalogue.

Shorelle looked at it without much interest. "That's grey."

As soon as she'd said it, it was true. "Bay of Fundy?" he suggested, tapping the card.

"Urgh."

"You barely looked at it."

"It only takes a second to hate something," she told him. "Imagine living with that for the next however-many years . . ."

Leroy consulted the couple of neighbours he knew to say hi to; they all agreed the current patch of Evening Sky was an eyesore.

Several suggested cream; he had to be polite enough to pretend to be considering it. He asked a guy going by with his short-haired poodle, and a woman from FedEx. Shorelle came out with Africa on her hip. "Timothy's going to drop by Monday morning," she announced.

"Oh yeah?" he said neutrally.

"I thought, if you're polling every passing dog, it's time to call in an expert."

"Rod's an expert," Leroy pointed out.

"No he's not; he's just some guy who happens to paint houses for a living. Décor is Timothy's business."

"Interiors," said Leroy, aware he was quibbling. "He'll probably suggest pistachio or cerise."

"Oh, for Christ's sake." She mouthed the swearword, so Africa wouldn't hear it. "You have got to get over your gay thing."

"Since when have I had a gay thing?"

"Since forever. You get all sulky like some rapper thug."

Leroy chewed his lip.

"Timothy's in the business; he knows about colour. We've got so stuck on this, I thought we could do with an objective opinion."

But there was no such thing as objectivity, Leroy was coming to realize. Colours were private passions and weaselly turncoats, bland-faced losers and enemies in disguise. His head ached from pursuing, through a forest of azures and cornflowers, cyans and midnights, the perfect slate blue.

On Monday he was sitting waiting for Rod on the gritty primed porch. "Hey," said the painter, getting out of his van. "You picked a colour?"

"I think so." He scanned the strip in his hand nervously, checked that he'd folded it so the right one showed. "It's not absolutely what we had in mind, but it seems the nearest to it, at least as far as we can tell." The *we* was a lie; the last time he'd brought out the brochures for a discussion, Shorelle had screamed and said she was going to put them down the Garburator.

The painter adjusted his baseball cap.

"It's called Distant Haze," said Leroy as he handed it over, immediately wishing he'd used its number instead.

Roy glanced at it and put it in his back pocket.

Was that it? No endorsement, after all this work? Leroy heard a car door open and looked over at the slim guy getting out of a black PT Roadster convertible. "Timothy!" he called, overdoing the enthusiasm. "Friend of Shorelle's," he told the painter in an apologetic undertone. "This'll only take a second—"

"Rod, my man!" Timothy and Rod were embracing.

Leroy blinked. Well, it was a bear hug, he supposed. "You know each other."

"Rod's done a lot of great work for me over the years. Looking good, man," said Timothy, giving the painter's shoulder something between a whack and a rub. "Where've you been?"

"Busy," said Rod, with a brief grin.

Leroy hadn't known the painter was capable of cracking a smile.

"I've got half an hour, you want to grab a coffee?"

"Why not," said Rod, heading for the convertible.

Leroy's jaw was throbbing. They weren't even going to ask him along. "Hey, what about the house, Tim?" He knew the guy hated to be called Tim. "That's the colour Shorelle likes," he added mockingly, pointing at the upper section of paintwork.

Timothy shook his head. "Stylish in itself, but not on a west-facing street."

Leroy should have felt vindicated.

Rod produced the folded chip from his back pocket. "That's their latest."

Timothy tilted it to the light. "Grey?"

Leroy stalked over. "It's slate blue; it's called Distant Haze. If you put it up against real grey—against the pavement, even—you can see how blue it is."

"OK," said Timothy, as if humouring a child. "Listen, tell Shorelle I'll call her later?" He made that annoying finger-and-thumb-spread gesture that meant a phone.

"So Tim, what would you do?" Leroy was leaning on the hood, aware he was holding them up, trying to sound casual.

"With this house?"

"Yeah."

"Cream, probably," said Timothy.

"Can't go wrong," said Rod.

"Classic."

Leroy waved them off with a rictus smile. He shut his eyes, saw hot and red.

The Cost of Things

Cleopatra was exactly the same age as their relationship. They found this very funny and always told the story at dinner parties. Liz would mention the coincidence a little awkwardly, then Sophie, laughing as she scraped back her curls in her hands, would persuade her to spit out the details. Or sometimes it would be the other way round. They prided themselves on not being stuck in patterns. They each had things the other hadn't—Liz's triceps, say, and Sophie's antique rings—but so what? Friends would probably have said that Sophie was the great romantic, who'd do anything for love, whereas Liz was the quiet dependable type, loyal to the end. But then, what did friends know—what could friends imagine of the life that went on in a house after the guests had gone home? Liz and Sophie knew that roles could be shed as easily as clothes; they were sure that none of their differences mattered.

They had met a few months before Cleopatra, but it was like a room before the light is switched on. After the party where they were introduced, Sophie decided Liz looked a bit like a younger

Diane Keaton, and Liz knew Sophie reminded her of one of those French actresses but could never remember which. At first, their conversations were like anybody else's.

Then, on one of her days off from the gardening centre, Liz had come round to Sophie's place to help her put up some shelves in the spare bedroom. Sophie insisted she'd pay, of course she would, and Liz said she wouldn't take a dollar, though they both knew she could do with the money. When the drill died down, they thought they heard something. Such a faint sound, Liz thought it was someone using a chain saw, several houses down, but then Sophie pointed out that it was a bit like a baby crying. Anyway, she held the second shelf against the wall for Liz to mark the holes. They were standing so close that Liz could see the different colours in each of Sophie's rings, and Sophie could feel the heat coming off Liz's bare shoulder. Then that sound came again, sharper.

They found the kitten under the porch, after they'd tried everywhere else. Its mother must have left it behind. Black and white, eyes still squeezed shut, it was half the size of Sophie's cupped hand. Now, Liz would probably have made a quick call to the animal shelter and left it at that. She didn't know then how quickly and completely Sophie could fall in love.

It knew it was on to a good thing, this kitten; it clung to Sophie's fingers like a cactus. They said *it* for the first few days, not knowing much about feline anatomy. It was hard to give a kitten away, they found, once the vet told you she was a she, and especially once you knew her name. They hadn't meant to name her, but it was a long hour and a half in the queue at the vet's and it started out as a joke, what a little Cleopatra she was, said Liz, because the walnut-sized face in the corner of the shoe box was so imperious.

Sophie was clearly staggered by the bill of two hundred dollars for the various shots, but soon she was joking that it was less than she spent on shoes, most months. Liz was a little shocked to hear that, but then, Sophie did wear very nice shoes. Sophie plucked out her Visa card and asked the receptionist for a pen, it having been her porch the kitten was left under. Liz, watching her sign with one long flowing stroke, decided the woman was magnificent. Her hand moved to her own wallet and she spent ten minutes forcing a hundred-dollar bill into Sophie's breast pocket, arguing that they had, after all, found the kitten together.

Cleopatra now belonged to both of them, Sophie joked as Liz carried the box to the car, or rather, both of them belonged to her. It was—what was the word?—*serendipitous.*

That first evening they left the kitten beside the stove in her shoe box with a saucer of milk, hoping she wouldn't drown in it, and went upstairs to unbutton each other's clothes. So, give or take a day or two, they and Cleopatra began at the same time.

These days she was a stout, voluptuous five-year-old, her glossy black and white hairs drifting through every room of the ground-floor apartment where Liz now paid half the rent, never having meant to move in exactly but having got in the habit of coming over to see how the kitten was doing so often that before she knew it, this was home. On summer evenings, when Sophie took out the clippers to give Liz a No. 3 cut on the porch, Cleopatra would abuse the fallen tufts as if they were mice. Cleopatra had commandeered a velvet armchair in the lounge that no one else was allowed to sit on, and in the mornings if they delayed bringing her breakfast, the cat would lift the sheet and bite the nearest toe, not hard but as a warning.

They had a fabulous dinner party to celebrate their anniversary, five years being, as Liz announced, approximately ten times as long as she had ever been with anybody else. Three of their guests had brought champagne, which was just as well, considering how hard Liz and Sophie were finding it to keep their heads above water these days. Sophie's hair salon had finally gone out of business, and Liz's health plan didn't stretch to same-sex partners.

Over coffee and liqueurs they were prevailed upon to tell the old story of finding the kitten the very day they got together, and then Sophie showed their guests the marks Cleopatra had left on her hands over the years. Sophie had bought appallingly expensive steel claw clippers at a pet shop downtown, but the cat would never let anyone touch her feet. Her Highness was picky that way, said Liz, scratching her under her milk-white chin.

They knew they shouldn't have let her lick the plates after the smoked salmon linguini, but she looked so wonderfully decadent, tonguing up traces of pink cream. That night when they had gone to bed to celebrate the best way they knew how, the cat threw up on the Iranian carpet Liz's mother had lent them. It was Sophie who cleaned it up the next morning, before she brought Liz her coffee. Cleopatra wasn't touching her food bowl, she reported. "She must still be stuffed with salmon, the beast," said Liz, clicking her tongue to invite Cleopatra through the bedroom door.

The next day she still wasn't eating more than a mouthful. Liz said it was just as well, really—Cleopatra could do with losing a few pounds—but Sophie picked up the cat and said that wasn't funny.

They'd been planning to take her to the new cat clinic down the road to have her claws clipped at some point anyway. It took a while to get her into the wicker travel basket; Liz had to pull her paws off the rim one by one while Sophie pressed down the lid an inch at a time, nervous of trapping her tail. The cat turned her mutinous face from the window so all they could see was a square of ruffled black fur.

The clinic was a much more swish place than the other vet's, and Liz thought maybe they should have asked for a list of prices in advance, but the receptionist left them alone in the examining room before she thought of it. Cleopatra could obviously smell the ghost aromas of a thousand other cats. She sank down and tucked everything under her except her thumping tail. The place was too much like a dentist's waiting room, but Liz, who knew that Sophie relied on her to be calm, read the posters aloud and pretended to find them funny. WHY YOUR FURRY FRIEND LOVES YOU, said one poster on the wall. IN SICKNESS AND IN HEALTH, began another. The two of them whispered to each other and gave the cat little tickles, as if this sterile shelf was some kind of playground.

Dr. McGraw came in then, spoke to the cat as if he was her best friend but stroked her in the wrong place, above her tail, which flapped like an enemy flag. When he took hold of her face, her paw came round so fast that she left a red line down the inside of his wrist. Liz and Sophie apologized over and over, like the parents of a delinquent child. Dr. McGraw, dabbing himself with disinfectant, told them to think nothing of it. Then he called in Rosalita to wrap the cat in a towel.

Swaddled in flannel, Cleopatra stared at the doctor's face as if memorizing it for the purposes of revenge. He put a sort of gun in her ear to take her temperature and bared her gums in an artificial smile to see if they were dehydrated. He squeezed her stomach and kidneys and bladder, and she made a sound they'd never heard before, in a high voice like a five-year-old girl's, but it was hard to tell if she was tender in the areas he was pressing, or just enraged.

Liz had to make out the check for fifty dollars as Sophie was already up to her Visa limit. They carried the basket to the car, Cleopatra's weight lurching from side to side. They joked on the way home that the vet wouldn't try calling her Sweetums next time.

That night on the couch Sophie yawned as she put down her book, let her head drop into Liz's lap, and asked in a lazy murmur what she was thinking. In fact, Liz had been fretting over her overdraft and wondering whether they could cancel cable as they hardly ever watched it anyway, but she knew that was not what Sophie wanted to hear, so she grinned down at her and said, "Guess." Which wasn't a lie. Sophie smiled back and pulled Liz down until her shirt covered Sophie's face, then they didn't need to say anything.

Cleopatra still wasn't eating much the next day, but she seemed bright-eyed. Sophie said the clinic had rung, and wasn't that thoughtful?

The following evening when Liz came home the cat wasn't stirring from her chair. Liz began to let herself worry. "Don't worry," she told Sophie as she dropped her work clothes in the laundry basket. "Cats can live off their fat for a good while."

The two of them were tangled up in the bath, rubbing lavender oil into each other's feet, when the phone rang. It was Rosalita from the clinic. Liz felt guilty for the cheerful way she'd answered the phone and made her voice sadder at once.

Rosalita was concerned about little Cleo, how was she doing?

Liz didn't like people who nicknamed without permission; she'd never let anyone call her Lizzy, except Sophie, sometimes. Not bad, she supposed, she told Rosalita; hard to tell, about the same really.

By the time she could put the phone down, her nipples were stiff with cold. She'd left lavender-scented footprints all the way down the stairs. When she got back to the bathroom, Sophie had let all the water out and was painting her nails purple. What did she mean, the cat was not bad? Sophie wanted to know. The cat was obviously not well.

Liz said she knew. But they could hardly take her for daily checkups at fifty dollars a go, and surely they could find a cheaper vet in the Yellow Pages.

No way, said Sophie, because Cleopatra had already begun a course of treatment with the clinic and they were being wonderful.

Liz thought it was all a bit suspect, these follow-up calls. The clinic stood to make a lot of money from exaggerating every little symptom, didn't they?

Sophie said one of the things she'd never found remotely attractive about Liz was her cynicism. She went down to make herself a cup of chamomile and didn't even offer to put on the milk for Liz's hot chocolate. When Liz came down, Sophie was curled up on the sofa with the cat on her lap, the two of them doing their telepathy thing.

Sophie was probably premenstrual, Liz thought, but she didn't like to say so, knowing what an irritating thing it was to be told, especially if you were.

She knew she was right about that the next day when Sophie came in from a pointless interview at a salon downtown and started vacuuming at once. In five years Liz had learned to leave Sophie to it, but Liz was only halfway down the front page of the paper when she heard her name being called, so loudly that she thought there must be an emergency.

Sophie, her foot on the vacuum's off switch, had dragged the velvet armchair out from the wall and was pointing. What did Liz call that? she wanted to know.

"Vomit, I guess," said Liz.

Why hadn't she said something?

"Because I didn't know about it," said Liz, feeling absurdly like a suspect. Yes, she'd been home all day, but she hadn't heard anything. A cat being sick was not that loud. Yes, she cared, of course she cared, what did Sophie mean didn't she care?

That night Sophie didn't come to bed at all. Liz sat up reading a home improvement magazine and fell asleep with the light on.

The next day Rosalita called at eight in the morning when Liz was opening a fresh batch of bills, before she'd had her coffee. Nerves jangling, Liz was very tempted to tell Rosalita to get lost. She wondered whether the clinic was planning to charge her for phone consultations. "Hang on," she said. "I'll be right back." She went into the kitchen to look at Cleopatra, who was lying on her side by the fridge like a beached whale and hadn't touched her water, even. Sophie was kneeling beside her on the cold tiles. Liz wanted to touch Sophie, but instead she stroked the cat, just how she usually liked it, one long combing from skull to hips, but there was no response.

Sophie went out to the phone and asked Rosalita for an appointment. "Please," Liz heard her say, her voice getting rather high, and then, after a minute, "Thanks, thank you, thanks a lot."

Liz took the afternoon off work and brought the car home by two, as promised.

That afternoon the two of them stood in the examining room at the clinic, staring at the neatly printed estimate. Rosalita had left them alone for a few minutes, to talk it all over, she had said with a sympathetic smile. The disinfected walls of the little white room seemed to close in around them. Cleopatra crouched between Sophie's arms. Liz was reading the list for the third time as if it were a difficult poem.

After a minute she said, "I still don't really get it."

Sophie, staring into the green ovals of Cleopatra's eyes, said nothing.

"I know she's sick. But surely she can't be as sick as all that," Liz went on. "Like, she still purrs."

Sophie scratched behind the cat's right ear. Cleopatra shook her head vehemently, then subsided again.

"It's not that I'm not worried." Liz's voice sounded stiff and theatrical in the tiny room. She went on, a little lower, "But eleven hundred dollars?"

It sounded even worse out loud.

"That's an extraordinary amount of money," said Liz, "and number one we haven't got it—"

At last Sophie's head turned. "I can't believe we're even having this discussion," she said in a whisper.

"We're not having it," said Liz heavily. "It's not a discussion till you say something."

"Look at her," pleaded Sophie. "Look at her eyes." There was a tiny crust of mucus at the corner of each. "They've never been dull before, like the light's been switched off."

"I know, sweetheart," said Liz. She stared at the crisp print to remember her arguments. "But eleven hundred dollars—"

"She's our cat," Sophie cut in. "This is Cleopatra we're talking about."

"But we don't even know for sure if there's anything serious wrong with her."

"Exactly," said Sophie. "We don't know. We haven't a clue. That's why I can't sleep at night. That's why we're going to pay them to test her for kidney stones and leukemia and FOP disease and anything else it could possibly be."

"FIP," Liz read off the page. "FIP disease. And it's a vaccine, not a test."

"Whatever," growled Sophie. "Don't pretend to be an expert; all you're looking at is the figures."

"Hang on, hang on," said Liz, louder than she meant to. "Let's look at it item by item. Hospitalization, intravenous catheter insertion . . . Jesus, sixty dollars to put a tube up her ass, that can't be more than thirty seconds' work. IV fluids, OK, fair enough. X-rays . . . why does she need three X-rays? She's less than two feet long."

Sophie was chewing her lipstick off. "I can't believe you're mean enough to haggle at a time like this."

"How can you call me mean?" protested Liz. "I just get the feeling we're being ripped off. This is emotional blackmail; they think we can't say no."

There was a dull silence. She tried to hear other voices from other rooms and wondered if Rosalita was standing outside the door, listening.

"Look," she went on more calmly, "if we left out these optional blood tests we could trim off maybe three hundred dollars. What the hell is feline AIDS anyway? Cleopatra's a virgin."

"I don't know what it is, but what if she has it?" asked Sophie. "What if two months down the road she's dying of it and you were too damn callous to pay for a test?"

"It's probably just crystals in her bladder," said Liz weakly. "The doctor said so, didn't he?"

Sophie curled over Cleopatra, whose eyes were half shut as if she was dreaming. Liz stared around her at the cartoon cats on the walls, with their pert ears and manic grins.

After a few minutes silence, she thought they'd probably got past the worst point of the row. Now if she could only think of something soothing to say, they'd be onto the homestretch.

But Sophie stood up straight and folded her arms. "So what is she worth then?"

"Sorry?"

"A hundred dollars? Two hundred?"

Liz sighed. "You know I'm mad about her."

"Yeah?"

"I can't put a figure to it."

"Really?" spat Sophie. "But it's definitely under eleven hundred, though; we know that much."

"We don't have eleven hundred dollars," said Liz, word by word.

"We could get it."

Liz was finding it hard to breathe. "You know I can't take out another loan, not so soon after the car."

"Then I'll sell my grandmother's fucking rings," said Sophie, slamming her hand on the counter with a metallic crack. "Or would it make your life simpler if we just had her put down here and now?"

"Give me the damn form," said Liz, pulling the estimate towards her and digging in her pocket for her pen.

Sophie watched without a word as Liz signed, her hands shaking.

Dr. McGraw carried Cleopatra away to the cages. The cat watched them over his shoulder, unforgivingly.

Out in the car, Sophie sat with the empty basket on her lap. Liz couldn't tell if she was crying without looking at her directly, but she had a feeling she was. Liz thought of their early days when they went to the cinema a lot and Liz always knew just when Sophie needed her to reach over and take her hand.

She drove home, taking corners carefully.

"I'm just curious," said Sophie at a traffic light. "What would you pay for me?"

"*What?*" Liz's voice came out like a squeal of brakes.

"If I was rushed into the emergency room and a doctor handed you an estimate. What would I be worth to you?"

Liz told her to shut the fuck up.

Rosalita rang the same evening, her voice bright. Crystals in the bladder, that's all it was. Little Cleo was doing fine, had taken well to the new diet, and they could pick her up the next morning. That would be just ninety-eight dollars.

So the cat came home, and for a while everything seemed like it ever was.

And when six months later Sophie left Liz for a beautician she met at the cosmetic academy and moved into the beautician's condo in a building with a strict no-pets policy, Liz used to hold on to Cleopatra at night, hold her so tight that the cat squirmed, and think about the cost of things.

Pluck

On rare occasions, over the years that followed, if he was having a few pints with a mate, Joseph thought of asking, *Would you break up with your girlfriend over a hair on her chin? Don't laugh,* he'd add, *it's not funny.*

But the question sounded impossible when he put it in words, so he never did ask it.

It was most unlike him, the whole thing. He'd always been glad Róisín didn't cover her fuzzy peach face with layers of foundation. He relished her bushy black eyebrows that almost met, like Frida Kahlo's. *Perfection Incarnate,* that was one of his names for her. They were in agreement that Róisín was not only the brains of the relationship but the beauty as well. Joseph was the pancreas, maybe, or the kneecap.

For seven years they'd lived in a skinny terraced house and had no problems. None that Joseph knew of, anyway. Then after a while they hadn't the time for problems, because they had Liam instead. Liam was never a problem; he was the opposite of all problems. So when Joseph was made redundant from a telesales job he'd hated anyway, they decided it was perfect timing: he'd stay home and mind the boy.

One Sunday, Liam was up till two with a tickly cough, so the next morning there wasn't a peep out of him. Joseph lay among the pillows, relishing the lie-in. He scratched his stubble and watched Róisín run in and out, power-dressing. Tights half up, she dipped into the wardrobe for a pair of heels and stubbed her forehead on the hinge. Then she stumbled over to the bedside table to scoop up her watch and earrings. Joseph leaned out far enough to hold her legs in a rugby tackle.

Róisín told him to get lost, but not as if she meant it.

"Stay home today," he offered, "and I'll kiss every inch of your body." He used to say that a lot in the old days, when they were students and every day was twice as long. She stooped down to kiss him now and he arched up like a turtle to meet her mouth.

It was then he noticed it. One dark bristle, just under her chin, a quarter of an inch long.

He must have let go of her legs, because she said, "What?"

Joseph shook his head as if he didn't know what she meant.

"You were looking funny."

He lay back against the pillows and denied it with a laugh.

"Dadda!" In the next room Liam sent up his wail. Róisín made a lunge for her briefcase, and Joseph struggled out of the sheets.

It wasn't like Joseph went round thinking about it all day every day after that; he wasn't some kind of Neanderthal, like his father. He'd been born in 1970, for god's sake. He could ask for Tampax Super Plus in the chemist without lowering his voice more than a notch. He'd never wanted Róisín to be some air-brushed pinup or Stepford Wife. He'd always liked the dark fuzz on her thighs, her crazy-paving bikini line, the scattered hairs that danced their way to her navel. He had a habit of burying his face in the spiral curls under her arms. So why would it bother him, one little hair on her chin?

But somehow he couldn't shed the childhood image of an old great-aunt with a full set of quivering whiskers, and how once when she'd tried to kiss him he'd run away screaming. And every night now when he read fairy tales to Liam, the book seemed to fall open to the same picture of a toothless, mole-studded, hairy-faced witch.

Joseph was aware he was overreacting; he knew he'd have to snap out of it soon. It wasn't that he brooded, exactly, only that being home all day left a lot of little chinks of time free for thinking.

One evening he was waiting up for Róisín and couldn't find the remote, so he flicked through a magazine she'd left on the coffee table. FREE YOURSELF FROM FACIAL HAIR FOREVER, a headline ordered. His eyes scuttled over the diagrams. The follicles looked like blueprints of mining shafts.

When he heard Róisín's key in the lock, Joseph stuffed the magazine down the side of the sofa.

She was still peeling off her coat in the hall when he rushed out and hugged her. Under cover of a kiss, he stroked her chin. But he couldn't feel a thing.

The next morning the demented chirp of the alarm clock woke Joseph first. Róisín's face was half immersed in the pillow. He bent over, very carefully, to see if the hair had grown at all. Was there really only one? How many could sprout below the line of her jaw before she'd notice?

Her eyes were very blue. He jerked back. She grinned up at him confusedly.

It wasn't a turnoff; it wasn't as simple as that. It was more that Joseph would be sitting beside Róisín on a park bench as she played clap-handies with Liam, say, and suddenly she'd turn her head a fraction and he'd see it. It interrupted the smooth curve of her chin. And a little frisson would go through him, like lust but not quite.

It had become a sort of tic, this habit of peering at his girl-friend's chin. The little hair there wasn't sharp like the ones that pushed out of his own skin overnight. It was so soft he could barely feel it when he found a pretext to stroke her face. It was just a wisp, really. There was no harm in it. So why did he long to take it between his nails and yank it out?

It was like an itch in his fingers, too deep to scratch. It disgusted him.

Another man might have simply asked her to pluck it.

But Joseph couldn't imagine saying those words. Not to Róisín. This sort of thing was a delicate matter; you didn't just tell a woman she was growing a beard. They were sensitive about these things. It would be best if it came up naturally in the course of conversation, but if he tried to lead their dinnertime conversation gradually round to female facial hair he knew he'd make a hash of it. She might be cross that he thought it was any of his business to tell her which bits of her body were acceptable. Or worse, she might be hurt; she might think he didn't fancy her anymore, now she wasn't twenty-one, now she had stretch marks and other proofs of a body that had been lived in.

Not that he was God's Gift to Womanhood himself. He never had been. Joseph stood at the bathroom mirror, these mornings, and stared at the hair matted on his brush. Had he always shed that much? His hairline seemed to be in the same place it had always been, but maybe the change was so infinitesimal he wouldn't notice until the day he woke up bald. He tried to laugh at that thought, but only managed the half grin of a stroke victim. He ran his fingers across his head, and another hair came away, wrapped round his thumb.

Maybe there were only a given number of hairs in the world, and they had to be shared out.

Surely Róisín would laugh if she knew what was scurrying through his mind, these days. It could become one of her running gags. "Be careful of Bearded Ladies, Jo-Jo," she might say. "They have a habit of running away with the circus."

The real question wasn't whether she would be hurt if he asked her to pluck it, Joseph realized. The real question was, What if she said no?

In the library he left Liam slamming Barbie and Ken's heads together and ducked round the corner. He thought it might take some research, but the first encyclopaedia told him all he needed, and more than he wanted to know.

It turned out that a hair was a filament or filamentous outgrowth that grew from the integument of an animal or insect. Joseph had never known he had an integument. He also learned that although in many cultures beards were a symbol of the dignity of manhood, there was nothing intrinsically masculine about facial hair at all. Native American and Chinese men didn't tend to develop much hair on their faces; Mediterranean women did. Even in the British Isles, the incidence of facial hair among women was much higher than was commonly supposed.

Joseph felt slightly breathless, at this point. He had been tricked. To think of all those hairy-chinned women out there on the streets, plucked and waxed and powdered down, going about their business with nobody knowing a thing . . .

He read on distractedly. Both men and women of high birth in ancient Egypt wore metal ceremonial hairpieces on their chins. Then there was Saint Uncumber, who prayed to God to deliver her from men and was delighted when he gave her a beard.

Joseph let the encyclopaedia sag shut. He edged round the

corner to Self-Help, where he found a book called *Women Are Cats, Men Are Dogs: Making Your Relationship Work.* He had to skim through Sexual Positions, Money Worries and In-law Trouble before he found the right section.

> *Instead of commenting negatively on her appearance, say "Honey, I'd like to treat you to a top-to-toe makeover. You deserve the best."*

Joseph tried out that line, under his breath, but it sounded like bad karaoke.

Down on his knees on the cork tiles, a few hours later, he tried to unclog the bath; the plunger made a violent gulp. He finally had to use his fingers in a tug-of-war with the long clot of soap and hair; more and more of it unreeled as if it grew down there. From the colour it looked more like his than hers. Queasy, he flicked it into the bin.

He was tidying up the living room after lunch when he noticed that Róisín's magazine was on the coffee table again. She must have found it stuffed down the side of the sofa cushion. She must have wondered. Joseph stared at the crumpled cover, wondering what exactly she'd have wondered. SIZZLING SUMMER SANDALS. PEACE OF MIND IN JUST TEN DAYS. HOW TO TELL IF HE'S CHEATING.

These days he was trying to ensure that sex wouldn't happen. Not that he didn't feel like it. But he knew that sex brought his guard down, and he was afraid that it would ruin some intimate moment if Róisín caught him staring fixedly at her chin.

He was just playing for time. He knew he had to tell her, whether it sounded reasonable or not. He had to say something at least, make a joke of it instead of a sore point. Otherwise he was going to lose his tiny mind.

They used to be able to tell each other anything, the two of them. That's what they'd boasted, in the early days. Everyone went round saying things like that at college. *Tell me. Honestly. I really want to know.*

Later that afternoon Joseph had a better idea. He ran upstairs to the bathroom and ransacked the cupboard like a burglar. He rooted through all Róisín's paraphernalia: eyelash crimpers, toenail sponges, an old diaphragm. Finally he recognized the tweezers. He was holding it up to the light to check its grip when he sensed he was being watched. He turned. Róisín in her stocking feet, arms piled high with files, staring.

"You're home early! Sorry about the mess," he said as if it was a joke.

"What are you doing with my tweezers?" she asked.

"Got a splinter, down the playground," Joseph improvised.

Róisín took hold of his hand and tugged him towards the window. She peered at the map of lines: head, heart, fate. "I don't see anything."

"It's tiny," said Joseph, "but it's driving me mad."

That evening he was watching some stupid quiz when Róisín came in and sat on the arm of the sofa. "You're in a funny mood these days," she said, so softly that he thought at first she was commenting on the program.

"Am I?" Joseph assured her he didn't know why he seemed that way. No, he didn't miss his old job; what was there to miss? No, Liam wasn't getting on his nerves, no more than usual. It was nothing.

At which point Róisín reached for the remote and muted the TV.

Joseph stared at the flickering images. He wasn't ready to look at her yet. He was choosing his words. "It's nothing that *matters*," he said at last, too cheerfully. "It's—"

"It's me," interrupted Róisín, "isn't it?"

And he turned to look at her then, because her voice was stripped down like a wire. Naked. The skin below her eyes was the blue of a bird's egg.

Joseph gathered her into his arms and lied with his whole heart. "Of course it's not you. Why would it be you? You're grand. You're Perfection Incarnate," he added, pressing his lips to her neck, trying to shut himself up.

She twisted her head. "But are you—"

"I'm just tired, love," he interrupted, so she couldn't finish the question. "I'm just a bit tired these days." He faked an enormous, apelike yawn.

It was two in the morning before he could be sure she was in deep sleep. He opened his eyes and sat up, feeling under the pillow for the pen torch and the tweezers.

Hovering over Róisín, he aimed the tiny light at her chin. His thumb pressed hard on the ridged plastic of the switch. Arms shaking, he caught the little hair in his narrow beam. With the other hand he reached out to close the tweezers on it. Please god he wouldn't stab her in the chin.

Just then Róisín stirred and rolled towards him, onto her face. Joseph lurched back and snapped off the torch. He shoved everything under his pillow and lay down flat. His heart was hammering like police at the door.

He lay quite still for a long time. Veils of darkness hung all round him. He was sinking.

Then Róisín spoke. "Can you not sleep?"

Joseph didn't answer.

In the morning he lay hollow-eyed, watching Róisín put on her lipstick in the bedroom mirror. She grabbed her bag and came over to give him a kiss.

She turned to open the door. He hauled himself upright and put on a casual voice. "Hey. You know that tiny wee hair under your chin?"

He waited for the world to crack apart.

"Which?" Róisín doubled back to the mirror without breaking stride. She stuck her jaw out and threw back her head. "Got it," she said in a slightly strangled voice. Her finger and thumb closed together and she made a tiny, precise movement. Like a conductor might, to finish a symphony.

She brushed her fingers together and gave Joseph a little wave on her way out.

STRANGERS

Good Deed

Sam had always thought of himself as a pretty decent guy, and who was to say he wasn't? While he was doing his MBA at the University of Toronto he'd been a volunteer on the Samaritans' phone line. These days he couldn't spare the time, but he made regular tax-free contributions to schemes for eradicating river blindness in sub-Saharan Africa and improving children's sports facilities in the Yukon. He always wore a condom (well, not always, just when he was having sex), and he never pushed past old ladies to get on a streetcar.

The day it happened, he was coming down with a head cold. Funny how such a petty thing could make such a difference. Not that it felt petty at the time; it was a January cold, one of those brutes that makes you screw up your eyes all week and cough wetly for the rest of the month. So Sam—sensibly enough—had left the office before rush hour in order to get home and take care of himself. He had his Windsmoor coat buttoned up to the throat as he hurried towards the subway station. His friends seemed to live in down jackets all winter, but Sam refused to abandon his

dress sense so he could look like a walking duvet. Today he did
keep his cashmere scarf looped over his nose and mouth, to take
the ice out of the air. With a hot whiskey and something mindless
like *Nip/Tuck* and an early night, he thought he could probably
head this cold off at the pass.

He walked right by the first time, like everyone else. It was a
common sight, these last few winters, street persons in sleeping
bags lying on the hot-air vents. The first time you saw it you
thought: *My god, there's a guy lying in the middle of the sidewalk,
and everyone's walking round him like he's invisible. How bizarre.
What a sign of the times.* But you got used to it—and, to be fair, it
was probably much warmer for the homeless, lying on the air
vents, than if they had to tuck themselves away against the wall of
a bank or a travel agency.

This particular guy near the intersection of Bloor and Bay
seemed pretty much like all his peers: a crumpled bundle with
eyes half closed and a not-entirely-unsatisfied expression. *Probably Native,* thought Sam, *but you should never assume.* It was
only when Sam had got as far as the crossing, blowing his nose on
his handkerchief with awkward leather-gloved hands, that his
brain registered what his eyes must have seen. Just as sometimes
by the time you ask someone to repeat themselves, you've realized
what they've said. Anyway, that's when Sam saw it in his mind's
eye, the little trickle of blood. He thought he must have imagined
it. *Classic white middle-class guilt hallucinations,* he said to himself. Then he thought: *So the guy's bleeding a little from the lip,
not necessarily a big deal, I sometimes chew my lips to shreds when
I'm working on a big presentation.*

The lights changed but something wouldn't let Sam cross. Instead, he clenched his jaw and waded back against the tide of commuters. He picked a place to stand, near enough to the street
person to get a good look at him, but not so near that anyone

would notice. Besides, if he stood too close, the guy might wake up and take offense and bite him or something. A significant percentage of them were mentally ill, Sam had read in the *Street Times,* and no wonder, considering. But there was no sign of this particular guy waking up anytime soon. The blood from his mouth had trickled all the way round and under his chin, now, like some kind of Frankenstein party makeup. He had a dirty white beard.

Sam had no idea what to do, and frankly, all he felt was irritation. Where were human feelings when you wanted them? The timing was so inappropriate. Why couldn't this have happened on another winter afternoon, when Sam wouldn't have had a cold and so would have been able to respond like the person he truly was?

His eyes were dripping; he thought they might freeze shut. He unfolded his handkerchief and mopped at his face. An unworthy thought occurred to him: *Why did I look round at all when I should have kept my head down and run for the subway?*

There was a foul reek of spirits coming off the guy when Sam bent nearer. It occurred to him to touch the guy, but he didn't know where. Or why, now Sam came to think of it. On a theoretical level, he knew that the rigours of life on the street would drive just about anyone to alcoholism, but he still couldn't help finding it gross.

"Excuse me?" he said, sniffing loudly so his nose wouldn't drip on the guy. "Sir?" How ludicrously genteel. "Mister? Are you OK?"

No answer. Sam's breath puffed out like white smoke. He made up a reply: *Sure I'm OK, mister; I love to spend my Friday nights lying on the sidewalk, bleeding from the mouth.*

Sam was crouched beside the guy now. Commuters kept streaming past; nothing interrupted the flow on Bloor and Bay.

They probably assumed Sam was some kind of weirdo friend of the guy on the ground, despite the Windsmoor coat—which was trailing in the gutter's mound of dirty old snow, he noticed, snatching up the hem. Now he wasn't upright and moving at speed, like the commuters, it was as if he'd left the world of the respectable and squatted in the mud. They'd probably think the coat was stolen. Damn them for a bunch of cold salaried bastards. It wouldn't occur to one of them to take the time to stop and—

And what, exactly? What was Sam going to do?

His nose was streaming now, and his legs were starting to freeze into place. He almost lost his balance as he rooted for his handkerchief. He ripped one leather glove off, reared up, and blew his nose. It made the sound of a lost elephant.

Quick, quick, think. What about first aid? Shit, he should have volunteered to go on that in-house course last year. Shreds of traditional advice swam giddily through Sam's mind. Hot sweet tea was his mother's remedy for everything, but it would be tough to come by; the nearest stall said ESPRESSO EXPRESS. Whiskey? Hardly the thing if the guy was full of alcohol already. Put his feet higher than his head? What the fuck was that about? Sam wondered.

The guy on the ground hadn't moved. The blood didn't seem to be flowing at speed, exactly. It hadn't dripped onto the pavement yet. In films, bleeding from the mouth always meant you were a goner; the trickle only took a few seconds to grow into a terrible red river.

Sam shifted from foot to foot to keep his circulation going, like a hesitant dancer at an eighties disco night. Maybe, it occurred to him with an enormous wave of relief, maybe the blood on this guy's face was an old mark he hadn't washed off. If you didn't have a mirror you probably wouldn't even know you had blood on your chin. Maybe a bit of bleeding was the natural result of drinking methanol or whatever the cocktail of choice was these days. Well, not choice; Sam didn't mean choice, exactly.

But the thing was, how could he be sure? How was a personnel officer with no medical experience to tell if there was something seriously wrong going on here? He shouldn't call 911 on a whim. If they sent an ambulance, it might be kept from some other part of the city where it was really needed. They got these false alarms all the time; hadn't he seen something on City TV about it? And the homeless guy probably wouldn't thank him for getting him dragged into the emergency room, either . . .

And then Sam looked at the guy on the ground, really looked for the first time; he felt a wave of nausea roll from the toes he could no longer feel, all the way to his tightening scalp. The man lay utterly still, not even shivering in the hard air that seemed liable to crystallize round them both any minute now. Sam was not repelled by the guy, exactly; what turned his stomach was the sudden thought that he himself, by some terrible knot of circumstances such as came down on successful people all the time, might someday end up lying on an air vent with people stepping round him and an overeducated ignorant prick in a Windsmoor coat standing round inventing excuses for not making the call that could save his life.

Sam reached for his cell phone, but the pocket of his coat was empty. At first he couldn't believe it; thought he'd been robbed. Then he remembered laying it down beside his computer after lunch. Today of all days! His head was made of mucus.

He dialed 911 from the phone box at the corner. He was afraid they wouldn't believe that it was an emergency—that they would hang up on him—so he sounded inappropriately angry, even when he was giving the address. "The guy looks seriously ill," he barked.

It hadn't occurred to Sam to wonder what he would do once he had made the call. He hovered outside the phone box, as if waiting for another turn. In a sense, there was nothing else to do now; the proper authorities had been called in, and Sam was just a passerby again, with every right to head home to his condo and nurse his cold. But in another sense, he thought with self-righteous gloom, he was the only connection. What if the ambulance never turned up? What if the medics couldn't see the guy on the ground because the human traffic was too thick?

A sneeze shook him like a blow from a stranger. With grudging steps he walked back to the guy on the ground, who hadn't stirred. It occurred to Sam for the first time that the guy might be dead. How odd that would be, for such a dramatic thing not to show on a human face, except by this discreet ribbon of blood and a certain blueness about the lips. He thought maybe he should see if there was any sign of life in the guy, but he couldn't decide which bit of dirty raincoat to lay his hand on. If he wasn't dead, Sam should keep him warm; yes, that was definitely to be recommended. Sam stared around to see if there was a department store on the block. He could buy a blanket, or one of those rugged tartan picnic rugs. He would be willing to pay up to, say, $100, considering the seriousness of the occasion; $125, maybe, if that was what it took. But the only stores in view sold lingerie, shoes, and smoked meats. He blew his nose again.

Take off your coat, Sam told himself grimly. He did it, wincing as the cold air slid into his armpits. He was wearing a wool-blend suit, but it wasn't enough. This was probably a crazy idea, considering his own state of health.

He laid the Windsmoor over the man; it was stagy, like a gesture from some Shakespearean drama. No response yet. What if the warmth made the guy wake up, and Sam had to make conversation? No sign of life, nor death, either. The coat lay too far up the guy's body, so it almost covered his head; it looked like the scene after a murder, Sam thought with a horrified inner giggle. He stooped again, took the coat by its deep hem and dragged it delicately backwards until it revealed the dirty white beard. Sam's keys slid out of a pocket and caught in a grating; he swooped to retrieve them. Jesus, imagine if he'd lost his keys on top of everything! Then he remembered his wallet and had to walk around the guy to reach the other pocket. Passersby might think he was picking the pockets of a dead man, like a scavenger on a battlefield.

He let out a spluttering cough. He could just feel his immune system failing. This cold would probably turn into something serious, like post-viral fatigue or something. He should sit down and try some deep breathing. But where? The heating vent in front of him would be the warmest, but it would look so weird, a guy in an $800 suit squatting on the sidewalk beside a bum. But then, who did he think would be looking at him? he asked himself in miserable exasperation. And why should he care?

Sam let himself down on the curb at last. It was so cold on his buttocks, through the thin wool, it felt like he had wet himself. He stood up and kept moving, jigging on the spot. He couldn't remember the last time he'd been out in January without a winter coat. Like one of those squeegee punks who lived in layers of ragged sweaters. Was that snow, that speck in his eye, or just a cold speck of dust? He rubbed his leather-gloved hands against his cheeks. His sinuses were beginning to pulse.

Twice he heard a siren and began preparing his story—which in his head sounded like a lie—and twice it turned out to be police, zooming by. After a quarter of an hour he no longer believed in the ambulance. His shoulders were going into tremors. For a moment he envied the guy on the vent, who looked almost cozy under the Windsmoor coat. He considered borrowing it back for a few minutes, just to get his core temperature up, but he was afraid of how it would look to passersby and afraid to touch the guy again, besides. *The bum probably brought this on himself,* he thought very fast. *What goes around comes around. These people get what they deserve.*

Sam knew this was madness; he must be running a fever. He blew his nose again, though his handkerchief was a wet rag.

He felt a moment of pure temptation, melting sugar in his veins. All he had to do was pick up his coat, shake it off, put it on, and walk away.

He very nearly cried.

Thirty-two minutes by his Rolex by the time the ambulance showed up. He wanted to be gruff with the paramedics, but his voice came out craven with gratitude, especially when they said no, the guy wasn't dead. He begged them to let him climb into the ambulance after the stretcher. They seemed to think this was a sign of his concern and reluctantly agreed, but the truth of the matter was that Sam was too cold to walk. He would have got into any heated vehicle, even with a psychopathic truck driver. Also there was the matter of his coat.

At the hospital the staff didn't tell him anything. The doors of the ward flapped shut. The last thing Sam saw was his coat, draped over the end of the trolley. It occurred to him to ask for it back, but he couldn't think how to phrase it.

It turned out they really did call people John Doe, like in the movies. The forms were mostly blank, even after Sam and the receptionist had done their best. Sam was staggered by all the things he didn't know about the guy and couldn't begin to guess: *age, nationality, allergies.* He left his own name and address, as well as a little note about his coat, and set off walking to the subway. He was streaming from the eyes, the nose, the mouth, even. The dark night wrapped round him.

He knew he should feel better now. He had been a civic-minded citizen; committed what his Scout Leader had called a Good Deed for the Day; displayed what editorials termed "core Canadian values." So why did he feel like shit?

"Bad day?" asked the owner of the corner shop as he sold Sam a carton of eggnog.

Was it written that plain on his face? Sam nodded without a word. Only halfway down the street did it occur to him that, compared with nearly dying on the pavement, his day had been almost a pleasant one.

Sam waited till Monday before calling the hospital. He went down into the park to call, so no one from the office would get curious about his query. No, said the receptionist—a different one—she was not authorized to report on the condition of a patient except to a party named as the next of kin. Sam explained over and over again about John Doe not having any known kin. "I'm as near to kin as anyone else. You see, I'm . . ." But what was he? "I called about him, originally. I called 911," said Sam in a voice that sounded both boastful and ashamed.

The receptionist finally figured out which particular John Doe they were talking about. She relented enough to say that the patient had discharged himself that morning.

"What does that mean?"

"I'm not at liberty to say, sir."

Sam let the phone drop back into place. Guilt, again, that twinge like whenever he went on the leg-curl machine at the gym. He should have visited the hospital yesterday. What would he have brought, though? Roses? Grapes? A bottle of methanol? And what would he have said? *Here I am, your saviour?*

Maybe in the back of his mind Sam had been thinking it would be like in the movies. An unexpected, heartwarming friendship of opposites; he would teach the street person to read, and in return would learn the wisdom of life in the rough. Who did he think he was kidding?

Sam went back to work with a poppy-seed bagel.

He got over his cold. He took up racquetball. He gave up on ever seeing his coat again, though he did keep one eye out for it on the various homeless guys downtown.

One evening, while watching the news, Sam dimly remembered something from Sunday School about having two coats and giving away one. On a whim, he got up and opened his closet. Twenty-six coats and jackets. He counted them twice and he still couldn't believe it. He thought of giving away twenty-five of them. A dramatic gesture; faintly ludicrous, in fact. Which one would he keep, a coat to clothe and protect him in all seasons? Which one outer garment would say everything that had to be said about him? Which was the real Sam?

He shut the closet.

Always after that he thought of the whole thing as the Coat Episode—as if it had happened on *Seinfeld.* It was like touching a little sore that wouldn't heal up, every time he remembered it. What good had he done? There was no such thing as saving someone's life. You couldn't make it easy for them to live or worth their effort. At most what you did was lengthen it by a day or a year, and hand it back to them to do the living.

At dinner parties, Sam liked to turn the petty happenings of his working day into funny stories. But never this one. Several times he found himself on the point of telling it—when the harshness of the winter came up as a topic, or provincial policy on housing—but he could never decide on the tone. He dreaded sounding pleased with himself, but he didn't want to beat his breast and have his friends console him, either.

What he would really have liked to tell them was his discovery: that it was all a matter of timing. If he'd been in the full of his health, that day, he was sure he'd have risen grandly to the occasion. His courage would have been instant; his gestures, generous and unselfconscious. Then again, if he'd felt a fraction worse—if he'd discovered that he'd lost his handkerchief, say—he knew he'd have scurried on by. What Sam used to think of as his conscience—something solid, a clean pebble in his heart—turned out to depend entirely on the state of his nose.

Five weeks later the hospital sent his Windsmoor coat back in a plastic bag. It smelt harsh, as if it had been bleached. Sam hung it in his closet, but whenever it occurred to him to wear it that winter, his hand skidded on by.

Finally he gave it to the Goodwill and bought a down jacket, like everybody else he knew.

The Sanctuary of Hands

After a messy ending, the thing to do is to get away. Put several hundred miles between yourself and the scene of the crime. Whether you call yourself victim or villain, the cure's the same: get on a plane.

I flew from Cork to Toulouse and rented an emerald green sports car that cost three times as much as I would have been willing to pay under normal circumstances. I knew that if I sat in some four-door hatchback, my self-pitying panic would well up like heartburn. The thing to do was to pretend I was in a film. French, for preference. I drove out of Toulouse like Catherine Deneuve. I wore very dark shades, a big hat, and an Isadora Duncan gauzy scarf, long enough to strangle me.

My plan was simple. I would spend fourteen days driving through the Pyrenees fast enough to drown out every sound and every thought, and if despite my best efforts there were any tears, the sun and the wind would wipe them off my face. In the afternoons I would find somewhere green and shady to read—at Heathrow Airport I'd picked up a silly novel about Mary Queen of Scots—and then in the evenings I'd round off my four-course table d'hôte with a large cognac and a sleeping pill. I didn't intend to talk to anyone during the next fortnight, so my schoolgirl French wouldn't have to stretch to more than the occasional *merci*.

On the seventh day, driving between one craggy orange hill and another, it came to me that I hadn't touched another human being for a week. I supposed my elbow in its linen sleeve must have brushed past someone else's in one of those painfully narrow hotel corridors, but no skin was involved. And, not knowing anyone, I was exempt from all the kiss-kissing the locals did. I looked down now at my hands on the steering wheel; they were clean and papery.

When I stopped for lunch, I remembered I'd finished my book the night before and left it by the bed. Over my espresso I could feel boredom beginning to nibble. No, not boredom: *ennui*, that was the word, it came back to me now. Much more film-starrish. Ennui was about sunshine like white metal and a huge black straw hat and simply forgetting the name of anyone who'd ever hurt you and anyone you'd ever hurt.

The next sign said CAVERNES TROGLODYTIQUES, over a shaky line drawing of a bear, so that's where I turned off the road. To be honest, I wasn't quite sure what trogloditic caverns were, but they sounded as if they might be cool, or cooler than the road, at least.

But after standing around at the mouth of the cave for a quarter of an hour with a knot of brown-legged Swedes and Canadians, I was just about ready to go back to the car. Then the old woman in the jacket that said GUIDE finally clambered up the rocks towards us, and behind her, a straggling crocodile of what I thought at first were children. None of them seemed more than five feet tall, and they wore little backpacks too high up, like humps. When I saw that they were adults—What's the phrase these days? *People with special needs?*—I looked away, of course, so that none of them would see me staring. That was what my mother always said: *Don't stare!,* hissed like a puncture.

Three or four of the Specials, as I thought of them, had smiles that were too wide. One of them peered into my face as if he knew me. They kept patting and hugging each other, and two men at the back of the group—quite old, with Down syndrome, I thought, hard to tell how old but definitely not young—were holding hands like kindergarten kids. I looked for the leader of the group—a teacher or nurse or whatever, someone who would be giving them their own little tour of the prehistoric caves—but then I realized that we were all going in together.

At which point I thought, *Fuck it, I don't need this.*

But we were shuffling through the cave mouth already, and to get out I would have had to shove my way back through the Specials, and what if I knocked one of them over? There was one girl, a bit taller than the rest, with a sort of helmet held on with a padded strap across her chin, as if she were going into outer space. Fits, I thought. We're about to descend into a trogloditic cavern with someone who's liable to fits. There was a balding man behind her in an old-fashioned grey suit. He seemed so pale, precarious, with his eyes half shut. I wondered if the same thing that had damaged their brains had stunted their growth, or maybe they hadn't been given enough to eat when they were children. You heard terrible stories.

As we left the sunlight behind us, I realized that my clothes were completely unsuitable for descending into the bowels of the earth. My sandals skidded on the gritty rock; my long silk sundress caught on rough patches of the cave wall, and what the hell had I brought my handbag for? The air was damp, and there were little puddles in depressions on the floor. Beside the little lamps strung up on wires, the stone glowed orange and red.

The guide's accent was so different from that of the nun who taught us French at school that I had to guess at every other word she spoke. She aimed her torch into a high corner of the cave now and pointed out a stalactite and a stalagmite that had been inching towards each other for what I thought I heard her say was eight thousand years. That couldn't be right, surely? In another twelve thousand, she claimed, they would finally touch. And then she launched into a laughably simplistic theory of evolution, for the benefit of the Specials, I supposed. Her words boomed in the cavern, and whenever she stopped to point something out, we all had to freeze and shuffle backwards so as not to collide. I couldn't remember the last time I'd been at such close quarters with a herd of strangers. There was perfume eddying round, far too sweet, and I'd have laid a bet it came from that girl behind me with the Texan accent.

Basically, the guide's story was that we used to be monkeys— *"Non! Non!"* protested one or two of the more vocal Specials, and *"Si, si!"* the guide cried. We used to be monkeys, she swore— speak for yourself, I wanted to tell her—but then one day we stood up and we wanted to use tools so what did we have to grow?

I peered at her blankly in the half-light. What did we have to *grow?*

"Les mains!" she cried, holding up her splayed right hand, and three or four of the Specials held theirs up, too, as if to play Simon Says, or to prove their membership of the species. The guide went on to explain—I could follow her better now that I was getting used to her accent—that everything depended on growing real hands, not paws; hands with thumbs opposite the fingers, for grip. She moved her wrinkled fingers like a spider, and one of the Specials wiggled his right back at her. They seemed irrationally excited to be here, I thought; maybe even a big damp cave was a thrill compared to their usual day.

I shivered where I stood and tucked my hands under my arms to warm them. It occurred to me that it must have been a sad day, that first standing up. I imagined hauling myself to my feet for the first time ever, naked apart from the fur. No more bounding through the jungle; now I'd have to stagger along on two thin legs. All at once my head would feel too heavy to lift, and the whole world would look smaller, shrunken.

One of the Specials giggled like a mynah bird, too close to my ear. I edged away from her, but not so fast that anyone would notice. They didn't know the rules, it occurred to me: how much space to leave between your body and a stranger's, how to keep your voice down and avoid people's eyes. They didn't seem to know about embarrassment.

The guide wasn't at all discomfited, either, not even when the Specials let out echoing whoops or hung off her hands. Now she was saying that the cave dwellers only lived half as long as people do nowadays and had much smaller brains than we do. I stared up at the dripping ceiling so as not to look at any of the Specials. Were they included in her *we*? Then the guide asked why we thought people had lived in these freezing old caves. After a few seconds she answered herself, in the gushing way teachers do: Because it was worse outside! Imagine thousands of years of winter, up there, she said, pointing through the rock; picture the endless snow, ice, leopards, bears . . .

I could feel the cold of the gritty floor coming up through my sandals. I tried to conjure up a time when this would have counted as warm. Jesus! Why they all hadn't cut their throats with the nearest flint scraper, I couldn't imagine. Funny thing, suicide; how rarely people got around to it. We seemed to be born with this urge to cling on. Like last Christmas when I gave my brother's newborn my little finger and she gripped it as if she were drowning.

The guide was leading us down a steep slope now, and the Specials swarmed around her. Except for the pale man with the half-shut eyes, who hung back, then suddenly stopped in his tracks so I bumped into him from behind. I backed off, but he didn't move on. I tried to think what to say that would be politer than *"Allez, allez!"* The guide looked over her shoulder and called out a phrase I didn't understand, something cheerful. But the man in front of me was shaking, I could see that now. His head was bent as if to ward off a blow. It was a big balding head, but not unnaturally big. I might have taken him for a civil servant, if I'd passed him in the street, or maybe a librarian. *"Peur,"* he said faintly, distinctly. *"J'ai peur."* He was afraid. What was he afraid of?

The guide shouted something. My ears were ringing. I finally understood that she was suggesting mademoiselle might be kind enough to hold—what was his name?—Jean-Luc's hand, just for the steep bit. I looked around to see whom she could mean. Then I felt the blush start on my neck. I was the only mademoiselle in sight, kind or otherwise—the Texans having dropped back to photograph a stalactite—so I held out my hand, a little gingerly, like a birthday present that might not be welcome. I thought of taking him by the sleeve of his jacket, the man she'd called Jean-Luc. But he looked down at my hand, rather than me, and slipped his palm into mine as if he'd known me all our lives.

To be honest, I'd been afraid his fingers might be clammy, like pickled cucumbers, but they were hot and dry. We walked on, very slowly; Jean-Luc took tiny, timid steps, and I had to hunch towards him to keep our hands at the same level. All I could think was, *Thank god it's dark in here.*

In hopes of distracting myself, I was trying to remember the last time I'd held hands with a stranger. A *céilí,* that was it, with my sister's boyfriend's cousin, and our palms were so hot with sweat we kept losing our grip in the twirls and apologizing over and over. I remember thinking at the time that hands were far too private to exchange with strangers. Those Victorians knew what they were doing when they kept their gloves on.

The Texan family was coming up behind now, their shadows huge as beasts on the cave wall. I could hear the girl giggle and mutter to her parents. My cheeks scalded with a sort of shame. I knew we probably looked like something out of Dickens, me with my big hat and Jean-Luc with his shiny head no higher than my shoulder: a monstrously mismatched bride and groom. Though really, why I should have cared what some small-town strangers thought of me, I couldn't say. The Texans didn't even know my name, and I'd certainly never see them again once we got out of this foul cave. Funny to think I'd come on this holiday to distract myself from serious things like tragedy and betrayal, only to find myself sweating with mortification at the thought that a couple of strangers might be laughing at me.

On an impulse I stepped sideways, flattening myself against the cave wall, jerking Jean-Luc with me. His pale eyes looked a little startled, but he came obediently enough. When the Texans had almost reached us I said rather coldly, "Go ahead," and let them squeeze past.

That was better. Now there was no one behind us and we could go at our own pace. The passage was getting more precarious, twisting down into the hillside. The roof was low; once or twice it scraped against my absurd straw hat. I had to walk with a stoop, lifting my dress out of my way like some kind of princess. Jean-Luc was saying something, I realized, but so quietly I had to bend nearer to make out the words—nearer, but not too near, in case my face brushed his. My heart rattled like a pebble in a can. I hadn't counted on conversation. What if he was asking me something, and I didn't understand his accent, and he thought it was because I didn't want to speak to him?

"La belle mademoiselle," that was it. That's all it was. *"La belle mademoiselle m'a donné la main. Elle m'a donné la main."* He wasn't talking to me at all, he was reassuring himself, telling himself the story of the pretty lady who gave him her hand. He had an amazing voice, deep like an actor's. For a moment I was absurdly warmed by the fact that he thought I was *belle,* even if he couldn't have much basis for comparison.

The floor was slick, now, and the passage had narrowed so much I had to walk ahead of Jean-Luc, twisting my arm backwards and waiting for him to catch up with me every couple of steps. I could feel his hand twitch like a rope. He was starting to wheeze, casting anxious glances at the craggy walls closing in on us. The air was dank. I couldn't hear the guide anymore, the group had left us so far behind. Damn her to hell, I thought.

The man's breath was coming faster and harsher in his throat. Had he any idea why he was being dragged down into these prehistoric sewers? I wondered. I supposed I should tell him there was nothing to be afraid of. He had a little wart on the edge of one finger, I could feel it, or maybe it was a callus. I gave his hand a small and tentative squeeze. Jean-Luc squeezed back, harder, and didn't let go. I could feel the fine bones shifting under his skin. Well that was all I needed, for this poor bastard to have a heart attack and die on me, twenty thousand leagues below the earth! The thought almost made me laugh. I wished I knew how old he was. Baldness didn't mean anything; I knew a boy who started losing his hair at twenty-two. I cleared my throat now, trying to think of something comforting to say. Every word of French had deserted me. *"Faut pas . . . Faut pas avoir peur,"* I stuttered hoarsely at last, praying I had my verb ending right. How would it translate? One should not be afraid. It is a faux pas to have fear.

I thought Jean-Luc might not have heard me or taken it in; he still stared ahead fixedly, as if anticipating a cave bear or mammoth around every corner. His eyes were enormous; the occasional beam of light showed their whites. But as we ducked under an overhang, I heard it like a mantra, under his breath: *"Faut pas avoir peur. Mademoiselle dit, 'Faut pas avoir peur.'"*

I grinned, briefly, in the dark. He was doing all right. Mademoiselle had told him not to be afraid. We'd get out of here in one piece.

When we came to a set of deep steps spiraling down in to the rock, I went first, so that at least if he slipped I could break his fall. But Jean-Luc held on to my hand like a limpet, and I didn't want to scare him by tugging it away, so I held on with the tips of my fingers, our arms knotted awkwardly in the air, as if we were dancing a gavotte. His arm was weaving and shaking; it was like wrestling a snake. My silk hem got under my feet, then, and the pair of us nearly crashed down on one of those stubby little stalagmites. Now that would be funny, if we snapped off ten thousand years' worth of growth and got sued by the French state.

The steps began to twist the other way, and I found my arm bent up behind my back as if I was being led to my death. This was ludicrous; I was going to dislocate something. I stopped for a second and switched hands as fast as I could. Jean-Luc stared at me, but held on to the new hand. *"Pas de problème,"* I said foolishly. No problem. Could you say that in French or did it sound American?

We found our rhythm again, and I could hear Jean-Luc behind me, repeating, *"Pas de problème, pas de problème,"* in a ghost's whisper. Our joined hands were the only spot of heat in this whole desolate mountain.

At last the path leveled out and we found ourselves in a huge cavern where the rest of the group stood watching the guide point out painted animals with her torch. A few faces looked over at us. I relaxed my grip, but Jean-Luc held on tight. For a moment I felt irritated. He wasn't afraid of falling anymore; he was just taking advantage. And then I almost laughed at the thought of this peculiar gentleman taking advantage of me. I stood with his warm cushioned hand in mine, the pair of us gazing forward like a bashful couple at the altar. I was cold right through, now, and my nipples were standing up against the silk of my dress; I angled myself a little away from Jean-Luc so he wouldn't see.

I tried to pay attention to the guide. I peered up at the rock walls: orange, greenish grey, and a startling pink. There were scrawl marks that looked as if they'd been done with fingers on a thousand long nights. The paintings were of horses and lions and bears, or so the guide said, and the Specials were laughing and pointing as if they could make them out, but to be honest the rusty overlapping squiggles on the rock all looked alike to me. Whatever the cave dwellers' powers of endurance, it occurred to me, they hadn't been able to draw for shite.

The guide said something I didn't catch, and then let out a surprisingly young laugh and flicked off the light switch. Blackness came down on us like a falling tent. Some of the Specials shrieked with excitement, but Jean-Luc cleaved to my hand as if it were a life belt. I tried to squeeze back, even though he was hurting my fingers. My eyes strained to find any speck of light in the darkness. It suddenly struck me that this was entirely normal behaviour for a troglodytic cavern. When the cold and the dark and the weight of a mountain pressed down on you, what made more sense than to grab the nearest living hand and hold on as tight as you could?

When the lights came back on, I blinked, relieved. A fat boy with a baseball cap on sideways edged back to us, and tried to take hold of Jean-Luc's other hand, but Jean-Luc shook him off, almost viciously. I looked away and bit down on my smile.

What did we think they ate, the cave dwellers? the guide was asking. Most of the Specials grinned back at her as if it were a joke rather than a question. Did they go to a supermarket, she suggested, and buy veal? One or two nodded doubtfully. No, she told us, there were no supermarkets! This claim caused quite a stir among the Specials. Now the guide was shining her torch on a painted animal; I couldn't tell what it was. She announced with grim enthusiasm that the cave dwellers hunted animals with sticks and cooked them in the fire.

"*Non!*"

"*Non!*"

"*Tuer les animaux?*"

A shock wave ran through the group as she nodded to say that yes, they killed the animals. A tiny woman with a squeezed-up face sucked in air. "*Manger les animaux?*" Yes, indeed, they ate the animals. The Specials' reactions were so huge and incredulous that I began to suspect them of irony. Had no one ever told them what sausages were made of?

That's what the cave dwellers did, the guide insisted. And they caught fish, too, she told us, in nets made out of their own hair. And they turned animal skin into leather by soaking it in their own urine, then chewing it till it was soft. At least, I feared that was what she said; the cave was a confusion of voices, now, and all I could think about was how cold I was. I was starting to shake as if I had a palsy. People must always have been cold in those days, it occurred to me. Maybe they knew no different, so they didn't notice it. Or, more likely, maybe they couldn't think about anything else. The minute you woke up, you'd have to start working as if your life depended on it, because it did: build up the fire, eat, keep moving, pile on more clothes, keep eating, never let the fire go out, even in your sleep. They'd all have slept in one big heap, the guide was saying now, putting her head on the shoulder of the girl in the helmet and miming a state of blissful unconscious; if you slept alone, she said, you'd wake up dead. Jean-Luc, by my side, must have heard this, because he let out a single jolt of laughter. I turned my head to smile at him, but he was looking down at his shoes again.

I thought the tour had to be nearly over by now—all I could think of was getting back up into the sunlight—but the guide led us through a little passage so tight we had to go in single file. Jean-Luc and I stayed knotted together like a chain gang. At last the group emerged into a chamber, the smallest so far. The guide mentioned that the man who had discovered these caverns called this one the Sanctuary of Hands.

Then she lifted her torch, and all at once I could see them; they sprang out to meet the light. Handprints in red and black, dozens—no, hundreds of them—daubed on top of each other like graffiti, pressed onto the rock as high as someone on tiptoes could reach. This was how you signed your name, about twenty-seven thousand years ago, said the guide with a casual swing of her torch. The prints glowed in the wide beam as if they were still wet. They were mostly left hands, I saw now, and smallish; perhaps the prints of women or even children. I stepped up to one for a closer look and Jean-Luc crept along behind me.

The handprint nearest us only had three and a half fingers. I recoiled, and the guide must have noticed, because she swung her torch round to where we were standing. I backed out of the blinding light. Yes, she said, many of these hands appeared to be missing a piece or two. This was a great mystery still. Some archaeologists said the cave dwellers must have lost fingers in accidents or because of the cold, but others thought the people must have cut them off themselves. For a gift, she said, almost gaily, did we understand? To give something back to the gods. To say *merci,* thank you.

Jean-Luc stared at the print on the wall a few inches from his head. He let go of my hand, then, and laid his own against the rock, delicately fitting his short pale fingers to the blood-red marks. He turned his head and looked at me then, for the first time, and his mouth formed a half smile as if he were about to tell me a great secret. But *"Touche pas!"* called the guide sternly. *"Faut pas toucher,* Jean-Luc!" Touching was forbidden; I should have told him that. His hand contracted like a snail, and I took it into mine again. It was chilled by the rock.

We followed the group up a long widening tunnel that seemed to have been dug out in modern times, and soon I could smell fresh air. After some very steep steps, we were all panting audibly, even the backpackers, and Jean-Luc's hand was hot in my grip again. He and I were the last to emerge, wincing in the sunlight like aged prisoners set free. The hills were a jumble of rocks on every side, and the half-reaped valley slid away below us. The sun warmed my face, and the air tasted sweet as straw.

Every year for a week or two there would be a sort of summer, the guide was explaining; the snow might shrink away just enough to let the cave dwellers come out and sit on the ground.

And what became of them in the end? someone asked her. Well, she said with a little shrug, one year they must have come out and found the snow gone and the sun shining. Then they walked down into the valley and never came back.

On the way down to the car park, I began to wonder when Jean-Luc was going to let go of my hand. I didn't want to have to wriggle it out of his grasp, but I could see the group leader waiting for them by the little bus. I hoped Jean-Luc didn't think I was coming home with the Specials. All of a sudden I felt appallingly sad. I wished I knew what to say to him, in any language.

But at the edge of the car park he disengaged his sticky fingers from mine and turned to face me, very formally. *"Au revoir, mademoiselle,*" he said, which I supposed could be translated as "Until we meet again," and I smiled and nodded and took up his hand again for a second to shake good-bye. He was puzzled by this, I could tell, but he let me shake it, as if it were a rattle.

"*Au revoir,* Jean-Luc," I repeated, more often than I needed to, and waved until he'd disappeared into the bus. I did look for his profile in the window, but the glass was white in the glare of the sun.

WritOr

Appalled by his credit-card debts, the writer succumbed to a one-year writer-in-residence job at a small college in the mountains. Until he sold the Great Novel for a hefty enough sum to pay the rent on his apartment for a few years, pragmatism seemed to be called for. In the distant past, the writer had tried every joe-job he could think of; he'd picked grapefruit and filed insurance applications, fried pancakes and sold fitness equipment door-to-door. Since then, he'd supplemented his royalties by other means that he was even less proud of: he'd written inane articles for in-flight magazines and lived two years too long with a doctor because it was just so damn handy not to have to worry about the rent. This year, at least, he would be making his living in a job which was, if not literature itself, then at least not unconnected with it.

As jobs went, the writer thought this would probably turn out to be a rather pleasant one. Interesting, even, at the human level as well as the intellectual one. Packing his possessions into the locker room at the self-storage facility, the day before his departure, he

tried to visualize the office that awaited him at the college, perhaps
with a view of the bluish mountains. He imagined himself mentor-
ing a few bright young poets and diffident, late-blooming novelists
whose brief visits to his office—Mondays and Fridays only—
would leave him ample time to work on the Great Novel.

> *Dear Mr. Writer-in-Residence (I'm afraid I don't know your
> Name),*
>
> *I would greatly like to Introduce Myself. My name is
> Herb Leland and I call myself a WritOr that is not just
> someone who Happens to write but who am a Storyteller
> from the very Depths of my Be-ing. The Truth is that I must
> WRITE OR DIE so to me the word WritOr which came to
> me during one long Sleepless Night eighteen months ago
> expresses this fully. I am sure you Understand being a
> Multi-Talented Wordsmith Yourself.*
>
> *I take great Pleasure in enclosure of the following two
> Book manuscripts The Long and Lonely Road that is a
> Memoir that follows Me from Ages one to fifty-three (my
> present age) and Serendipity a Novel about my character
> Lee Herbert's Journey from Naivete through Confusion to
> an (eventually) sense of Atuneness with Everything around
> him. I have been working on them for Ten Years and they
> are now done.*
>
> *I look forward to our Appointment on Friday next 6
> September at 9:15 am when You will be able to give a full
> Critique of my Works's strengths and any Possible short-
> comings. There are so few Kindred Spirits in this town so I am
> Most excited at the prospect of being able to Share with you.*

Herb Leland's epistle—written in looped, purple letters—
made the writer laugh out loud. He was tempted to pin it to the

corkboard in his office, but he supposed that wouldn't be nice. Perhaps his year's sojourn among small-town eccentrics would bring out a new humour and warmth in his writing, a sort of Sarah Orne Jewett quality.

His office was narrower than he had expected; the high walls were stubbled with the ubiquitous cream paint. The framed prints he'd shipped from home looked minute. One wall was occupied by a vast set of dark bookshelves; he filled a few inches of one with his complete works—three slimmish volumes—then reconsidered and turned them face out, so they took up half a shelf. Proof that he was a professional, a "published writer" as Marsha the secretary of English kept calling him.

"I'm curious," he asked the self-professed WritOr at their first meeting, "about why you use so many capital letters. Are you trying for a Germanic effect?"

Herb Leland's white, swollen face looked back at him in puzzlement. "The capitals are for added meaning," he confided, "and emphasis."

"Ah," said the writer. "You know, Herb, in my view, it's best to let the emphasis . . . grow out of the choice of words. When you capitalize something, it doesn't really add to its meaning. As such."

The middle-aged man's face split into a broad smile.

The writer grinned back at him nervously.

"That's exactly what the last three writers-in-residence said," marveled Herb.

The writer shrugged, as if to say that life was full of coincidence.

At the end of that first Monday, tired but still amused, he strolled home to the cheapest ground-floor apartment he had been able to find. (He was intending to live simply this year, saving most of his stipend to reduce his debts.) The rooms smelled of something cooked, something he couldn't identify even when he sniffed the air and free-associated, as he'd learned to do many years ago in a workshop on overcoming writer's block.

He sent a flippant e-mail to all his friends. *Currently ensconced in college community in small-town America. Pray for me!*

What should he call them, he wondered, the unknowns lined up in his day planner? "My writers" seemed a little optimistic. "My visitors" sounded like a hospital. "My students," maybe, except that Marsha had given him to understand that very few of the locals who had made appointments to see him would turn out to be enrolled at the college. "The student body here are into football," she told him regretfully. On his corkboard someone—probably Marsha—had pinned an article from the *Campus Calendar* in which the provost was quoted as saying, "The Writer-in-Residence is our college's ambassador to the wider community—a way for us to reach out the window of our so-called Ivory Tower and truly touch the lives of those we live and work alongside."

By the second week the writer was seeing ten of them a day.

He worked late into the night on the manuscripts they left in his pigeonhole; he made extensive notes for his own reference. He read Christian magazine columns and chapters of legal thrillers, bits of action screenplays and one twenty-page piece entitled "Absurdist Collage Poem." Instead of scribbling anything in the margins—that would be too schoolteacherish, he thought—the writer typed out long lists of tentative suggestions under the headings Micro (spelling, grammar) and Macro (genre, plot, theme).

"Jonas," he asked, one morning, "could you read me this sentence here?"

The boy looked at where the writer was pointing. He cleared his throat raspingly. *"It was then immeasurably time for it to be enacted, the action that required to be carried out as aforesaid."*

The writer let the words hang on the air for a few seconds. "Do you see what I mean about how your vocabulary in this story tends slightly to the abstract, rather than the concrete? How it could possibly be hard for some readers to tell what's actually going on?"

Jonas scratched a spot on his chin. "No."

An hour later the writer was struggling with Mrs. Pokowski. "When you say on page one that 'The savages recognized the White Man as lord of their dark and mysterious jungle,'" he quoted neutrally, "don't you think perhaps some readers might be bothered by that?"

She furrowed her brow. "You mean the word *savages*?"

"Ah, yes, for one thing . . ."

"Well, I didn't want to put *niggers*," she said virtuously.

After lunch (a tuna sandwich at his desk) came Pedro Verdi with his genetic-engineering near-future fantasy. "OK," said the writer, taking a peek at his notes to refresh his memory, "so the opening scene takes place in a hospital?"

A shrug from the bank teller. "Well, you think it's hospital."

"Yes," said the writer, not wanting to seem stupid. But after a minute, he couldn't help asking, "Isn't it?"

"Yeah, yeah, it's hospital," Pedro conceded, "but I no want my readers to be too sure, you know?"

"Don't worry, they won't be," said the writer heavily. "Now"— trying to read his own handwriting—"there's some ambiguity about the newborn daughter."

"Aha. Yes. There has been mix-up," articulated Pedro, leaning forward with his elbows on his knees. "Only it's no really mix-up, but you don't find it out till after."

"Mr. Verdi." The writer meant to sound stern, rather than petulant. "By my count there are three newborn babies in this book."

"Pedro, please." The bank teller loosened his Bart Simpson tie.

"Fine. Pedro. Now, which baby is the genetically modified telepath?"

"Me, I prefer to leave that open. Tell you the truth, I no decided yet," said Pedro, lying back and gazing out the window.

Three hours later the tiny office was feeling full. Maybelline Norris had brought her mother, a weighty woman introduced only as "my mom, she's my best friend," who sat with her chair several feet behind Maybelline's.

"Who's your favourite poet?" the writer asked, to put off discussion of Maybelline's own work.

"Dunno. Jewel, I guess," the girl said. "If I like stuff, I don't pay much attention to who actually wrote it, you know?"

The writer couldn't think of any other general questions. His eyes flickered between the two Norris women.

"So hey, do you like my poems?" Maybelline asked brightly.

"They're very interesting," he lied. "I like some . . . more than others."

The girl's mother squinted at him disapprovingly.

His eyes fell to the manuscript on his lap, and he silently reread a verse at random.

> *Hurts hurts*
> *like   crazy*
> *My emotionality*
> *crushingly hemmed in*
> *like   cactus flowers*
> *Utterly longing   for the monsoon*

"Have you ever tried . . . redrafting any of your poems?" he suggested.

"Oh no," Maybelline reassured him. "I wouldn't want to mess with the magic. I don't know where they come from; I just shut my eyes and it flows. I call up my mom and I say, 'Mom, I've just written another poem,' and she says, 'Wow, that's so wonderful! You're so talented!'"

The writer's eyes veered to the mother, just for politeness, but she only nodded.

"I showed a bunch of them to my teacher back in eleventh grade and she said, 'Wow, you can write. You can really write!'"

It astonished the writer, how tiring it was, this listening business.

"I've got about maybe a thousand of them at home! But these ones are like the crème de la crème," said Maybelline, her eyes resting fondly on the manuscript. "I showed them to my swim coach and she said, 'Wow, this stuff deserves to be published.'"

The writer allowed his eyebrows to soar up, as if in encouragement rather than disbelief.

The girl's mother leaned forward then. "But then there's copyright, ain't there?" she said darkly.

This took him aback.

"Yeah," said Maybelline regretfully. "My mom thinks, what if I send my poems to like a magazine or something, and they get stolen?"

"Stolen?" the writer repeated.

"Yeah, you know, published under another name. Like the editor's, maybe."

His throat was dry; he suddenly longed for a martini. "No one would ever do that," he said faintly.

"Really?" said Maybelline, smiling.

"Trust me. It's never going to happen."

Even on the days when he didn't have office hours, he found it hard to get much of his own work done; this job was so distracting, somehow. But when he did manage a page, at least he approved of what he wrote. It might not be Faulkner, but it was a damn sight better than Herb Leland.

His office collected sounds, he found. Chain saws outside where the dead trees were coming down; gurgles in the ducts as the heating revved up at the start of October; high-pitched giggling in the corridors. Sometimes he imagined that students were pausing to read the résumé pasted to his office door, and laughing at it. He wished he'd left out the line about the *New York Times Book Review* calling his work "profoundly promising"; it would mean something only if he were still twenty-four.

He stared at his shelf, the few inches his slim hardbacks took up. His name in three different typefaces, repeated, as if it were a phrase that meant something. So sweet to his eyes; so insubstantial.

He rather wished he hadn't pinned a head shot on his door, either. Now people recognized him in the corridors and took him by the elbow to ask one of the four FAQs of the trade:

"Did you always want to be a writer?"
"Where do you get your ideas?"
"How many hours a day do you write?"
"How can I get published?"

But when the writer did a lunchtime reading from his poetry collection, only eleven people showed up. To think that on the plane, flying down here, he had worried about his privacy, how to keep people from prying into every detail of his life! As if they gave a damn. Nobody was remotely curious about him as a person except for Herb Leland, who seemed to have formed an unconscious crush. And Herb's questions were hardly probing, either; they were more along the lines of "Do you realize how Honoured we feel to have You Living here among us?"

Most nights the writer read detective novels and ate microwaved macaroni.

"I guess I'm a would-be writer," one housewife introduced herself coyly.

After that, in his head he called them all "my would-be's," meaning that they perhaps would have been writers if they'd been born with a tittle of talent. It never occurred to them to supplement their high school education by consulting a dictionary. They seemed to feel—like Humpty Dumpty but without his powers—that words should mean what they wanted them to mean: that *un-usual* was a brand-new coinage, that it was possible to *riposte* someone, that drunks fell down *unconscientious* in the street.

By mid-October the writer realized that he shouldn't waste his energy trying to teach the would-be's about literature or anything else. His job was to listen. And it was not just casual nodding along that was required, either, but an intense, full-frontal, eyes-locked kind of attention.

The would-be's claimed they longed for honest criticism. "Be brutally honest with me, man," said BJ, a trainee electrician and spare-time rapper who was writing a novel about his recent adolescence and owned seventeen how-to-get-published books. "Hit me with it!" But BJ didn't really mean it; none of them did, the writer discovered.

"Should I chuck the thing in the stove?" one grandmother asked, her eyes watery and fearful, but it was obviously a rhetorical question.

To be honest was to hurt. Even a mild remark like "I'm not a big fan of limericks" could make a would-be's face implode.

But to be kind was to lie. The days he said things like "It's wonderful you've written a whole novel," he went home feeling greasy with deceit.

This had to be how therapists felt, he realized one long Monday afternoon, when Doug McGee—fifty-something, with eczema—began yet again to unravel the story of how his parents, teachers, and so-called friends had crushed his self-esteem from an early age. The writer crossed and recrossed his legs.

His next visitor, Meredith Lopez Jones, was in love with her writer's block—or *blockage,* as she called it, as if were in her colon. "I still don't have anything to show you," she murmured proudly. "I suffer from SAD, did I tell you? I withdraw from the world right after the equinox. I just curl up like a seed in the earth all winter, that's all I do."

Apart from coming in to bore the pants off me twice a week, the writer added mentally.

"Last summer I stayed up all night and tried to get it all down on paper, everything, the whole universe, you know? But my head was so full of images I thought it might burst! I burnt it all the next day, of course."

The writer pursed his lips as if regretting this.

Meredith pressed her cheekbones so hard she left white fingerprints. "I'm so afraid of writing something mediocre! That's always been my problem. Probably because I was raised as a woman in this society. The scars run deep. No matter how many people have told me I'm an amazingly talented person, I can't quite believe it."

The writer nodded, unable to quite believe it, either.

Clearly, writing was not an ordinary hobby like wine making or kung fu. It attracted the most vulnerable people; the strange, the antisocial, the sad. Some were struggling with addictions or mysterious debilitating illnesses; others wrote endless versions of their childhood traumas. One quite young, balding man called Jack had been divorced five times already; "Got no knack for picking 'em, I guess." His memoir-disguised-as-a-short-story was full of phrases like "there going to blame me" and "their's no way out." The writer stared at the page exhaustedly, wondering if it was worth correcting the grammar.

He had come to dread his office hours. He relied on certain basic survival techniques. He kept an enormous bag of gourmet brownie bites in his filing drawer. After each visit he'd gobble one to lift his spirits, or at least his blood-sugar level. A visit from Stinking Steve—who had a bloated, sun-browned face and always wore the same Disney World sweatshirt—merited two brownie bites. When the writer's aunt sent him a homemade pomander for his office—a beribboned orange studded with cloves—he didn't laugh at it. He hung it on his desk lamp and pressed his nose to it between sessions. It made him feel like a medieval troubadour in a world of serfs.

It occurred to him to ask Marsha to tell the would-be's that his appointment diary was all filled in for a fortnight, but somehow he couldn't bring himself to do it. Besides, she seemed like a woman of integrity, and she might report him to the dean of arts.

He was not doing much with the Great Novel these days. He feared the terrible writing of the would-be's might be contagious. Whenever he wrote a sentence, he had to stop and check it for mixed metaphors. All the fatuous rules he'd been spouting this term looped through his head. *Write what you know,* he thought. *Show, don't tell. Verbs and nouns are stronger than adjectives and adverbs.* This was painting by numbers; it felt like a uniquely pointless way to spend the rest of his life. *Avoid the passive voice.* He tried to remember, when was the last time he'd written anything in the white heat of inspiration?

There was just one café in town that roasted its own beans. The writer tried going there with his laptop to have a go at chapter three over a latte, but people stared, and he got a croissant crumb lodged between Q and W.

He went back the next day with paper and pen and ordered a bracing shot of wheatgrass. He'd composed just half a sentence when two blond girls whose names he couldn't remember came over to say how awesome it was to find him here, and would he mind looking at their essay plans? The topic was Believing in Ourselves.

He e-mailed his friends: *Making whoopee in the mountains. My office gets the best sunsets. Oh, the life of a state-subsidized sybarite! Great Novel coming along nicely. Miss you all, naturally, but not enough to come home.*

He knew this was a stupid policy—he could hardly keep up this pretense forever—but right now he couldn't bear to tell anyone what a mistake he had made.

As an experiment, he started working to rule. He no longer read any of the manuscripts jammed into his pigeonhole. The would-be's never seemed to notice.

"Why don't you tell me the overall story in your own words," he murmured, eyes shut, to Tzu Ping.

Off she went: "Well, it starts when I'm—I mean when my character—is in second grade . . . ," and soon her time was up.

Later the same day, Mrs. Pokowski frowned at the pristine manuscript he handed back to her. "Did you like chapter three?"

"Very much," said the writer. "But"—here he flicked through the pages and picked out a line at random—"I'm a little confused by the metaphors in this sentence: *'A fragile essence of deep buried undigested resentments were locked away behind a veil of stone.'*"

"What's to confuse?" asked Mrs. Pokowski coldly.

With Linda Shange, he only ever had to glance at the first paragraph. "Linda," he said, "you see the way you keep telling us how nice your protagonist is? Here, for instance: *'She was a sweet and kind person who never killed mice.'*"

"Yes, she really was, in real life," said Linda beatifically.

"The danger is," he told her, "you might actually put some readers off."

She looked shocked.

"We don't need to like your protagonist all the time," he told her, yet again, "we just need to care what happens to her."

One week, every story presented to him seemed to contain some reference to child abuse. He was irritated by this craven following of literary fashion. "Lenny," he said to the golden-haired boy majoring in English, "couldn't you pick a more original angle? The hard-drinking, big-fisted Daddy is kind of a stereotype. And isn't it rather implausible that it would be the *eldest* boy he'd rape?"

"But that's what happened," said Lenny.

The writer stared at him.

The boy gave an awkward little grimace and pushed his blond fringe out of his eyes. "If I slept in the bed nearest the door, you know . . . he'd come in and do it to me and leave the younger ones alone."

The writer covered his mouth with his hand. He found himself unable to give the standard speech about the distinction between fiction and autobiography. In an unsteady voice, for the last five minutes of the session he talked about Lenny's excellent use of nature imagery.

So he cultivated compassion. He started practicing meditation again. *You don't need to like these people,* he told himself over and over, *you just need to care what happens to them.*

He taught himself to sit there opposite the would-be's and vary his smiles and nods, crinkle his eyebrows and say "Mmm" at the right bits. He kept his hands folded—priestly—and let the would-be's talk about whatever they needed to talk about. Some of them never mentioned writing at all. Others eventually revealed that they hadn't written a word since high school, but they were somehow convinced that they could if they tried. "Because I've had such an interesting life and I've a lot to teach the world."

"Because I'm retired now and I want to make some vacation money."

"Because my doctor said it might help."

One day the writer didn't say a word for thirty-five minutes while Maybelline Norris yammered on about how talented everybody said she was. If he'd been inventing a character for his novel, he couldn't have come up with such a combination of egotism and naked need. He looked at the girl's surprisingly bad teeth and wondered if she was bulimic. He would have liked to put his hand over her mouth, to hush and comfort her, but that was hardly possible with Mrs. Norris sitting implacable, two feet behind her daughter.

Only in one session did he come close to nodding off, and it wasn't his fault. Mrs. Pokowski was describing a self-hypnosis technique she'd learned "for so as to unleash creativity," as she said in her mosquito-drone voice. She took him through it step by step—"Now I'm falling down the hole, and I'm falling down deeper, and deeper, and now what do I see, I see another tunnel, so what do I do, I go down that one . . ."

The world began to melt; he had to writhe on his chair and bite the inside of his cheek to stay awake.

In the second week of November the writer turned sullen. He stopped practicing meditation; he couldn't see the point in spending twenty minutes a day sitting very still on his couch while the entire lyric oeuvre of David Bowie raced through his head. He gave up on compassion.

He had cruel private names for most of the would-be's by now: as well as Stinking Steve there was Jawless Jennifer (whose face seemed to fall away below the nose), Mr. Hypochondria, and Dottie-Date-Rape. He was just an ear to this pack of social rejects, an official representative of Literature who had to listen to their grievances and explain why they'd never been let into the club, why publishers invariably returned their fat single-spaced manuscripts with the floral designs on the cover page.

"I have to tell you, I just love this poem, I just think it says everything I've ever wanted to say in my life," Meredith Lopez Jones told him, wet-eyed, her hand fondling the page.

I am so glad to have had this Opportunity to have Shared the story of Running Fox with you, wrote Herb Leland. *I take no credit for Running Fox, she germinated and Marinated in my head for many Moons then gave birth to herself in tune with the rhythms of her People's Spirituality. To have Helped bring her into this World makes me Proud.*

These people were philistines, pariahs, parasites. They haunted the writer's nights and stalked his days. When he tried going for a run along the riverbank to work off his tension, who should he meet but Herb Leland, who had the gall to lurch along behind him, rhapsodizing about the Crisp Fall Keatsian Air.

In fact, human beings in general repelled him these days. Marsha with her fat wrists; George W. Bush blustering at press conferences; even his old friends, who had taken to sending him irritating Internet jokes.

As for language—his former lover, his enigmatic deity—these days, it slunk through his office like a diseased cat. Language had a limp, a scab, a tumour, a death wish. Words on the page were a helpless leakage, a human stain.

In his tiny apartment, he opened the file called GREAT NOVEL and tinkered with the punctuation of a single sentence, then stared at the wall until his computer went into sleep mode to save energy. He sniffed the air. Parsnips? he wondered. Or cumin? Damp under the carpet?

He lay on the couch all evening watching the Home Shopping Network. They always seemed to be advertising some gadget that sealed things into plastic bags. Cubes of broth, apple pies, cashmere sweaters, silver spoons—just about everything, they said, would be cleaner and safer if stored in a vacuum pack.

He fell asleep on the couch and woke in the middle of the night with a crooked neck. He had been dreaming that he lured the would-be's, with their griefs and their odours and their terrible ambitions, into a giant plastic bag and sealed them all away.

The next morning he had a raging headache. He lay staring at the ceiling for some hours before he called Marsha to say, in an exaggeratedly gravelly voice, that he feared he was coming down with something, and could she reschedule all his appointments?

He moped around all week, dozing on the couch in the afternoons, staying close to home in case anybody saw him and reported he wasn't sick.

He went back into college on Monday, before Marsha could call and ask him for a doctor's note. But this time he was determined not to let the bastards grind him down.

He indulged in cruelty; it passed the time. He started reading the manuscripts again and marking them in red pen—a big circle round every mistake—not because he thought the would-be in question would really benefit, but simply as punishment. He made his marginalia deliberately intimidating. *Inexplicable P.O.V. slippages,* he would scribble, or *I suspect the irony of this double entendre is not intentional?,* or *See identical errors pp. 2, 3, 9, 15, passim.* Whereas in the early weeks he had used kind euphemisms like *A little overfamiliar?* he now wrote *CLICHÉ* in large red capitals.

He slouched in his office chair. "Sharon, would you agree that the prevailing mood of this piece is self-pity?"

"Dr. Partridge, you describe the mother's smile as *viscous.* Were you referring to a metaphorical oiliness about it, or failing to spell *vicious*?"

Dear Mr. McCullen, he wrote on English department notepaper, *Thank you for your letter. I have read your manuscript, which appears to be largely based on* Gone with the Wind, *though lacking that novel's strengths. For your future reference, plagiarism has a better chance of going undetected when the source text is not one of the bestselling novels of the twentieth century.* Then his hand started to shake, so he tore the letter up.

Insomniac at four a.m., the writer fantasized about going one step further and speaking the plain truth. *No, Jonas,* he might say to the spotty boy, *this isn't a poem. These are pretentious words from an online thesaurus, typed out in no particular order.*

Maybelline, forget what your swim coach said. You have no talent. Zero. Zip!

Herb, we are not Soul-Friends, as you put it in your last note. You are suffering from a midlife homoerotic infatuation, and I only talk to you because I'm being paid.

People, give it up! he could bawl at them all. *Get over it! Try extreme sports, masturbation, anything. Stop violating the language I used to love.*

The worst thing the writer ever actually said was at the end of a long Friday. BJ came in with gold shades on, radiant. "I did what you told me, man."

"Really," said the writer, trying to remember what he had told BJ.

"I made all those changes you asked for. And I'm gonna go for it."

"For what?"

"The big time!" BJ delivered the line in rapper style, using his hands. "You know how I was telling you John Grisham sold his first book out of his truck? Well, Wal-Mart's gonna let me set up a table."

The writer's mind was foggy this morning. "Is this about . . . self-publishing?"

"That's right, man." BJ was only a little sheepish. "I made a few calls, found a guy that'll do me five hundred copies for two grand. Charlene is gonna lend me most of it."

The writer considered whether to tell BJ that to print five hundred copies of his so-called coming-of-age novel was a criminal waste of trees as well as his ex-girlfriend's money. That it would never get reviewed, stocked, or bought. Instead he dragged the dog-eared manuscript towards him and opened it at random. "This sentence doesn't have a verb."

The gilt shades looked back at him blankly.

"If you don't know what a verb is, BJ, why the fuck do you imagine you can write a novel?"

Tears skidded down BJ's face. The young man tried to speak; his Adam's apple jerked. He bent over as if he'd been stabbed. There were salt drops on the writer's desk, on the manuscript.

"I'm sorry," the writer said, breathless, "I'm so sorry—"

But BJ didn't seem to hear him. "I just, you know," he sobbed at last, "I guess it was different for you 'cuz you're like a genius. I just think, I've spent so long on this thing, I just want it to be over and out there." The breath rasped in his throat. "If I could only see my name—I'd know I'd done something. On a book. Any kind of book of my own. My name on it. You know?"

The writer did know.

He flew home for the weekend and slept on a friend's futon. He wandered round town the way he always used to, and he felt sick, as if something were punctured in his stomach. The seats in his favourite café were all taken. In his local bookstore, the massed titles faced him down.

He sat on a park bench, bundled up against the December cold. It would be easy enough to tender his resignation on health grounds. Depression, he could call it, or a breakdown. He could send the rest of the money back, ask Marsha to box up his possessions and shred any papers in his office.

Three slim hardcovers proved nothing about him. There

were hundreds of thousands of new books published every day. He thought about other ways of earning a living. He'd been quite good at selling fitness equipment, he seemed to remember. *WritOr Die,* he repeated in his head, *WritOr Die.* Was there any truth in that? Did he have a real gift, a sacred vocation? Maybe he was just as much of a self-deceiver as any of the would-be's. Maybe he'd be happier being a salesman.

The fact that he took the last flight back on Sunday night and was in his office at nine o'clock the next morning rather puzzled him afterwards. But he needed to get the job done.

That Monday was quiet. He surprised himself by writing a four-page scene for chapter four of his novel. Nothing that would change the course of literary history, but still, not bad: well-constructed, workmanlike, entirely readable.

A knock. It occurred to him not to answer. He wasn't visible through the smoky glass. How could anyone know he was there?

"Are you, like, the writer?" the girl asked when he opened the door.

"So they say," he answered.

She stepped into the office. She held out a single sheet with flittered edges, ripped off from a refill pad.

"All writings have to be given in a week in advance," he said automatically.

"Yeah, the secretary said, but I just happened to be passing through this building, I never usually do. I only got this done last night; it's sort of a poem."

He repressed a wince. He waved to indicate that she should sit down while he looked at it.

After he'd read the short lyric for the first time he turned towards the window, in his swivel chair, so he could be unobserved. He didn't want to have to worry about his face. He read it again, more slowly, then once more. Yes, his first impression hadn't deceived him. It wasn't just wishful thinking after all these awful months.

"So?" the girl asked, sounding a little bored.

He turned round, and gave a little shrug. "It's . . . entirely beautiful." He sounded hoarse.

She stared back at him for a second, then let out a hiccup of laughter. She was an ordinary, not-very-good-looking girl. "Cool," she said, and reached out to take her page back.

"No, but listen," the writer told her, holding on to it. "You have a rare talent."

"Nice of you to say so." The girl was strapping her bag across her shoulder blade.

"If you leave this copy with me—"

"Sorry, no can do," she said, holding out her hand for it again; "I send them to my boyfriend, he's in the Marines, though I don't know does he like them really, though he says he does."

"But this poem must be published."

"Get out," she said, sheepish.

"I'm quite serious," the writer told her. "I know the editor of a marvelous little magazine . . ."

She shook her head. "I wouldn't really be into that. I just like writing them."

"You don't want to be published?" His voice was shrill.

"Not really. My friends would think it was kinda dumb. I mean, no offense," she corrected herself.

He could feel his face contort. "So why did you come here?"

"Gee, I'm sorry if I've wasted your time. I just thought, you know, as I was passing, I'd see what you had to say."

"Well, I'm telling you, this poem is superb. So simple and so powerful. I don't know how you did it. I—" He made the great effort. "I've never written anything that good in my life."

She gave him an odd, pitying look. "Hey, keep it, then. See ya," she added, backing out the door.

Alone in his office, he read the poem twice more before realizing there was no name on the page. He called Marsha, but she didn't know who the girl was, either.

He kept the poem pinned to his corkboard. He read it once, at the end of every day, till the end of the year. It kept him dangling somewhere between hope and despair.

DESIRE

Team Men

That was the kindest thing Saul could say about anyone, that he was a real team man. "Jonathan," he used to tell his son over their bacon, eggs, sausage, and beans, "a striker's not put up front for personal glory. You'll only end up a star player if you keep your mind on playing for the good of the team. Them as tries to be first shall be last and vice versa."

Jon just kept on eating his toast.

Saul King believed in fuel, first thing in the morning, when there was plenty of time ahead to burn it up. "Breakfast like a legend, dine like a journeyman, and sup like a sub." That made him cackle with laughter.

The boy was just sixteen and nearly six foot tall. Headers were his strong point. When the ball sailed down to him he could feel his neck tighten and every bit of force in his body surge towards the hard plate at the front of his skull. The crucial thing was to be ready for the ball; to meet all its force and slam it back into the sky. On good days Jon felt hard and shiny as a mirror. He knew that if the planet Mars came falling down, he could meet it head-on and rocket it into the next galaxy.

But by now he had learned to pay no attention to his dad before a game. If Jon let the warnings get through to him, he couldn't swallow. If he didn't eat enough, he found himself knackered at halftime. If he flagged, he missed passes, and the goalmouth seemed ten miles away. If the team lost, his dad took it personally and harder than a coach should. Once when Jon fluffed a penalty kick, Saul hadn't spoken a word to him for a week.

"Nerves of steel," the greying man said finally, as they sat at opposite ends of the table waiting for Mum to bring a fresh pot of tea.

Jon's fork clinked against his plate. "What's that, Dad?"

"If a striker hasn't got nerves of steel when they're needed, he's no right to take a penalty kick at all."

His son listened and learned. As if he had a choice.

The lads were already having a kickabout on the pitch when the Kings drove up. Saul got out; the car door steadied in his hand as he watched the lads over his shoulder. "Well, well," he said, "who have we here?"

One unfamiliar coppery head, breaking away from the pack. "Oh yeah, Shaq said he might bring someone from school," Jon mentioned, hauling his kit bag out of the backseat.

"Now there's a pair of legs," breathed Saul. He and his son stood a foot apart, watching the new boy run. He was runt-sized, but he moved as sleekly as cream.

"A winger?" hazarded Jon.

"We'll see," said Saul, mysterious.

Davy turned out to be seventeen. Up close he didn't look so short; his limbs were narrow but pure muscle. The youngest of eight; one of those big rackety Irish families. His face went red as strawberries when he ran, but he never seemed to get out of breath; his laugh got a bit hoarser, that was all. He was a cunning bastard on the pitch. Beside him Jon felt lumbering and huge.

In the dressing room after that first practice Davy played his guitar as if it were electric. He sang along, confidently raucous.

> *Get knocked down*
> *But I get up again . . .*

"Best put a bit of meat on those bones," observed Saul, and loaded Davy down with five bags of high-protein glucose supplement. It turned out Davy lived just down the road from the Kings, so Saul insisted on giving him a lift home.

After a fortnight Davy was pronounced a real team man. He was to be the new striker. Jon was switched to midfield. "It's not a demotion," his father repeated. "This is a team, not a bloody corporation."

Jon looked out the car window and thought about playing on a team where the coach wouldn't be his dad, wouldn't shove him from one position to another just to prove a point about not giving his son any special treatment. Jon visualized himself becoming a legend in some sport Saul King had never tried, could hardly spell, even—badminton, maybe, or curling, or luge.

The thing was, though, all he'd ever wanted to play was football.

Jon was over the worst of his sulks by the next training session. He had every reason to hate this Davy, but it didn't happen. The boy was a born striker, Jon had to admit; it would have been nonsense to put him anywhere else on the pitch. He wasn't a great header of the ball, but he was magic with his feet.

And midfield had its own satisfactions, Jon found. "You lot are the big cog in the team's engine," Saul told them solemnly. "You slack off for a second, the game will fall apart."

Pounding along with the ball at his feet, Jon saw Davy out of the corner of his eye. "With ya!" Jon passed the ball sideways, and Davy took it without even looking. Only after he'd scored did he spin round to give Jon his grin.

"Your dad's a laugh. I mean," Davy corrected himself in the shower, "he's all right. He knows a lot."

"Not half as much as he pretends," said Jon, soaping his armpits.

"Is it true what Shaq says about him, that he got to the semi-final of the 1979 FA Cup?"

Jon nodded, sheepish.

Davy, under the stream of water, sprayed like a whale. "Fuck. What did he play?"

"Keeper." On impulse, Jon stepped closer to Davy's ear. "Dad'd flay me if he knew I told you this. He's never forgiven himself."

"What? What?" The boy's eyes were green as scales.

"He flapped at it. The winning goal."

Davy sucked his breath in. It made a clean, musical note.

In October the days shortened. One foul wet afternoon Saul made them run fifteen laps of the field before they even started, and by the time he finally blew the whistle, they had mud to their waists and it was too dark to see the ball. Naz tripped over Jon's foot and landed on his elbow. "You big ape," moaned Naz; "you lanky fucking ape-man."

The other lads thought this was very funny.

"You can't let them get to you," Davy said casually, afterwards, while they were warming down.

"Who?" said Jon, as if from a million miles away.

Davy shrugged. "Any of them. Anyone who calls you names."

Jon chewed his lip.

"I've got five big brothers," Davy added, when he and Jon were sitting in the back of the car, counting their bruises. "And my sisters are even worse. They've always taken the piss out of me. One of them called me the Little Stain till she got married."

A grin loosened Jon's jaw. He stared out the window at his father, who was collecting the training cones.

"Just ignore the lads and remember what a good player you are."

"Maybe I'm not," said Jon, looking down into Davy's red hair.

"Maybe you're what?" Davy let out a yelp of laughter. "Jonboy, you're the best. You've got a perfect footballing brain, and you're a sweet crosser of the ball."

Jon was glad of the twilight, then. Blood sang in his cheeks.

Davy came round every couple of days now. Mrs. King often asked him to stop for dinner. "That boy's not getting enough at home," she observed darkly. But Jon thought Davy looked all right as he was.

Jon's little sister Michaela sat beside Davy at the table whenever she got the chance, even if she did call him Short-arse. She was only fifteen, but she looked old enough. As she was always reminding Jon, girls matured two years faster.

Davy ended up bringing Michaela to the local Hallowe'en Club Night and Jon brought her friend Tasmin. While the girls were queuing up for chips afterwards, Davy followed Jon into the loos. Afterwards, Jon could never be sure who'd started messing round; it just happened. It was sort of a joke and sort of a dare. In a white stall with a long crack in the wall they unzipped their jeans. They kept looking down; they didn't meet each other's eyes.

It was over in two minutes. It took longer to stop laughing.

When they got back to the girls, the chips were gone cold and Michaela wanted to know what was so funny. Jon couldn't think of anything, but Davy said it was just an old Diana joke. Tasmin said in that case they could keep it to themselves because she didn't think it was very nice to muck around with the dead.

After Hallowe'en, some people said Davy was going out with Michaela. Jon didn't know what that meant exactly. He didn't think Davy and Michaela did stuff together, anyway. He didn't know what to think.

Saul King expressed no opinion on the matter. But he'd started laying into Davy at practice. "Mind your back! Mind your house!" he bawled, hoarse. "Keep them under pressure!"

Davy said nothing, just bounced around, grinning as usual. "Where's your bleeding eyes?"

"Somebody's not the golden boy anymore," commented Peter to Naz under his breath.

Saul said he had errands to do in town, so Jon and Davy could walk home for once.

"Your dad's being a bit of a prick these days," commented Davy as they turned the first corner.

"Don't call him that," said Jon.

"But he is one."

Jon shook his heavy head. "Don't call him my dad, I mean." "Oh."

The silence stretched between them. "It's like the honey jar," said Jon.

Davy glanced up. His lashes were like a cat's.

"I was about three, right, and I wanted a bit of honey from the jar, but he said no. He didn't put the jar away or anything—just said no and left it sitting there about six inches in front of me. So the minute he was out of the room I opened it up and stuck my spoon in, of course. And I swear he must have been waiting because he was in and had that spoon snatched out of my hand before it got near my face."

"What's wrong with honey?" asked Davy, bewildered.

"Nothing."

"I thought it was good for you."

"It wasn't anything to do with the honey," said Jon, dry-throated. "He just wanted to win."

Davy walked beside him, mulling it over.

They went the long way, through the park. When they passed a gigantic yew tree, Davy turned his head to Jon and grinned like a shark.

Without needing to say a word, they ducked and crawled underneath the tree. The dark branches hung down around them like curtains. Nobody could have seen what they were up to; a passerby wouldn't even have known they were there. Jon forgot to be embarrassed. He did a sliding tackle on Davy and toppled him onto the soft damp ground. "Man on!" yelped Davy, pretending to be afraid. They weren't cold anymore. They moved with sleek grace, this time. It was telepathic. It was perfect timing.

"For Christ's sake, stay onside," Saul bawled at his team.

Davy's trainers blurred like Maradona's, Jon thought. The boy darted round the pitch confusing the defenders, playing to the imaginary crowd.

"Don't bother trying to impress us with the fancy footwork, Irish," screamed Saul into the wintry wind, "just try kicking the ball. This is footie, not bloody Riverdance."

Afterwards in the showers, Jon watched the hard curve of Davy's shoulder. He wanted to touch it, but Naz was three feet away. He took a surreptitious glance at his friend's face, but it was shrouded in steam.

Saul never gave Jon and Davy a lift home from practice anymore. He said the walk was good exercise and lord knew they could do with it.

"I don't know why, but your dad is out to shaft me," said Davy, on the long walk home.

"No he's not," said Jon weakly.

"Is so. He said he thought I might make less of a fool of myself in defense."

"Defense?" repeated Jon, shrill. "That's bollocks. Last Saturday's match, you scored our only goal."

"You set it up for me. Saul said only a paraplegic could have missed it."

Jon tried to remember the shot. He couldn't tell who'd done what. On a good day, he and Davy moved like one player, thought the same thing at the same split second.

"I don't suppose there's any chance he knows about us?"

Jon was so shocked he stopped walking. He had to put his hand on the nearest wall or he'd have fallen. The pebble dash was cold against his fingers. *Us*, he thought. There was an *us*. An *us* his dad might know about. "No way," he said at last, hoarsely.

Jon knew there were rules, even if they'd never spelled them out. He and Davy were sort of mates and sort of something else. They didn't waste time talking about it. In one way it was like football—the sweaty tussle of it, the heart-pounding thrill—and in another way, it was like a game played on Mars, with unwritten rules and a different gravity.

The afternoons were getting colder. On Bonfire Night they took the risk and did it in Jon's room. The door had no lock. They kept the stereo turned up very loud so there wouldn't be any suspicious silences. Outside the bangers went off at intervals like bombs. Jon's head pounded with noise and terror. It was the best time yet.

Afterwards, when they were slumped in opposite corners of the room, looking like two ordinary postmatch players, Jon turned down the music. Davy said, out of nowhere, "I was thinking of telling the folks."

"Telling them what?" asked Jon before thinking. Then he understood, and his stomach furled into a knot.

"You know. What I'm like." Davy let out a mad chuckle.

"You're not . . ." His voice trailed off.

"I am, you know." Davy still sounded as if he were talking about the weather. "I've had my suspicions for years. I thought I'd give it a try with your sister, but *nada,* to be honest."

Jon thought he was going to throw up. "Would you tell them about us?"

"Only about me," Davy corrected him. "Name no names, and all that."

"You never would."

"I'll have to sometime, won't I?"

"Why?" asked Jon, choking.

"Because it's making me nervous," explained Davy lightly, "and I don't play well when I'm nervous. I know my family are going to freak out of their tiny minds whenever I tell them, so I might as well get it over with."

He was brave, Jon thought. But he had to be stopped. "Listen, you mad bastard," said Jon fiercely, "you can't tell anyone."

Davy sat up and straightened his shoulders. He looked small, but not at all young; his face was an adult's. "Is that meant to be an order? You sound like your dad," he added, with a hint of mockery.

"He'll know," whispered Jon. "Your parents'll guess it's me. They'll tell my dad."

"They won't. They'll be too busy beating the tar out of me."

"My dad's going to find out."

"How will he?" said Davy reasonably.

"He just will," stuttered Jon. "He'll kill me. He'll get me by the throat and never let go."

"Bollocks," said Davy, too lightly. "We're not kids anymore. The sky's not going to fall in on us. You're just shitting your shorts at the thought of anyone calling you a faggot, aren't you?"

"Don't say that."

"Touchy, aren't you? It's only a word."

"We're not, anyway," he told Davy coldly. "That's not what we are."

The boy's mouth crinkled with amusement. "Oh, so what are we then?"

"We're mates," said Jon through a clenched throat.

One coppery eyebrow went up.

"Mates who mess around a bit."

"Fag-got! Fag-got!" Davy sang the words quietly.

Jon's hand shot out to the stereo and turned it way up to drown him out.

Next door, Michaela started banging on the wall. *"Jonathan!"* she wailed.

He turned it down a little, but kept his hand on the knob. "Get out," he said.

Davy stared back at him blankly. Then he reached for his jacket and got up in one fluid movement. He looked like a scornful god. He looked like nothing could ever knock him down.

Jon avoided Davy all week. He walked home from the training sessions while Davy was still in the shower. In the back of his mind, he was preparing a contingency plan. *Deny everything. Laugh. Say the sick pervert made it all up.*

Nobody else seemed to notice the two friends weren't on speaking terms. Everyone was preoccupied with the big match on Saturday.

At night Jon gripped himself like a drowning man clinging to a spar.

Saturday came at last. The pitch was muddy and badly cut up before they even started. The other team were thugs, especially an enormous winger with a moustache. From the kickoff, Saul's team played worse than they'd ever done before. The left back crashed into his central defender, whose nose bled all down his shirt. Jon moved like he was shackled. Whenever he had to pass the ball to Davy, it fell short or went wide by a mile. It was as if there was a shield around the red-haired boy and nothing could get through. Davy was caught offside three times in the first half. Then, when Jon pitched up a loose ball on the edge of his own penalty area, one of the other team's forwards big-toed a fluke shot into the top right-hand corner.

"You're running round like blind men," Saul told his team at halftime, with sorrow and contempt.

By the start of the second half, the rain was falling unremittingly. The fat winger stood on Peter's foot, and the ref never saw a thing. "Look," bawled Peter, trying to pull his shoe off to show the marks of the studs.

The other team found this hilarious. "Wankers! Faggots!" crowed the fat boy.

Rage fired up Jon's thudding heart, stoked his muscles. He would have liked to take the winger by the throat and press his thumbs in till they met vertebrae. What was it Saul always used to tell him? *No son of mine gets himself sent off for temper.* Jon made himself turn and jog away. *No son of mine,* said the voice in his head.

Naz chipped the ball high over the defense. Jon was there first, poising himself under the flight of the ball. It was going to be a beautiful header. It might even turn the match around.

"Davy's," barked Davy, jogging backwards towards Jon.

Jon kept his eyes glued to the falling ball. "Jon's."

"It's mine!" Davy repeated, at his elbow, crowding him.

"Fuck off!" He didn't look. He shouldered Davy away, harder than he meant to. Then all of a sudden Jon knew how it was going to go. He wasn't ready to meet the ball; he didn't believe he could do it. He lost his balance, and the ball came down on the side of his head and crushed him into the mud.

Jon had whiplash.

Saul came home from the next training session and said Davy was off the team.

"You cunt," said Jon.

His father stared, slack-jawed. Michaela's fork froze halfway to her mouth. "Jonathan!" appealed their mother.

Above his foam whiplash collar, Jon could feel his face burn. But he opened his mouth and it all spilled out. "You're not a coach, you're a drill sergeant. You picked Davy to bully because you knew he's going to be a better player than you ever were. And now you've kicked him off the team just to prove you can. So much for team-fucking-spirit!"

"Jonathan." His father's face was dark, unreadable. "It was the lad who dropped out. He's quit the team and he's not coming back."

One afternoon at the end of a fortnight, Davy came round. Jon was on his own in the living room, watching an old France '98 video of England versus Argentina. He thought Davy looked different: baggy-eyed, older somehow.

Davy stared at the television. "Has Owen scored yet?"

"Ages ago. They're nearly at penalties." Jon kept his eyes on the screen.

Davy dropped his bag by the sofa but didn't sit down, didn't take his jacket off. In silence they watched the agonizing shoot-out.

When it was over, Jon hit rewind. "If Beckham hadn't got himself sent off, we'd have demolished them," he remarked.

"In your dreams," said Davy. They watched the flickering figures. After a long minute he added, "I've been meaning to come round, actually, to say, you know, sorry and all that."

"It's nothing much, just a bit of whiplash," said Jon, deliberately obtuse. He put his hand to his neck, but his fingers were blocked by the foam collar.

"You'll get over it. No bother."

"Yeah," said Jon bleakly. "So," he added, not looking at Davy, "did you talk to your parents?"

"Yeah." The syllable was flat. "Don't worry, your name didn't come up."

"I didn't—"

"Forget it," interrupted Davy softly. He was staring at the video as it rewound; a green square covered in little frenzied figures who ran backwards, fleeing from the ball.

That subject seemed closed. "I hear you're not playing, these days," said Jon.

"That's right," said Davy, more briskly. "Thought I should get down to the books for a while, before my A-Levels."

Jon stared at him.

"I'm off to college next September, touch wood." Davy rapped on the coffee table. "I've already got an offer of a place in Law at Lancaster, but I'll need two Bs and an A."

Law? Jon nodded, then winced as his neck twinged. So much he'd never known about Davy, never thought to ask. "You could sign up again in the summer, though, after your exams, couldn't you?" he asked, as neutrally as he could.

There was a long second's pause before Davy shook his head. "I don't think so, Jon-boy."

So that was it, Jon registered. Not a proper ending. More like a match called off because of a hailstorm or because the star player just walked off the pitch.

"I mean, I'll miss it, but when it comes down to it, it's only a game, eh? . . . Win or lose," Davy added after a moment.

Jon couldn't speak. His eyes were wet, blinded.

Davy picked up his bag. Then he did something strange. He swung down and kissed Jon on the lips, for the first time, on his way out the door.

Speaking in Tongues

"Listen," I said, my voice rasping, "I want to take you home but Dublin's a hundred miles away."

Lee looked down at her square hands. I couldn't believe she'd only spent seventeen years on this planet.

"Where're you staying?" I asked.

"Youth hostel."

I mouthed a curse at the beer-stained carpet. "I've no room booked in Galway and it's probably too late to get one. I was planning to drive back tonight. I have to be at the office by nine tomorrow."

The last of the conference goers walked past just then, and one or two nodded at me; the sweat of the *céilí* was drying on their cheeks.

When I looked back, Lee was grinning like she'd just won the lottery. "So is it comfortable in the back of your van then, Sylvia?"

I stared at her. It was not the first time I had been asked that question, but I had thought that the last time would be the last.

She was exactly half my age, I reminded myself. She wasn't even an adult, legally. "As backs of vans go, yes, very comfortable."

The reason I got into that van was a poem.

I'd first heard Sylvia Dwyer on a CD of contemporary poetry in Irish. I'd borrowed it from the library to help me revise for the Leaving Cert that would get me out of convent school. Deirdre had just left me for a boy, so I was working hard.

Poem number five was called "Dhá Theanga." The woman's voice had peat and smoke in it, bacon and strong tea. I hadn't a notion what the poem was about; you needed to know how the words were spelt before you could look them up in the dictionary, and one silent consonant sounded pretty much like another to me. But I listened to the poem every night till I had to give the CD back to the library.

I asked my mother why the name sounded so familiar, and she said Sylvia must be the last of those Dwyers who'd taken over the Shanbally butchers thirty years before. I couldn't believe she was a local. I might even have sat next to her in Mass.

But it was Cork where I met her. I'd joined the Queer Soc in the first week, before I could lose my nerve, and by midterm I was running their chocolate-and-wine evenings. Sylvia Dwyer, down from Dublin for a weekend, was introduced all round by an ex of hers who taught in the French department. I was startled to learn that the poet was one of us—a "colleen," as a friend of mine used to say. Her smooth bob and silver-grey suit were intimidating as hell. I couldn't think of a word to say. I poured her plonk from a box and put the bowl of chocolate-covered peanuts by her elbow.

After that I smiled at her in Mass once when I was home in Shanbally for the weekend. Sylvia nodded back, very minimally.

Maybe she wasn't sure where she knew me from. Maybe she was praying. Maybe she was a bitch.

Of course I had heard of Lee Maloney in Shanbally. The whole town had heard of her, the year the girl appeared at Mass with a Sinéad O'Connor head shave. I listened in on a euphemistic conversation about her in the post office queue but contributed nothing to it. My reputation was a clean slate in Shanbally, and none of my poems had gendered pronouns.

When I was introduced to the girl in Cork she was barely civil. But her chin had a curve you needed to fit your hand to, and her hair looked seven days old.

On one of my rare weekends at home, who should I see on the way down from Communion but Lee Maloney, full of nods and smiles. Without turning my head I could sense my mother stiffen. In the car park afterwards she asked, "How do you come to know that Maloney girl?"

I considered denying it, claiming it was a case of mistaken identity, then I said, "I think she might have been at a reading I gave once."

"She's a worry to her mother," said mine.

It must have been after I saw Sylvia Dwyer's name on a flyer under the title DHÁ THEANGA/TWO TONGUES: A CONFERENCE ON BILINGUALISM IN IRELAND TODAY that my subconscious developed a passionate nostalgia for the language my forebears got whipped for. So I skived off my Saturday lecture to get the bus to Galway. But only when I saw her walk into that lecture theatre in her long brown leather coat, with a new streak of white across her black fringe, did I realize why I'd sat four hours on a bus to get there.

Some days I have more nerve than others. I flirted with Sylvia all that day, in the quarter hours between papers and forums and plenary sessions that meant equally little to me whether they were in Irish or English. I asked her questions and nodded before the answers had started. I told her about Deirdre, just so she wouldn't think I was a virgin. "She left me for a boy with no earlobes," I said carelessly.

"Been there," said Sylvia.

Mostly, though, I kept my mouth shut and my head down and my eyes shiny. I suspected I was being embarrassingly obvious, but a one-day conference didn't leave enough time for subtlety.

Sylvia made me guess how old she was, and I said, "Thirty?" though I knew from the program note that she was thirty-four. She said if by any miracle she had saved enough money by the age of forty, she was going to get plastic surgery on the bags under her eyes.

I played the cheeky young thing and the baby dyke and the strong silent type who had drunk too much wine. And till halfway through the evening I didn't think I was getting anywhere. What would a woman like Sylvia Dwyer want with a blank page like me?

For a second in that Galway lecture hall I didn't recognize Lee Maloney, because she was so out of context among the bearded journalists and wool-skirted teachers. Then my memory claimed her face. The girl was looking at me like the sun had just risen, and then she stared at her feet, which was even more of a giveaway. I stood up straighter and shifted my briefcase to my other hand.

The conference, which I had expected to be about broadening my education and licking up to small Irish publishers, began to take on a momentum of its own. It was nothing I had planned, nothing I could stop. I watched the side of Lee's jaw right through a lecture called "Scottish Loan-Words in Donegal Fishing Communities." She was so cute I felt sick.

What was most unsettling was that I couldn't tell who was chatting up whom. It was a battle made up of feints and retreats. As we sipped our coffee, for instance, I murmured something faintly suggestive about hot liquids, then panicked and changed the subject. As we crowded back into the hall, I thought it was Lee's hand that guided my elbow for a few seconds, but she was staring forward so blankly I decided it must have been somebody else.

Over dinner—a noisy affair in the cafeteria—Lee sat across the table from me and burnt her tongue on the apple crumble. I poured her a glass of water and didn't give her a chance to talk to anyone but me. At this point we were an island of English in a sea of Irish.

The conversation happened to turn (as it does) to relationships and how neither of us could see the point in casual sex, because not only was it unlikely to be much good but it fucked up friendships or broke hearts. Sleeping with someone you hardly knew, I heard myself pronouncing in my world-weariest voice, was like singing a song without knowing the words. I told her that when she was my age she would feel the same way, and she said, Oh, she did already.

My eyes dwelt on the apple crumble disappearing, spoon by spoon, between Lee's absentminded lips. I listened to the opinions spilling out of my mouth and wondered who I was kidding.

By the time it came to the poetry reading that was meant to bring the conference to a lyrical climax, I was too tired to waste time. I reached into my folder for the only way I know to say what I really mean.

Now, the word in Cork had been that Sylvia Dwyer was deep in the closet, which I'd thought was a bit pathetic but only to be expected. However.

At the end of her reading, after she'd done a few about nature and a few about politics and a few I couldn't follow, she rummaged round in her folder. "This poem gave its name to this conference," she said, "but that's not why I've chosen it." She read it through in Irish first; I let the familiar vowels caress my ears. Her voice was even better live than on the CD from the library. And then she turned slightly in her seat, and, after muttering, "Hope it translates," she read it straight at me.

> *your tongue and my tongue*
> *have much to say to each other*
> *there's a lot between them*
> *there are pleasures yours has over mine*
> *and mine over yours*
> *we get on each other's nerves sometimes*
> *and under each other's skin*
> *but the best of it is when*
> *your mouth opens to let my tongue in*
> *it's then I come to know you*
> *when I hear my tongue*
> *blossom in your kiss*
> *and your strange hard tongue*
> *speaks between my lips*

The reason I was going to go ahead and do what I'd bored all my friends with saying I'd never do again was that poem.

I was watching the girl as I read "Dhá Theanga" straight to her, aiming over the weary heads of the crowd of conference goers. I didn't look at anyone else but Lee Maloney, not at a single one of the jealous poets or Gaelgóir purists or smirking gossips, in case I might lose my nerve. After the first line, when her eyes fell for a second, Lee looked right back at me. She was leaning her cheek on her hand. It was a smooth hand, blunt at the tips. I knew the poem off by heart, but tonight I had to look down for safety every few lines.

And then she glanced away, out the darkening window, and I suddenly doubted that I was getting anywhere. What would Lee Maloney, seventeen last May, want with a scribbled jotter like me?

I sat in that smoky hall with my face half hidden behind my hand, excitement and embarrassment spiraling up my spine. I reminded myself that Sylvia Dwyer must have written that poem years ago, for some other woman in some other town. Not counting how many other women she might have read it to. It was probably an old trick of hers.

But all this couldn't explain away the fact that it was me Sylvia was reading it to tonight in Galway. In front of all these people, not caring who saw or what they might think when they followed the line of her eyes. I dug my jaw into my palm for anchorage, and my eyes locked back onto Sylvia's. I decided that every poem was made new in the reading.

If this was going to happen, I thought, as I folded the papers away in my briefcase during the brief rainfall of applause, it was happening because we were not in Dublin surrounded by my friends and work life, nor in Cork cluttered up with Lee's, nor above all in Shanbally where she was born in the year I left for college. Neither of us knew anything at all about Galway.

If this was going to happen, I thought, many hours later as the cleaners urged Sylvia and me out of the hall, it was happening because of some moment that had pushed us over an invisible line. But which moment? It could have been when we were shivering on the floor waiting for the end-of-conference céilí band to start up, and Sylvia draped her leather coat round her shoulders and tucked me under it for a minute, the sheepskin lining soft against my cheek, the weight of her elbow on my shoulder. Or later when I was dancing like a berserker in my vest, and she drew the back of her hand down my arm and said, "Aren't you the damp thing." Or maybe the deciding moment was when the fan had stopped working and we stood at the bar waiting for drinks, my smoking hips armouring hers, and I blew behind her hot ear until the curtain of hair lifted up and I could see the dark of her neck.

Blame it on the heat. We swung so long in the *céilí* that the whole line went askew. Lee took off all her layers except one black vest that clung to her small breasts. We shared a glass of iced water and I offered Lee the last splash from my mouth, but she danced around me and laughed and wouldn't take it. Up on the balcony over the dance floor, I sat on the edge and leaned out to see the whirling scene. Lee fitted her hand around my thigh, weighing it down. "You protecting me from falling?" I asked. My voice was meant to be sardonic, but it came out more like breathless.

"That's right," she said.

Held in that position, my leg very soon began to tremble, but I willed it to stay still, hoping Lee would not feel the spasm, praying she would not move her hand away.

Blame it on the dancing. They must have got a late license for the bar, or maybe Galway people always danced half the night. The music made our bones move in tandem and our legs shake. I tried to take the last bit of water from Sylvia's mouth, but I was so giddy I couldn't aim right and kept lurching against her collarbone and laughing at my own helplessness.

"Thought you were meant to be in the closet," I shouted in her ear at one point, and Sylvia smiled with her eyes shut and said something I couldn't hear, and I said, "What?" and she said, "Not tonight."

So at the end of the evening we had no place to go and it didn't matter. We had written our phone numbers on sodden beermats and exchanged them. We agreed that we'd go for a drive. When we got into her white van on the curb littered with weak-kneed céilí dancers, something came on the radio, an old song by Clannad or one of that crowd. Sylvia started up the engine and began to sing along with the chorus, her hoarse whisper catching every second or third word. She leaned over to fasten her seat belt and crooned a phrase into my ear. I didn't understand it—something about "bóthar," or was it "máthar"?—but it made my face go hot anyway.

"Where are we heading?" I said at last, as the hedges began to narrow to either side of the white van.

Sylvia frowned into the darkness. "Cashelagen, was that the name of it? Quiet spot, I seem to remember, beside a castle."

After another ten minutes, during which we didn't meet a single other car, I realized that we were lost, completely tangled in the little roads leading into Connemara. And half of me didn't care. Half of me was quite content to bump along these lanes to the strains of late-night easy listening, watching Sylvia Dwyer's sculpted profile out the corner of my right eye. But the other half of me wanted to stretch my boot across and stamp on the brake, then climb over the gear stick to get at her.

Lee didn't comment on how quickly I was getting us lost. Cradle snatcher, I commented to myself, and not even a suave one at that. As we hovered at an unmarked fork, a man walked into the glare of the headlights. I stared at him to make sure he was real, then rolled down the window with a flurry of elbows. "Cashelagen?" I asked. Lee had turned off the radio, so my voice sounded indecently loud. "Could you tell us are we anywhere near Cashelagen?"

The man fingered his sideburns and stepped closer, beaming in past me at Lee. What in god's name was this fellow doing wandering round in the middle of the night anyway? He didn't even have our excuse. I was just starting to roll the window up again when "Ah," he said, "ah, if it's Cashelagen you're wanting you'd have to go a fair few miles back through Ballyalla and then take the coast road."

"Thanks," I told him shortly, and revved up the engine. Lee would think I was the most hopeless incompetent she had ever got into a van for immoral purposes with. As soon as he had walked out of range of the headlights, I let off the hand brake and shot forward. I glanced over at Lee's bent head. The frightening thought occurred to me: *I could love this girl.*

The lines above Sylvia's eyebrow were beginning to swoop like gulls. If she was going to get cross, we might as well turn the radio back on and drive all night. I rehearsed the words in my head, then said them. "Sure who needs a castle in the dark?"

Her grin was quick as a fish.

"Everywhere's quiet at this time of night," I said rather squeakily. "Here's quiet. We could stop here."

"What, right here?"

Sylvia peered back at the road and suddenly wheeled round into the entrance to a field. We stopped with the bumper a foot away from a five-barred gate. When the headlights went off, the field stretched out dark in front of us, and there was a sprinkle of light that had to be Galway.

"What time did you say you had to be in Dublin?" I asked suddenly.

"Nine. Better start back round five in case I hit traffic," said Sylvia. She bent over to rummage in the glove compartment. She pulled out a strapless watch, looked at it, brought it closer to her eyes, then let out a puff of laughter.

"What time's it now?"

"You don't want to know," she told me.

I grabbed it. The hands said half past three. "It can't be."

We sat staring into the field. "Nice stars," I said, for something to say.

"Mmm," she said.

I stared at the stars, joining the dots, till my eyes watered.

And then I heard Sylvia laughing in her throat as she turned sideways and leaned over my seat belt. I heard it hissing back into its socket as she kissed me on the mouth.

When I came back from taking a pee in the bushes, the driver's seat was empty. I panicked, and stared up and down the lane. Why would she have run off on foot? Then, with a deafening creak, the back doors of the van swung open.

Sylvia's bare shoulders showed over the blanket that covered her body. She hugged her knees. Her eyes were bright, and the small bags underneath were the most beautiful folds of skin I'd ever seen. I climbed in and kneeled on the sheepskin coat beside her, reaching up to snap off the little light. Her face opened wide in a yawn. The frightening thought occurred to me: I could love this woman.

"You could always get some sleep, you know," I said, "I wouldn't mind." Then I thought that sounded churlish, but I didn't know how to unsay it.

"Oh, I know I could," said Sylvia, her voice melodic with amusement. "There's lots of things we could do with a whole hour and a half. We could sleep, we could share the joint in the glove compartment, we could drive to Clifden and watch the sun come up. Lots of things."

I smiled. Then I realized she couldn't see my face in the dark.

"Get your clothes off," she said.

I would have liked to leave the map-reading light on over our heads, letting me see and memorize every line of Lee's body, but it would have lit us up like a saintly apparition for any passing farmer to see. So the whole thing happened in a darkness much darker than it ever gets in a city.

There was a script, of course. No matter how spontaneous it may feel, there's always an unwritten script. Every one of these encounters has a script, even the very first time your hand undoes the button on somebody's shirt; none of us comes without expectations to this body business.

But lord, what fun it was. Lee was salt with sweat and fleshier than I'd imagined, behind all her layers of black cotton and wool. In thirty-four years I've found nothing to compare to that moment when the bare limbs slide together like a key into a lock. Or no, more like one of those electronic key cards they give you in big hotels, the open sesame ones marked with an invisible code, which the door must read and recognize before it agrees to open.

At one point Lee rolled under me and muttered, "There's somewhere I want to go," then went deep inside me. It hurt a little, just a little, and I must have flinched because she asked, "Does that hurt?" and I said, "No," because I was glad of it. "No," I said again, because I didn't want her to go.

Sylvia's voice was rough like rocks grinding on each other. As she moved on top of me she whispered in my ear, things I couldn't make out, sounds just outside the range of hearing. I never wanted to interrupt the flow by saying, "Sorry?" or "What did you say?" Much as I wanted to hear and remember every word, every detail, at a certain point I just had to switch my mind off and get on with living it. But Sylvia's voice kept going in my ear, turning me on in the strangest way by whispering phrases that only she could hear.

I've always thought the biggest lie in the books is that women instinctively know what to do to each other because their bodies are the same. None of Sylvia's shapes were the same as mine, nor could I have guessed what she was like from how she seemed in her smart clothes. And we liked different things and took things in different order, showing each other by infinitesimal movings away and movings towards. She did some things to me that I knew I wanted, some I didn't think I'd much like and didn't, and several I was startled to find that I enjoyed much more than I would have imagined. I did some things Sylvia seemed calm about, and then something she must have really needed, because she started to let out her breath in a long gasp when I'd barely begun.

Near the end, Sylvia's long fingers moved down her body to ride alongside mine, not supplanting, just guiding. "Go light," she whispered in my ear. "Lighter and lighter. Butterfly." As she began to thrash at last, laughter spilled from her mouth.

"What? What are you laughing for?" I asked, afraid I'd done something wrong. Sylvia just whooped louder. Words leaked out of her throat, distorted by pleasure.

At one point I touched my lips to the skin under her eyes, first one and then the other. "Your bags are gorgeous, you know. Promise you'll never let a surgeon at them?"

"No," she said, starting to laugh again.

"No to which?"

"No promise."

When Sylvia was touching me I didn't say a single one of the words that swam through my head. I don't know was I shy or just stubborn, wanting to make her guess what to do. The tantalization of waiting for those hands to decipher my body made the bliss build and build till when it came it threw me.

There was one moment I wouldn't swap anything for. It was in the lull beforehand, the few seconds when I stopped breathing. I looked at this stranger's face bent over me, twisted in exertion and

tenderness, and I thought, Yes, you, whoever you are, if you're ask-
ing for it, I'll give it all up to you.

In the in-between times we panted and rested and stifled our
laughter in the curve of each other's shoulders and debated when
I'd noticed Lee and when she'd noticed me, and what we'd noticed and what we'd imagined on each occasion, the history of this
particular desire. And during one of these in-between times we
realized that the sun had come up, faint behind a yellow mist,
and it was half five according to the strapless watch in the glove
compartment.

I took hold of Lee, my arms binding her ribs and my head
resting in the flat place between her breasts. The newly budded
swollen look of them made my mouth water, but there was no
time. I shut my mouth and my eyes and held Lee hard and there
was no time left at all, so I let go and sat up. I could feel our nerves
pulling apart like ivy off a wall.

The cows were beginning to moan in the field as we pulled
our clothes on. My linen trousers were cold and smoky. We did
none of the things parting lovers do if they have the time or the
right. I didn't snatch at Lee's foot as she pulled her jeans on; she
didn't sneak her head under my shirt as I pulled it over my face.
The whole thing had to be over already.

It was not the easiest thing in the world to find my way back
to Galway with Lee's hand tucked between my thighs. Through
my trousers I could feel the cold of her fingers, and the hardness
of her thumb, rubbing the linen. I caught her eye as we sped round
a corner, and she grinned, suddenly very young. "You're just using
me to warm your hand up," I accused.

"That's all it is," said Lee.

I was still throbbing, so loud I thought the car was ringing
with it. We were only two streets from the hostel now.

I wouldn't ask to see her again. I would just leave the matter open and drive away. Lee probably got offers all the time; she was far too young to be looking for anything heavy. I'd show her I was generous enough to accept that an hour and a half was all she had to give me.

I let her out just beside the hostel, which was already opening to release some backpacking Germans. I was going to get out of the car to give her a proper body-to-body hug, but while I was struggling with my seat belt, Lee knocked on the glass. I rolled down the window, put *Desert Hearts* out of my mind, and kissed her for what I had a hunch was likely to be the last time.

I stood shivering in the street outside the hostel and knocked on Sylvia's car window. I was high as a kite and dizzy with fatigue.

I wouldn't ask anything naff like when we were likely to see each other again. I would just wave as she drove away. Sylvia probably did this kind of thing all the time; she was far too famous to be wanting anything heavy. I'd show her that I was sophisticated enough not to fall for her all in one go, not to ask for anything but the hour and a half she had to give me.

When she rolled down the window, I smiled and leaned in. I shut my eyes and felt Sylvia's tongue against mine, saying something neither of us could hear. So brief, so slippery, nothing you could get a hold of.

The Welcome

Women's Housing Coop Seeks Member. Low Rent, Central Manchester. Applicants Must Have Ability to Get On With People and Show Comittment To Cooperative Living. All Ethnic Backgrounds Particularly Welcome To Apply.

I tore stripes off Carola when I noticed that ad, taped up in the window of the newsagent's next door to our house. She said I could hardly complain if I'd missed the meeting where the wording of the ad was agreed on, but I should feel free to share my feelings with the policy group anyway. "They're not feelings," I said, "they're facts."

Dear Policy Group, I typed furiously.

Re: Recruitment Ad. I suggest we use a hyphen in Co-op, if we don't want the Welcome Co-operative to be confused with a chicken coop. Some other problems with this ad: "Seeks Member" sounds like we don't have any members yet. Do you

*mean "Seeks New Member"?—and, besides, it sounds rather
like a giant dildo. Also, I'm just curious, why should the
applicants HAVE "Ability To Get On With People" (and is
People a euphemism for Women, by the way, given that this is
a women-only co-op?), but only SHOW "Commitment To Co-
operative Living" (commitment being spelled with two m's
and one t, not vice versa, by the way, in case anyone cares)?
Or are you suggesting that an applicant might claim to
HAVE such a commitment but needs to be forced to SHOW it,
e.g. through housework? And if so, why not say so?*

*The way I see it, there's not a lot of point having policies
on Equal Opportunities and Accessibility and Class and Race
Issues if we're going to keep on writing our ads in politically
correct gobbledygook that would put off anyone who's not
doing a Ph.D. And speaking of Race Issues, what on earth
does it mean to say that ALL ethnic backgrounds (members
of all ethnic groups, I think you mean) are "Particularly
Welcome To Apply"? Who's not-so-particularly-welcome,
then? Or do you mean white people don't count as an ethnic
group? I can't believe one four-line ad can give such an
impression of confusion, illiteracy, and pomposity all at once.
Why can't we just say what we mean?*

My hands were shaking, so I left it at that and printed out the
page. *Yours, Luce,* I'd added at the bottom, as if it weren't obvious
who'd written the letter from vocabulary alone. As Di was always
telling me, "It's like you've got the *Oxford English Dictionary* hidden up your arse." She had a point; some days I sounded more
like eighty than eighteen. I suppose I'd read too many books to be
normal.

It was only when I was sealing the letter into the envelope that
I remembered: in my absence, at the last co-op meeting, they'd de-

cided to rotate me from the maintenance crew to the policy group, because, as I'd been pointing out for ages, my syntax was a lot better than my plumbing. I was meant to replace Nuala, who was moving back to Cork, and if Rachel made up her mind to go off for three months to that organic farm in Cornwall, it occurred to me now, there'd be no one left in the policy group but myself and Di, and I'd end up handing her my letter like some mad silent protestor. Or if Di happened to be away that evening, on one of those Buddhist retreats her boyfriend ran, it would be just me having a one-person meeting, and I'd have to read my own letter aloud and make snide comments about it.

Arghhhh. The joys of communal living. After two years in the Welcome Co-op, I could hardly remember living any other way.

I ripped the envelope open and went downstairs. In the kitchen I pinned my letter up on the corkboard over the oven—the only place you could be sure everyone would see it. I went back down for a prawn cracker five minutes later and found Di reading it as she stirred her miso. "The ad was appalling," I said defensively.

"Yeah. Carola wrote it after the rest of us had gone down the pub. You know you use the word 'mean' four times in the last paragraph?" she asked, grinning.

I ripped the thing down and stuffed it into the recycling bin.

"Temper, temper," she said, tucking away a pale curl that had come out of her bun.

I licked my prawn cracker. "What's wrong with me these days, Di?"

"You know what's wrong with you."

"Apart from that." I shifted uncomfortably against the wooden counter.

"There is no apart from that, Luce. You've been a virgin too long."

My head was hammering; I rubbed the stiff muscles at the back of my neck. "Why does every conversation in this house have to come back to the same-old same-old?"

"Well Jesus, child, take a look at yourself."

I glanced down as if I'd got food on my shirt.

"You came out at fifteen, but you haven't done a thing about it yet. For years now you've seen every kind of woman pass through these doors, and you haven't let one of them lay a hand on you. No wonder you've got a headache!"

I was out the door and halfway up the garden by then. Di was fabulous, but I could do without another of her rants about regular orgasms being crucial to health. Nurses were all like that.

The June sun was slipping behind the crab apple tree. My courgettes were beginning to flower, a wonderful pale orange. I picked a couple of insects off them. When I'd moved into the Welcome, the week after my sixteenth birthday—the date chosen to ensure my mother would have had no legal way of dragging me back home, if she'd tried, not that she did—anyway, at first I found the constant company unbearable. I'd been used to spending all my after-school time locked in my bedroom with a book, living in the world of the Brontës or Jung or Isabel Allende; just about any world would do so long as it wasn't the one my mother lived in. And now all at once I was supposed to become part of some bizarre nine-woman feminist family. The housing co-op was what I'd chosen but it freaked me out all the same. In the early weeks, digging the garden was the only thing that kept me halfway sane. The vegetable plot had been strictly organic ever since I'd taken it over, but sometimes I got the impression that most of my sweat went into providing a feast for the crawlies.

Di was sort of right. I was a pedant, a twitching spinster, dried up before my time, and I'd only just finished secondary school! Sixty-seven fortnightly co-op meetings (I'd counted them up, recently) had frayed me to a thread: all those good intentions, all that mind-numbingly imprecise jargon. These days even typos in the *Guardian* made me itch. When I was old, I knew I wouldn't wear purple, like in the poem; instead I'd limp around under cover of darkness, correcting the punctuation on billboards with a spray can. Rachel said I should become a proofreader and make a mint, instead of starting political studies at the university this October and probably ending up politically somewhere to the right of Baroness Thatcher. On my eighteenth birthday, when Di gave me a T-shirt that read DOES ANAL RETENTIVE HAVE A HYPHEN?, I was too busy considering the question to get the joke.

It wasn't that I didn't like the idea of sex, by the way. I was just picky. And somehow, the more free-floating fornication that went on in the Welcome—the louder the shrieks from Carola's attic room, the more often I walked into the living room and found anonymous bodies pillowing the sofa—the less I felt like attempting it. Besides, there was never enough privacy. At my birthday party I got as far as kissing a German acupuncturist, and by breakfast the next morning my housemates had given me: (*a*) a pack of latex gloves (Di), (*b*) much conflicting advice about sexual positions (Rachel, Maura, Iona, and the two Londoners whose names I was always getting wrong way around), and (*c*) a paperback called *Safe Space: Coping with Issues around Intimacy* (Carola, of course). The acupuncturist left me a message, but I never rang back. Collectively my housemates had managed to put me right off.

So Nuala went back to Cork, and that's how it all began. The Welcome's rent was so low, it was never hard to fill a place. We interviewed seven women, one endless hot Saturday at the end of June. I was the one who volunteered to tell JJ she was the lucky winner.

"I wasn't sure was it all right to ring at nearly midnight—," I told her, down the phone.

"Yeah, no problem. That's . . . excellent." Her voice was as deep as Tracy Chapman's, and hoarse with excitement.

"Well, we're all really glad," I added, somehow not wanting the call to be over so soon.

I could hear JJ let out a long breath of relief. "I never thought I'd hear from you people again, actually. I made such a cock-up of the interview."

"Not at all!" I said, laughing too loudly.

"But I hardly said a word."

"Well, we figured you were just shy, you know. All the others were brash young things who got on our nerves."

Di, passing through with a tray of margaritas for her hospital friends who were partying on the balcony, raised one eyebrow.

It was kind of a lie; we hadn't been at all unanimous. Carola had voted for a ghastly woman from Leeds who claimed to be very vulnerable after a series of relationships with emotionally abusive men and wanted to know did we do co-counseling after house meetings? But in the end I played the race card, like the hypocrite I was; I told Carola that if we were serious about Particularly Welcoming and all that—if we wanted to improve the co-op's representation of women of colour from none in nine to one in nine— then we had to pick JJ.

Not that her being black had anything to do with it, for me. I wanted JJ because her fingers were long and broad and made me feel slightly shaky.

The day she was to move in, I came downstairs to find the living room transformed. There was a Mexican blanket slung over the back of the pink couch, an African head scarf wrapped around the lampshade, and my framed print of Gertrude Stein appeared to have metamorphosed into a dog-eared poster of a woman carrying a stack of bricks on her head that said OXFAM IN INDIA: EMPOWERMENT THROUGH EDUCATION.

Rachel, Di, and Iona claimed to know nothing about the changes. Carola said she was only acting on the advice of a book called *Anti-Racism for Housing Co-ops*. She was trying to make the atmosphere more inclusive, less Anglo-Saxon.

"Gertrude Stein was an American Jew!" I protested.

"She lived on inherited wealth," said Carola, spooning up her porridge.

"So?"

"So I just don't think we should cover our walls with images of women of privilege; it sends out the wrong signals."

"Gertrude Stein only covered about three square feet of the wall!"

Carola rolled her pale blue eyes. "You're being petty, Luce. I wonder why you've got so much invested in the status quo?"

"Because the status quo was a pretty stylish living room. And you know what signals this room is sending out now, Carola? Embarrassingly obvious, geographically muddled, white guilt signals!"

She pointed out that we all had feelings around these issues.

"Feelings about," I corrected her, "not around, *about*," and it all went downhill from there, especially when I pulled down the Oxfam poster and a corner tore off. Di had to intervene, and it took hours of "feelings around" before we reached a grudging compromise: yes to the Mexican blanket, no to the lampshade wrap, and OK to a laminated poster of dolphins that none of us liked.

I'd been planning to do some weeding that afternoon because my eyes were sore from reading Dostoevsky in a Victorian edition with tiny print, but I was afraid I wouldn't hear the front door. I pottered around in my room instead, and when I heard the bell I ran downstairs to help JJ carry up her stuff. But she didn't have much in the way of stuff, it turned out: two backpacks, a duvet, and a rat.

I backed away from the cage.

"Ah, yeah, his name's Victor," she said nervously, clearing her throat. "I forgot to mention him at the interview."

"Oh, I'm sure everyone'll love him," I told her, grabbing the cage by its handle and frantically thinking, *Hamster, it's more or less a hamster.* I managed to carry the cage all the way upstairs without looking inside.

I was going to offer to help JJ unpack, but somehow I lost my nerve. There was something private about the way she dropped her bags in the corner beside Victor's cage and stood looking out the window. "This room gets the sun in the late afternoons," I told her; "I lived here, my first year in the co-op," but she just nodded and smiled a little, without looking back at me.

That night we had a communal dinner in JJ's honour, even though when the nine of us sat down together there was barely elbow room to use a fork. I talked too much, ate too much of Melissa's sushi and Kay's gooseberry fool, and felt rather ill. JJ seemed to listen attentively to the conversation—which covered global warming, how to eat a lychee, the government's treachery, what we wanted done with our bodies when we died, and (the inevitable topic) female ejaculation—but she said even less than she had at her interview, though I wouldn't have thought that was possible. I wondered whether we sounded peculiar to her, or ranty, or Anglo-Saxon.

Iona carried in the tray of coffee, chai, peppermint tea, and soy shake. "So tell us, JJ," said Carola with a sympathetic smile, "is it going to make you feel at all uncomfortable, d'you think, being the only woman of colour in the co-op?"

Di rolled her eyes at me, but it was too awful to be funny. I stared out the window at my tomato plants, mortified.

But JJ just shrugged and sipped her coffee.

Carola wouldn't let it rest, of course. "How old would you say you were, like, when you first became aware of systemic racism?"

"Carola!" Di and I groaned in unison.

This time JJ let out a little grunt that could have been the beginning of a laugh. Then she muttered something that sounded like "Bodies are an accident."

If I hadn't been sitting right beside her, I mightn't have caught that at all. Startled, I looked down at myself. A short, skinny, pale, post-adolescent Anglo-Saxon body; a random conglomeration of genes.

Afterwards JJ volunteered to wash up, so I said she and I would do it and everybody else was to get out of the kitchen. Some went to bed, and some went out to smoke dope by the bonfire, and I got to stand beside JJ, watching how gently she handled the plates. I took them dripping from her big hands, one by one, and wiped them dry.

Her hundreds of skinny plaits gleamed; I wondered how she kept them like that. Under her army surplus shirt her shoulders were wider than anyone's I knew. She had all she needed to be a total butch and didn't seem to realize it.

"So how did you pick the name?" she asked at last, jerking me out of my daze.

"What, Luce? Well, I was christened Lucy, but I've always—"

"No," she interrupted softly, "the co-op's name, the Welcome."

"Oh," I said, with an embarrassed laugh.

"Is it, like, meant to sound like everyone's welcome?"

"No, actually, it's named after some defunct co-op down in London, on Welcome Street," I told her. "When they folded they passed the leftover money to a group in Manchester that was just starting up. Before my time."

"So are you really only eighteen?"

I almost blushed as I nodded.

JJ had to be in her twenties, herself, but she didn't specify. In fact she hadn't volunteered any information about herself yet, it occurred to me now.

The whole time I'd lived in the Welcome—with all the guff that got talked about acceptance and non-judgmentalism—I'd never met anyone half as accepting as JJ. Her tolerance even crossed the species barrier; it didn't seem to have occurred to her, for instance, that a rat wasn't a suitable pet. (And Victor did turn out to be a total charmer.) Like a visitor from Mars, JJ displayed no fixed opinions about race, class, or any other label. Though she'd chosen to live in a women-only housing co-op, I never heard her make a single generalization about men (unlike, say, Iona, whose favourite joke that summer was "What's the best way to make a man come?"—"Who the fuck cares!").

When various of our housemates talked as if all the world was queer, JJ didn't join in, but she didn't make any objection, either. She listened with her head bent, wearing what Di called her "wary Bambi" look. At JJ's interview, I remembered, it was Rachel who'd come out with the usual uncomfortable spiel about "This co-op has members of a variety of sexualities," and instead of giving either of the two usual responses—"Oh, but I have a boy-friend" or "Fab!"—JJ had just nodded, eyes elsewhere, as if she were being told how the washing machine worked.

Shy people annoyed Di; she thought it was too much hard work, digging conversation out of them, and the results were rarely worth it.

"But is she or isn't she, though?" I begged Di.

"How should I know, Luce?"

"Didn't they teach you how to assess people at nursing school?"

Di laughed and flicked her hair back from her soup bowl. She blew on her spoon before she answered me. "Only their health. All I can tell you is the woman seems in good shape, apart from a bit of acne and a few stone she could afford to lose."

I felt mildly offended by that—JJ being the perfect shape, in my book—but I stuck to the point. "Yeah, but is she a dyke?"

Di twinkled at me. "What do you care, Miss Celibate?"

Not that I thought I had much of a chance, whatever kind of sexuality the woman had, but I needed to know anyway. Just to have some information on JJ. Just to find out whether it was worth letting her into my dreams.

One evening when I came in after the news, JJ told me, "The government are cutting housing benefit," and before I could stop myself, I said, "The government *is*."

Her thick black eyebrows contracted.

"Sorry. It's just—"

"Yeah?"

"It's a collective noun," I muttered, mortified. "It takes the singular. But it doesn't matter." I suddenly heard myself: what an unbearably tedious teenager!

But JJ's bright teeth widened into a grin. "You like to classify things, don't you, Luce?" she said. "Everything in its little box."

"I suppose so." I thought about how good my name sounded in her husky voice.

"Do you classify people, too?"

"Sometimes," I said, trying to sound cheeky, now, rather than obnoxious. "Like, you, for instance, I'd say . . ." I was bluffing; I tried to think of something she'd like to hear. "I'd say you're some-one who's at peace with yourself, I suppose," I told her. "Because you only speak when you've something to say. Unlike someone like me, who rabbits on and on and on all the time." I shut my mouth, then, and covered it with my hand.

The light was behind JJ; I couldn't read her eyes. "That's how you'd describe me, is it, Luce? At peace with myself?"

"Yeah," I said doubtfully.

She put her throat back and roared. Her deep laughter filled the room.

"What's the joke?" asked Rachel, sticking her head in the door, but I just shrugged.

Well, at least JJ found me funny, I told myself. It was better than nothing.

I still hadn't gathered a single clue about her sexual orientation. Some mornings, I woke with the clenched face that told me I'd been grinding my teeth again. To me, the fact that I was a dyke had been clear as glass by my thirteenth birthday, but then, precision was my thing. Maybe JJ was one, too, and didn't know it yet, would never know it till my kiss woke her. Or maybe she was one of those "labels are for clothes" people, who couldn't bear to be categorized. She dressed like a truck driver, but so did half the straight girls nowadays. With anyone else I would have pumped her friends for information, but JJ didn't seem to have any friends in Manchester. She worked long shifts at the Pizza Palace, and she never brought anyone home.

We got on best, I found, when we just talked about day-to-day matters like the colour of the sky. No big questions, no heavy issues. The sweetest times that summer were when she came out to help me with the vegetables. After a long July day we'd each take a hose and water one side of the garden, not speaking till we met at the end by the crab apple tree. Sometimes she brought Victor's cage down from her room for an airing. If Iona—who called him *that rodent*—wasn't in the garden, JJ would let him out for a run; once I even fed him a crumb from my hand.

We got talking once about why I wanted to do politics at college in the autumn. "I just think it'll be interesting to find out how things work," I said.

"What things?"

"Big things," I said, trying to sound dry and witty. "Countries, information systems, the global economy, that sort of thing. What goes on, and why."

JJ shook her head as if marveling and bent down to rip up some bindweed. I waited to hear what she thought; you couldn't rush her. "I dunno," she said at last, "I find it hard enough to understand what's going on inside me."

I waited, as I trained the hose on the tomato patch, but she didn't say another word.

Some days that summer I had this peculiar sense of waiting, from when I first rolled out of my single bed till long after midnight when I switched off my light; my stomach was tight with it. But nothing momentous ever happened. JJ never told me what I was waiting to hear—whatever that was.

She lavished care on Victor the rat, stroking his coat and scratching behind his ears with a methodical tenderness that softened me like candle wax. But she never touched another human being, that I could see. She wouldn't take or give massages; instead of good-bye hugs, she nodded at people. It was just how JJ was. I knew I shouldn't take it personally, but of course I did.

Iona didn't like her one bit, I could tell. Iona specialized in having enough information to take the piss out of anyone; pinned to her bedroom wall was a sprawling multicoloured diagram of who'd shagged who on the Manchester women's scene since 1990. One evening a few of us were in the living room, and JJ was stroking Victor all the way down his spine with one finger, very slowly and firmly. Iona walked in and said, "I get it! You don't fancy humans at all, just rats."

JJ threw Iona one unreadable look, scooped Victor back into his cage, and disappeared up the stairs.

The room was silent. "Aren't you ever going to give up?" I asked, without looking up from my book.

"Oh, she's probably just another repressed virgin," Iona threw in my direction.

But it didn't even have to be questions about sex that made JJ bolt, I discovered. She was prickly about the slightest things. For instance, one Sunday morning, most of us were lying around in the garden, half naked. JJ was wrapped up in her huge white flannel dressing gown, as usual. Rachel, bored of the newspapers, started teasing me about waxing my moustache off.

"What are you talking about?"

"I saw your little box of wax strips in the bathroom, Luce. Trying to get all respectable before you start college, are you?"

JJ lurched out of her deck chair so fast she knocked it over. She stomped off into the house, her dressing gown enveloping her like a ghostly monk. We all stared at each other.

"Which particular sore point was that?" snapped Rachel.

I shrugged uncertainly. "Maybe the wax is hers."

"Who cares if it is?" Iona butted in. "I've got pubes down to my knees, for god's sake!"

Di spoke from behind her magazine. "Hands up who didn't need to know that."

Di, Kay, and I put our hands in the air. Maura let out a yelp of laughter.

"Well, one reason I moved in here," growled Iona, "was to get away from that crap about what should and shouldn't be talked about. Nothing's unmentionable!"

"Yeah, well you can mention what you like as long as you leave JJ alone." That came out more loudly than I meant it to. I kept my eyes on the article on permaculture I was skimming. In the silence I could almost hear the others exchange amused glances. Nothing was ever private in the Welcome.

It troubled me that JJ would be so embarrassed about something petty like having a slight, faint moustache. Hadn't anybody ever told her what a handsome face she had? Now I came to think about it, she couldn't bear praise. "*Seriously* cute," I'd let myself say once when she'd come in wearing a new pair of combat trousers—that was all, two words—and she'd glanced down as if she'd never seen herself before and froze up. Could it be that she didn't like her body—the solid, glorious bulk that I let myself think of only last thing at night, in the dark?

Di was doing the pressure points in my neck one night during the news; she said I felt like old rope.

"Sleek and flexible?"

"No, all hard with salt and knotted round itself."

I stared glumly at the TV pictures.

"Jesus, Luce," asked Di out of nowhere, "why her?"

My head whipped round.

Di pushed it back into place gently. "And don't say 'who?' You're so obvious. Whenever JJ's in the room you sit with your limbs sort of *parted* at her."

My face scalded. "No I don't."

"Even Kay's noticed, and Kay wouldn't register the fall of a nuclear bomb."

I hid my face in my hand.

"Of all people to fall for!" said Di crossly.

"What's wrong with her?" I asked.

"JJ's an untouchable, honey."

I flinched at the word.

"You know it's true. That rat is the only one let into her bed. You'll never get anywhere with her in a million years. Don't take it personally; nobody could get past that force field."

"I think she cares about me," I said, very low. "When I had bad cramps, last month," I added in what I knew was a pathetic voice, "she left a tulip outside my door."

"Of course she cares about you," said Di pityingly. "Leave it at that."

But she didn't know how it was. JJ and I stayed up late sometimes; after the others had all gone to bed, we raided the fruit bowl and watched any old rubbish that was on television. Once, in the middle of a rerun of *Some Like It Hot,* my hand was lying on the couch about half an inch from hers, but no matter what I told myself, I couldn't bring myself to close the gap. JJ stared at the flickering screen, quite unaware.

I couldn't sleep, too many nights like that one, wondering what it would be like. Just the back of her hand against mine, that's all I imagined. I had a feeling it would be hot enough to burn.

August came in hot and cloudy. The tomatoes hung fat but green in the humid garden. Di and I were peeling carrots one morning. She was looking baggy-eyed after a bad shift in the emergency room. "Your problem is, Luce," she began out of nowhere, "you're too picky. You'll never find everything you're looking for in one woman."

"What if I already have?" I muttered, mutinous.

She let out a heavy sigh to show what she thought of that.

I knew I shouldn't push it, but I couldn't stop. "What if JJ's my ideal woman?"

"Your ideal fantasy, you mean. Listen, next time try picking someone who's willing to sleep with you. Call me old-fashioned, but it's a big plus!"

Irritated, I gave my finger a bad scrape on the peeler.

"You should have copped off with someone your first week in this house," said Di.

"With whom, exactly?" I asked, sucking the blood off my knuckle.

"I don't know," she said, "someone old and wise and relaxed

who wouldn't have put you through any of this angst. Someone like me," she added, lopping off a carrot top.

I stared at her through my sweaty fringe. "You're not serious," I told her.

"Well, no," said Di with one of her dirty laughs. There was a pause. "But I might have been, two years ago," she added lightly, "when you were all fresh and tempting."

"It's a bit bloody late to tell me now!" My voice was shrill with confusion.

"Oh, chop your carrots, child."

We worked on. I thought about Di and about her current boyfriend, Theo, quite a witty guy who remembered to put the seat down and, judging by the retreats he ran, which involved sitting cross-legged on a mat for six hours a day and Understanding the Pain, he seemed to have more staying power than her others. "Besides," I said at last, getting my thoughts in order, "you're straight."

She laughed again and did her *Star Trek* voice. *"Classification Error Alert!"*

I was sad then, and Di could tell.

"Don't worry about it, Luce," she said gently, shoveling the chopped carrots into the pot. "In the long run, you know, if two people matter to each other, it doesn't make much difference whether they've ever actually done the business or not."

She meant her and me, but in the weeks that followed I tried applying her words to me and JJ. I repeated them to myself whenever JJ left the room. If it was love, it should be enough on its own.

On the August bank holiday the weather was so sticky I felt like my skin was crawling. It was too unpleasant to work in the garden, even. JJ was at the Pizza Palace all day; I just hoped they were paying her time and a half. I sat in the shady living room and did a cryptic crossword with 108 clues. Whenever any of the others wandered by they offered to help, but they only gave stupid answers.

At ten that evening, Carola came downstairs to watch some grim documentary about child abuse. I kept on struggling with the crossword. JJ walked in at half ten, limp, with her uniform still on. I offered her cold mint tea from my herb patch; she grinned and said she'd love some, after her shower. I decided it was going to be a good night after all.

It still would have been, if Iona hadn't been such a maladjusted bollocks. She and her latest, Lynn, were sitting round on the balcony drinking beer. They came downstairs just as JJ was emerging from the bathroom, swaddled in her white dressing gown as usual. She looked cool and serene now; there were tiny flecks of water caught in her dreadlocks. She stood back against the wall to let Iona and Lynn go by; that was the kind of person she was, gentlemanly.

But Iona caught her by the lapel of her dressing gown and said, "Hey, Lynn, have you met JJ? She's the house prude!"

JJ didn't smile. She just kept a tight hold of the neck of her thick robe.

Lynn was giggling, and Iona wouldn't leave it at that. She wasn't even drunk, she was just showing off. "Jesus, woman," she said in JJ's face, "how hot does it have to get before you'll show a little flesh?" She put on a parodic games-mistress voice: "We're all gells here, y'know!" As she spoke she hauled on the dressing gown, and it fell open, and the next thing I knew Iona was on the floor, clutching her face.

JJ, knotted into her robe again, had backed against the door. "She hit me," howled Iona. "The bitch hit me in the eye!"

The next hour was the most awful I'd known in the Welcome. Rachel left her curry on high in the kitchen and ran in with the naturopathic first aid kit. After dabbing Iona's eyelid with arnica, she wanted to take her off to a hospital to have it checked out, "in case the co-op's legally liable," but Di told her not to be such a fuckwit. Every time one of the housemates came down to ask what all the noise was about, this time of night, the story had to be told all over again, in its various competing versions. JJ just sat on the edge of the couch with her face hidden in her hands, except when she was muttering, "Sorry, I overreacted, I'm so sorry," over and over again.

But Carola was the worst. It was as if, for the five years she'd been attending co-op meetings and volunteering to go off to weekend workshops, she'd been in training for this. She got the Policy Book out of the kitchen drawer and read out clause 13 about "unreasonable and unacceptable behaviour."

"*Behaviour* means longer than half a second," I spat at her.

"Violence is unacceptable no matter how long it lasts," she said smoothly.

Kay burst into tears and said she'd come to this co-op to escape male aggression (which was the first any of us had heard of it). "I thought I'd be safe with women," she snuffled.

"You are safe," said Di coldly. "Nothing's happened to you. You were upstairs watering your plants till ten minutes ago."

"And besides," I said incoherently, "what about Iona's aggression? She started it. She tried to rip JJ's dressing gown off."

"I did not," growled Iona from behind the bag of frozen peas Lynn was holding to her face.

"You did so. You're the most aggressive person I've ever met, male or female," I bawled at her.

At which point Di tried to calm us all down. "OK, OK," she said, "let's agree that Iona . . . violated JJ's bodily integrity"—I could see her mouth twitch with laughter at the phrase—"and that JJ . . ."

"Made a totally inappropriate response." Carola was icy.

"Oh come on." I was pleading with her now. "Who's to say what's an appropriate response? These things happen. You can't make rules for everything."

But I was wrong, apparently. Carola had the Policy Book open to another page, and she was reading aloud. "Step one, a formal letter of caution will be sent to Member B to instruct her to cease the offending behaviour—"

"She has ceased!" I looked over at JJ, who was bent over on the couch as if she had cramps.

"Or not to repeat it."

There was a long pause. I drew breath. Well, who cared about a formal letter anyway? It would all blow over. We'd be laughing at this by next weekend.

"We don't know that she won't repeat the behaviour," said Kay, quavering.

JJ stood up, then. Her hands hung heavy by her sides. "That's right," she said hoarsely. "You all don't know the first thing about anything."

The silence was broken by Carola, reading from the Policy Book again. "In the case of an act of violence, the co-op may proceed directly to step three, eviction."

Everyone stared at her. None of us had noticed the smell, till then, or the smoke fingering its way along the corridor. Only when the alarm began to squeal did we come to our senses.

In the kitchen the cork notice-board over Rachel's curry pot had gone up in flames. Di threw a bowl of water at it, putting out the fire and soaking Kay's pajamas. The smell was hideous. Phone messages, recycling schedules, minutes of meetings, a postcard from an ex-housemate in Java, and a pop-up card I'd got for my eighteenth birthday were all black and curled as feathers.

The eviction clause was never put to the test. JJ gave her notice the next day.

I was so full of rage I couldn't uncurl my fingers. "You could have stayed," I told her in her bedroom, not bothering to keep my voice down. "Why do the petty bureaucrats always have to win? It's Iona we should have kicked out, or Carola. All you did was defend yourself for half a second. Why is physical violence so much worse than the emotional kind, anyway?"

JJ said nothing, just carried on stowing away her rolled-up socks in the bottom of her backpack.

"My father hit my mother once," I told her, "and you know what?"

That made her look up.

"She deserved it. The things my mother used to say, I should have hit her myself." Now the tears were snaking down my face.

"Ah, Luce," said JJ. "Don't cry."

I sobbed like a child.

"I'd like to have stayed," she told me. "But I just don't feel welcome anymore."

"You are! Welcome to me, anyway," I choked, ungrammatically.

JJ came over to hug me then. I didn't quite believe she was going to do it. She hunched, a little, as if her back was hurting her. She took me by the shoulders and warily laid her heavy head on my neck. I could feel her hot breath. She smelt of jasmine.

A mad idea came to me then. "Well, I'll move out, too," I said brightly. "We can find a flat to share."

I could see her answer in her face, even before she shook her head.

My ribs felt cold and leaden. "Where are you going, though? You don't have anywhere else to go. Listen, why don't I ring round some of the letting agencies for you? I've nearly a thousand pounds in my account. You can have it."

Her head kept gently swinging from side to side, saying no to everything. "I'll be OK," she whispered.

And then I saw in the back of her dark eyes that she did have somewhere to go, she just wasn't telling me. So I took a step backwards and put my hands by my sides.

The taxi took her away. " 'Keep in touch," I shouted—a meaningless phrase, because JJ and I had never touched in our lives except for about five seconds, just before she left.

I didn't stay long at the Welcome myself, as it happened. Once I started college in the autumn, it seemed to make more sense to live in a student residence so I wouldn't have to trek across town.

The letter didn't reach me for months, because by then Di was off in Tibet and the others at the Welcome claimed to have mislaid my new address. I finally read it the day after Christmas, sitting on a park bench in the college grounds.

If I say hi, this is John, you won't know who I mean, will you? I used to think if anybody found me out, it would be you, Luce. Sometimes you used to look at me so intensely, like there was something on the tip of your tongue, I thought maybe you knew. But I was probably just kidding myself so I'd feel less guilty about bullshitting you all.

They said the hormones would be hard. But what I've found much worse is not quite belonging anywhere and having to lie all the time. Not that I ever had to actually claim to be a woman, because none of you ever asked.

And I am one, you know. Inside. Not where people usually mean by inside, but farther inside than that. I've

*known since I was four years old. I'm not John anymore,
except on my birth certificate; I don't think I ever really was.
I've been JJ for a long time now. That's why it wasn't exactly
a lie, what I let you all think. To have said "Hi, my name is
John" would have been the biggest lie.*

*But the body I've got is mostly wrong, still, and the
doctors won't give me the operation because they say I'm
not serious enough about wanting it. According to their
classifications, I should wear makeup and tights and get a
boyfriend. I have to keep telling them that's not the kind of
woman I am. I spent too many years pretending already, to
want to start all over again.*

*I did like living in the co-op, more than I showed,
probably. Most days I was able to forget about the whole man/
woman business and just be one of the girls. I'm sorry I
cocked it all up in the end (no pun intended).*

*I just wanted to tell you something, Luce, that's why I'm
writing. I just wanted to say (here goes), if I had the right
body—if I had any kind of body I was wanting to show or
share, or if I could feel much of anything these days—then it
would be you I'd want to do it with. You'd be welcome. That's
all. I just thought I'd tell you that, because what the hell.*

It all happened years ago. I wouldn't believe how many years,
except for the date on the letter, which I keep folded up small in a
sandalwood box with a couple of other important things, like my
grandfather's pipe and an iris from the bouquet Di chucked me at
her and Theo's wedding.

These days I have a very normal happy life, in a two-dykes-
and-their-dogs-and-their-mortgage kind of way. I'm not quite so
picky anymore, and I don't let myself correct people's grammar, at
least out loud. Last I heard, the Welcome was still going, though I

don't know anyone who lives there. I wonder are the potatoes still sprouting down the back of the garden, the ones I watered with JJ? I thought I saw her at Pride one year—or the back of her neck, anyway—but I might have been imagining it.

In case this sounds like some kind of doomed first-love story, I should admit that I was grateful there was no return address on that letter. I was young, that summer—younger than I knew, it occurs to me now. JJ must have known that I wouldn't have been able to write back; that I'd have had no idea what to say.

Her letter has gone all shiny at the folds. I don't read it for nostalgia; I prefer not to read it at all. It brings back that bruised, shivery feeling of being in love and making one mistake after another, of waking up to find myself in the wrong story. I keep the letter in my box for anytime I catch myself thinking I know the first thing about anything.

DEATH

The Dormition of
the Virgin

Fiorenze (Florence), Stazione Rifredi, Monday, Day 1.
Caffe Latte.

George had a brown leather notebook to record his impressions so that he could tell his friends at college exactly what Italy was like, rather than blabbing on vaguely. The caffe latte was much weaker than in the college café in Loughborough, but subtler, more authentic. He was killing half an hour in Stazione Rifredi, which had turned out not to be the main Florence station; because it had said FIORENZE on the sign, he'd leapt off the train like a twat, so now he had to wait for a local train to take him south to Stazione di Santa Maria Novella, which was the real one. He thought the Italians should label things more clearly.

They eat and drink standing up at the counter, very
odd—meant to be laid-back Mediterranean people?

People kept leaving the door of the buffet open and the February air skated in. But the guidebook said you really had to come off-season if you wanted to see the art without peering over stinky hordes.

As soon as he got to Florence proper, George went into Santa Maria Novella, the first church on his list.

Said to be finest Gothic church in Tuscany. Stripy b/w
facade, not at all like Gothic at home.

The wheels of his suitcase squeaked embarrassingly on the church's flagstones. It was hard to see in the chapels, but he'd brought his small torch, as the guidebook had suggested. He leaned against the wall and penciled in some notes.

Lots of martyrdoms (St. Lawrence on his griddle, St.
Catherine? with breasts on plate, St. Sebastian stuck
with arrows) and a raising of Drusiana, who she?

George had picked out the Hotel Annunziata because the guidebook said it was cheap, five minutes from Ponte Vecchio, and had lashings of atmosphere. It was three floors up over a posh wineshop. The Signora who ran the place could have been anything between sixty and ninety; despite his Linguaphone course, he couldn't understand a word she said, and he thought she must be speaking some kind of heavy Tuscan dialect. She uncurled a hand at the frescoes in the lounge, then led him down a skinny corridor to indicate the toilet and the shower. The Signora took George's passport away to her own apartment for a few minutes, leaving him standing round gazing at the frescoes, and then she came back with a police form for him to sign. He wondered whether all tourists had to do that or just young guys, potential troublemakers.

Unpacking in his bare square room, it occurred to George

that he might be the only person staying there. He hadn't heard any voices, but maybe the others would come in later. This place was like something from another century—the pensione from *A Room with a View*.

> *No view but what can expect for €49 a night? What's that in sterling?—must check. Hallway's got stucco putti, I think probably real. For lunch had pasta in gritty squid ink (not good), outside because there was a bit of sun but pretty cold.*

George had been planning this trip ever since he was seven and saw a film about the Medicis. He was doing social studies at Loughborough but was thinking of changing to art history. His Florence itinerary was only provisional; he knew he probably wouldn't get to all these churches and museums, but he meant to try, because for all he knew he'd never be here again. (His aunt had always wanted to go to Bali, but now she had emphysema.) If he started to flag, he could always have an espresso.

George knew the statues outside Orsanmichele were nearly all copies, but he had decided that looking at the full-size copies in their original setting was actually more authentic than looking at the originals (brought inside to escape the acid rain) in the museum, and besides, the museum was shut on Mondays.

> *The guidebook says most tourists rush right past Orsanmichele wh. is prob. single most important series of early Renaissance statues. I know I'm one too (a tourist) but they repel me (tourists, not statues). E.g. trying to soak up ancient atmosphere in this little piazza Santa something-or-other but scooters keep roaring by and there's two girls at the next table with Liverpool accents.*

The guidebook said the closed museum also had an excellent *Transition of the Virgin*.

There's just as much art about Mary as about JC, really, they're like his 'n her deities. What was she transitioning from, I wonder? Sounds like a sex change.

George just wanted to know, so that the art would make sense; he wasn't into any of that stuff personally. He'd stopped going to church when he was thirteen, and his parents hadn't seemed bothered.

In the Baptistery he craned up at the ancient mosaics. There was Jesus, twenty feet high, with under him all the sarcophagi opening and the dead crawling out, the ones on the left being escorted away to heaven by huge trumpeting angels,

and the poor buggers on the right being grabbed by devils like something out of Star Trek, *leathery bat wings, and enormous Satan munching them two at a time!*

The Baptistery doors were those famous ones Ghiberti had won the competition for in 1401, and George stood with his arms folded and tried to examine the panels closely, but tourists kept pushing past him to get in and out.

In a tiny *osteria* he ordered *pasta e fagioli,* thinking it was pasta with beans, but it turned out to be a bean soup with a few bits of pasta in it, and he was still hungry afterwards. He read his guidebook in bed and thought of asking the Signora for another pillow. There was a bell beside the door to her private apartment, but he didn't want to hassle her; she was probably down on her arthritic knees saying the rosary or something (though, actually, her radio was on). His phrase book didn't have *pillow* in it; he would have to mime the concept, or bring along the one pillow he had and point to it, and then she might think he was allergic to it. Never mind, he could sit cross-legged and lean back against the wall.

Tuesday, Day 2. I know it sounds pretentious, but this isn't a holiday — it's a pilgrimage.

George stood flinching under the shower, fiddling to try to find something between scalding and icy. His hair was still wet as he hurried past the Duomo. He felt like Michelangelo, on his way to choose a block of perfect translucent Carrara marble by the dawn light. Passing a tour party who were emitting the usually clicking and whirring sounds as they squinted up at Brunelleschi's orange dome, George was gratified that he'd decided to leave his camera in his room in Loughborough. This way he would really see things and really remember.

Standing in Piazza della Signoria beside gigantic statues, e.g. Donatello's Judith cutting off the head of Holofernes, noticed I was standing on a purple circle which turned out to be a disc of porphyry to mark where Savonarola (the hellfire-spouting, bonfire of the vanities priest) got burnt alive on 23 May 1498. Fuck!

Every inch of Florence meant something; there were no blank bits. It was slightly exhausting.

At the Uffizi he saw a Greek statue which had once been known as *The Knife Grinder,* but scholars had now established that it was a Scythian preparing his blade in order to flay Marsyas. There was another statue of a man hanging upside down and laughing, only he wasn't laughing, he was howling, and that was Marsyas again. *Gladiator* was nothing to this, George thought queasily. But he definitely preferred art in which something was happening: a fight or a miracle or a death or something. He was already bored with all those pictures of the Madonna tickling the Bambino under his chin.

When he's got his crown of thorns on it's called Ecce
Homo, then the Deposition is when his friends lift
him down off the cross (NB you never see them taking
the nails out with pliers, maybe it would look too
undignified). A Lamentation can also be called Dead
Christ or Piéta (he's not always on Mary's lap,
sometimes just propped up by angels, looking sick or
hungover rather than actually dead, hard to tell).

Back at the Annunziata, his bed had not been made; maybe that was the difference between a pensione and a hotel? Anyway, he liked the privacy; he wouldn't fancy the Signora shuffling round pawing through his stuff. She seemed to keep the radio on all the time; it was a bit sad. George stared at the picture over his bed, the one that looked like two wrestlers going in for a clinch. After he'd taken it down and cleaned the glass on the bedspread, it turned out to be a Visitation of Mary and Elizabeth; they were touching each other's pregnant stomachs. He was starting to recognize all the scenes, now; it was like a code, and he was cracking it.

Wednesday, Day 3. Never never go on holiday with only
one pair of shoes if they're suede. Pissing down all day
and I'm soaked to the ankles, my feet feel like dead fish.

George sat in a cafeteria eating a calzone out of a napkin. He was tempted to go back to the counter and complain that it was cold in the middle, but he'd left his phrase book in his room. He flicked through his notes, trying to figure out whether the Virgin Mary had died or not. In several churches he'd seen paintings called *The Death of the Virgin,* where she was lying there like a normal dying person with grieving relatives (including Jesus holding a baby—maybe his childhood self?). There were other pictures called the "Transition" or "Assumption," which showed Mary floating up to Heaven, looking pretty alive. As far as George could tell, Jesus "ascended" (actively) whereas Mary "was assumed," but what was the difference, apart from grammar? Could you say God assumed her? No, that sounded like he took her for granted. Maybe JC flew up by his own will, whereas Mary was sort of sucked up as if by aliens?

George hadn't time to obsess over these arcane details; he was two-thirds of a day behind on his itinerary. Reckless, he crossed off all the Baroque churches—the Renaissance was more than enough to be going on with—and squelched off to Santa Spirito, which bore a huge, crass sign proclaiming that its restoration was being funded by Gucci. The Church of the Ognissanti meant the "Church of All the Saints"; that was a good way to hedge your bets, George thought a little cynically. He saw a postcard of a painting that used to be there but was now in Berlin: a Giotto from 1310 called *The Dormition of the Virgin.*

Now what the hell's a dormition? Abstract word for sleep? Mary looks comatose in the picture (and about eight feet long), people are standing beside her bed, one guy is hugging her, but you can't tell if her eyes are open.

All the saints died, and so did Jesus (even if he rose again), so if Mary hadn't actually died, that would make her the only human being ever who had avoided it. Not that any of this stuff was actually true, George had to remind himself.

*Some gravestones say "fell asleep" meaning died, but it's
a stupid phrase, I bet they're totally different feelings.
Unless you happen to die in your sleep, which a lot of
people claim they'd like, but I think it's cowardly, I'd
rather be hit by a lorry and look it in the face. The thing
is, whatever's happening, to be totally AWARE and
AWAKE.*

He was starting to shake with cold; he'd have to go back for
dry socks. Passing a bookshop, he had a brain wave. In the English section he found a dictionary of religious terms and looked
up *dormition*. He turned away so the girl at the counter wouldn't
see him taking notes and scribbled in his leather journal.

*Turns out Mary died in the ordinary way, then three
days later Archangel Michael brought her soul back down
to reunite it with her body, Jesus and everybody was
clapping, then she got assumed into heaven again!*

It was very satisfying to sort out the full story.

At the Annunziata, George was suddenly knackered and let
himself get under the sheets. He wished the Signora would turn
her radio off the odd time; all that Western stuff wrecked the atmosphere. Well, of course, Italy was the West, but they could still do
better than Eminem.

When he woke up after an hour, he wanted to borrow an iron,
so he looked it up in his phrase book and knocked on the Signora's door, but she didn't answer; maybe she'd gone out in the
rain. George decided to wear his crumpled jacket for dinner;
who'd be looking at him, anyway?

Thursday, Day 4. My last day, arghhhhh!

George almost ran from church to church that morning, ticking
them off on his list. He had to fend off dozens of leather-jacket
salesmen to get into San Lorenzo. Donatello's late-period pulpit
was the grimmest George had seen, even the *Ascension* panel, with
a wrecked-looking Jesus trying to float off into the sky, but sinking
back down.

> So many of these guys seemed to start out all idealistic
> but got burnt out. Suppose life in Cinquecento would do
> that—plagues, revolutions, etc. Whereas now everything's
> easy and comfortable, no mysteries left, life comes pre-
> packaged by Disney or the Gap, we just drift along and
> nothing ever really happens compared with back then.

In a café, flicking through his highlights of the Uffizi book, he
came across a little panel by Fra Filippo Lippi called *Predella of
the Barbadori: Announcement of the Death of the Virgin*. He
didn't know how he could have missed it when he'd done the Uffizi; maybe because it was so small.

> It looks like an Annunciation at first, because she's
> standing up (not old or anything), and the angel's
> handing her something like a magic wand, or a tall gold
> candle. Wow. Imagine if we all got told when we were
> about to snuff it—like an e-mail, on the day, telling you
> to pack your bags.

Speaking of which, time to go. George headed reluctantly
back to the Hotel Annunziata via a cash machine.

When he'd zipped up his case, he went to the door of the Signora's apartment and knocked a few times, quite loudly. Her radio
was playing "Nights in White Satin"; she had to be a bit deaf, he

thought, though she hadn't seemed it on Monday. *"Bon giorno?"* he called a few times, then, almost shouting, "Signora?" She knew he'd be checking out this afternoon, didn't she?

George was beginning to panic about missing his train. He tried the door handle and walked down the narrow hall. "Signora?" There was an armchair with an ancient-looking radio playing beside it, and an empty espresso cup. He felt it, in case she'd just popped out, but it was cold. He wanted to turn the music down— something old of Sheryl Crow's—but he didn't dare. He got out his wad of cash and counted it, €196; that way he could wave it at her if she appeared, so she'd see why he'd barged in on her.

No one in the tiny kitchen. George's armpits were damp. If you were running a pensione or whatever, you just couldn't behave that way, even if it was off-season. It would serve the old bag right if he walked off without paying. Then it occurred to him to leave the money beside the radio with a note, but he'd packed his pen away with his journal. He put his head into the bedroom to see was there any sign of a ballpoint. It was very dim in there, with the curtains shut, but when George's eyes got used to it, he saw her on the bed.

He dropped some of the money on the floor, and when he bent down to pick it up he thought he might keel over. The Signora could have been asleep; she could have taken a pill or something. But it didn't look like sleep, the way she was lying quite straight on top of the bedspread with her shoes turned up. And he couldn't be sure in the bad light but he thought her eyes were open; he saw some kind of glimmer that had to be an eye. He ran back out to the room with the frescoes and sat on his case to catch his breath. He put the money back in his pocket; one of the notes had stuck to his hand and he had to peel it off.

George knew he should probably go back to check. He hadn't

smelled anything, but it was pretty cold in her room. It could have been days she'd been lying there.

In the end, he crept back into the apartment, just as far as the phone. He had to turn the radio off. He rang 999, but of course that was the British number; what a moron! There wasn't a phone book that he could see, so he had to go back out to his room to find the guidebook. The Italian emergency number turned out to be 113, not very memorable at all, he thought. George didn't make much sense on the phone; all he could say was *"Signora vecchio morte!"*, which was partly French, but the woman on the other end spoke some English and in the end she managed to get the address from him.

After he'd opened all the doors upstairs and downstairs in the lobby, too—he dreaded that he mightn't hear the bell—George waited in the hall with the stucco, and he tried to pass the time by figuring out what all the little *putti* in the frescos were doing. He felt sick. If he never saw another picture again as long as he lived it would be soon enough for him.

When the ambulance guys walked in, George jumped up and started crying, more out of embarrassment than anything else. They didn't seem bothered by this; after all, he told himself, Continental men cried more anyway. There were policemen, too, but not swaggering and fierce, as George had been imagining. He realized that he'd been afraid they'd suspect him of killing the Signora for her heirlooms (the frescoes? the stucco? it was absurd). But it hardly counted as an interrogation; they only took down his name and address from his passport and asked him in English when he had last seen the Signora. "About twenty minutes ago," he said stupidly, and then realized they meant *alive*. "Monday," he told them, "and since then there's only been the radio." Then he thought they might ask him, *Did you not wonder, boy, did you not*

*think it was strange that an old lady would play her radio all day
and all night for three days?*

As soon as the draped stretcher had been carried out, George
was told that he could go.

At the train station he queued up at the ticket office to explain,
but the girl behind the counter seemed bored; she said, "Next
train to Paris, 16:22," and he gathered that his old ticket would
still work. They were very casual about these things here. Of
course he didn't have a couchette on the next train, so he had to sit
up all night.

It got cold. About three in the morning, George realized that
what was digging into his leg was his rent money. He took it out
and felt like a criminal. It occurred to him to post it back from
London, marked *For the heirs and assigns of the Signora of Hotel
Annunziata, Florence.* But what would be the point of that? They
were about to inherit a prime bit of Florentine property even
though they clearly never gave enough of a shit about their grandmother (or whatever she was) to come round and see her, once in
a while. She could have been eaten by dogs, if she'd had dogs!

George wondered why he was getting so angry. For all he
knew, the Signora didn't have any heirs and assigns. He'd been the
last person to see her, and for three days, all he'd done was wish
she'd turn the bloody music off.

He put the money back in his pocket. He took out his notebook.

Left Florence, night train.

He couldn't think what else to put. He thought he should
probably get some sleep, and he put his head back against the
cracked leather of his seat and shut his eyes, but he didn't feel
sleepy, not at all.

Enchantment

Pitre and Bunch knew each other from the old time. They were Louisiana crawfishermen, at least as long as the crawfish were biting. These days, what with global warming and so forth, the cages were mostly empty, and it was hardly worth the trouble of heading out to Mudd Swamp every morning.

The two men were having a smoke at the Bourdreaux Landing one May evening, and discussing whether there was any such thing as a coloured Cajun, which is what Bunch claimed to be. Pitre mentioned, not for the first time, that what flowed in his own veins was one hundred percent French wine. "Every ancestor I ever have was a full-blood Acadian. Cast out of Nova Scotia back in 1755 at the point of a British gun."

"Maybe so," said Bunch, grinning, "but you were born in the state of Texas."

"About one inch over the border," growled Pitre. He was twenty years older than Bunch, and his reddened scalp was grizzled like a mouldy loaf.

"Well, whatever, you know, I'm a live-and-let-live sort of Cajun, my friend," said Bunch, sucking the last from his Marlboro. "I was born and reared in these swamps, but I'm willing to call you brother."

"Brother!" snorted Pitre. "You're a black Creole with a few Sonniers for cousins; that's not the same thing at all."

Just then a candy-apple red Jeep came down the dirt road. Four old ladies spilled out and started taking photographs of the boats. Pitre asked them in French if they wanted to buy some crawfish, then mumbled it again in English; he hauled a cage out of his boat and held it up, with a few red creatures waving inside. The ladies just lengthened their zoom lenses for close-ups.

"Are you fishermen?" one of them asked excitedly, and Bunch said, "No, ma'am. We're federal agents." They peered at his dark, serious face and twittered even more, and one of them asked if she could have her picture taken with him, and afterwards she tipped him ten dollars.

"I don't think the Bureau's gonna approve, *cher*," commented Pitre as the tourists drove off waving through their shiny windows.

"I'll put it in the Poor Box on Sunday," said the younger man.

Pitre let out a sort of honk through his nose, got back in his boat, and said something about checking that alligator bait he'd left hanging off a tree.

"You marinade the chicken good?"

"It stinks worse than your wife," Pitre assured him, and drove off, the snarl of his engine ripping the blue lake like paper.

When the older man got to the other side of the cypress swamp, the shadows were lengthening. His gator bait dangled, untouched except by the hovering flies. Pitre cut the rope down and hung it from another tree at the south edge of the basin, where he'd seen a big fellow the year before, thirteen feet if he was an inch. Pitre wondered how much gators were going for an inch, these days. You could sell the dried jaws to tourists, too. Tourists would buy turds if you labeled them A LITTLE BIT OF BON TEMPS FROM CAJUN COUNTRY.

It was cool, there under the trees, with the duckweed thick as guacamole, making the water look like ground you could stretch out on. All the other guys had gone home; Mudd Swamp was his own. Pitre leaned back against an empty crawfish cage and rested his eyes. The air was live with small sounds: a bullfrog, the tock-tock of a woodpecker, the whirr of wings.

He thought it had only been a minute or two, but when he opened his eyes they were crusted at the corners, and the evening was as dark as a snakeskin around him. He was somewhat ashamed of dozing off like that, like an infant or an old man. He couldn't read his watch by the faint light of the clouded moon. He supposed he was hungry, though he couldn't feel it; his appetite had shrunk with the years. Maybe he could fancy some fried oysters. The outboard motor started up with a cough, and Pitre maneuvered his way through the flooded forest. He veered right by the big cypress with the wood-duck box nailed onto it, then picked up some speed.

The stump reared up beneath his boat like a monster. Pitre flew free. The water swallowed him with a cool, silken gulp; it filled his eyes, his ears, plugged his nostrils, and got under his tongue. Pitre couldn't figure which way was up. He reared, shook the duckweed off his face, retched for breath. The water was no higher than his waist. You could drown in a couple of inches. He tried to take a step, but one of his legs wasn't working, damn the thing.

He told himself to stop splashing around. Gators were drawn to dogs, or to anything that moved like a dog. Pitre was shuddering with cold now; it sounded like he was sobbing. He turned his face up to the mottled sky. *Que Dieu me sauve.* A tag from a prayer his grandmother used to say. *Que Dieu me sauve.*

The moon came out like the striking of a match. Vast and pearly, it slipped through the branches of a willow tree and lit up the whole swamp. Pitre looked round and saw exactly where he was. His boat was only the length of a man behind him, not even overturned. He crawled over, got himself in after a couple of tries. There was a water hyacinth caught in the bootlaces of his smashed leg. He heard himself muttering, *Merci merci merci.* The motor started on the first try.

Before Pitre was off his crutches he'd started putting up signs. The ones nailed to electricity poles along the Interstate said simply SWAMP TOURS EXIT NOW. Along the levee road they went into more detail: EXPLORE THE WONDERS OF MUDD SWAMP 2 + ½ MILES FARTHER, or PITRE'S WILDLIFE TOURS TWICE DAILY NEXT LEFT.

Bunch rode the older man pretty hard for it. "What makes you think anybody want to get in your beat-up skiff and go round a little swamp no one's ever heard of? When they could be cruising in comfort in Atchafalaya Basin or Lake Martin?"

"If you build the signs, they will come." Pitre pursed his chapped lips and banged in another nail.

Bunch snorted. "And what's that marker you've hung up on the big willow that says 'Site of Miracle'?"

"You may mock," said Pitre, fixing Bunch with his small eyes, "but I know what I know."

"What do you know, *mon vieux*?"

"I know I was saved."

"Here we go." Nearly dying was a funny thing; Bunch had seen it take one of his aunts the same way: she kept her rosary knotted round her fingers like some voodoo charm.

"And now," said Pitre, wiping his forehead, "I've been called by the Spirit of the Lord to turn away from killing."

"Killing? Who've you been killing?" asked Bunch, pretending to be impressed.

"Crawfish, I mean."

The younger man let out a whoop of delight.

"I've been called to lead tours of the wonders of creation," said Pitre, thrusting a blurred photocopied leaflet into Bunch's hands.

Bunch read it over smothered chicken at his uncle's Cracklin' Café in Eunice. It made him snigger. Old Pitre couldn't spell, for one thing. *"I will tell you and show you also, a great variety of mammals, fish, and foul."*

As he drove back to the Bourdreaux Landing that afternoon to check his cages, he noticed that FRENCH SPOKEN had been added in fresh paint to all the signs.

By the beginning of June there was a little queue of tourists at the landing, most mornings. They shaded their eyes and gawked at the glittering blue sky, the lushly bearded trees. They were from Belgium and Mississippi, Seattle and Quebec, all over the map. They giggled and flicked dragonflies out of each other's hair.

"Hey, Pitre," Bunch called, as he drove up in his truck one day.

The other man walked over, counting twenties.

"I've got to hand it to you, my friend, you've drummed up more trade than I ever thought you could. You or the Spirit of the Lord!"

Pitre nodded guardedly.

"How many tours a day you and your heavenly buddy doing now?"

"If you're going to mock—"

Religion was one of those points folks couldn't bear to be pricked on, but how could Bunch resist? He put his hand on his heart. *"Mon vieux,* you've known me since I was a child. You probably got liquored at my christening! Don't you know mocking's my nature? It's him upstairs that made me that way," he added, straight-faced.

"Or the other guy," said Pitre, turning on his heel.

"So how many tours?" Bunch called after him.

"Four. Maybe five."

Bunch whistled sweetly. "Five tours a day at two hours long? What say I give you a hand, before these tourists wear you out, your time of life?"

But age was another of those sensitive points. "I'll manage," growled Pitre, and walked back to his boat.

In the middle of the night Bunch had a bright idea. He picked up a five-dollar box of pecan pralines in Grand Coteau, scattered them over tissue paper in his wife's old sewing basket, and sold them to the Mudd Swamp Tour queue at two dollars a pop. When he turned up the following day with a tray of alligator jerky, a party was staggering off Pitre's boat, their eyes bright with wonder. "It's so green out there," said one of them, and her friend said, "I've never been anywhere so green."

Bunch had sold a fistful of jerky by the time Pitre came over, his burnt-brick arms tightly crossed. "Get away from my clientele."

"Your what?" laughed Bunch.

"You heard me. Parasite!" Pitre cleared his throat wetly. The next boat party, filing past, were all agog. "I'm trying to do the Spirit's work here, like I've been called to—"

"You've been called, all right, old man. Called to make a fast buck!"

Pitre turned his back and jumped in the boat, surprisingly lithe. It bobbed in the water, and the tourists squealed a little.

By the time he got them out under the cypresses, he'd recovered his temper. The sun was a dazzling strobe, and the sky was ice blue. Iridescent dragonflies skimmed the water, clustered in a mating frenzy. "Lookit there, folks," Pitre said quietly, pointing through the trees at a great white egret on a log, its body one slim brushstroke.

"Is that a swan?" shrieked one little girl. At the sound, the bird lifted off, its huge snowy wings pulling it into the sky.

Pitre's visitors knew nothing about the wonders of creation. He considered it the least he could do to teach them the names of things. He showed them anhinga and glossy ibis; "Go to the state prison, you'll find twenty guys serving time for shooting ibis, that's the tastiest meat," he said sorrowfully. He pointed out water hyacinths in purple bloom, a turtle craning its neck on a stump, and a baby nutria wiping its face with its paws.

"So where's the alligators?" asked a New Yorker with a huge camera round his neck.

"Well, as I told you the start of the tour, I can't guarantee one," said Pitre. "They mostly look like logs. Yesterday's tour we saw three, but it's colder today; they don't come up much till it's sixty degrees or thereabouts."

"There!" yelped a small boy, pointing at a log.

Just then Bunch roared by in his boat, which was ten years newer than Pitre's, with a fancy air-cooled outboard on the back. Cutting the motor, he floated within ten feet of the tour. "Morning, all."

"Crawfish biting?" asked Pitre, cold.

"Some," said Bunch with his gleaming smile. "You folks seen that big-fella gator over there by the houseboat?"

It sounded like bullshit to Pitre, but of course his party clamoured to be taken over there right away, where the nice young man had said. Pitre spent fifteen minutes edging the boat round the shoreline, peering at dead wood and doing slow hand claps to attract any gators in the vicinity. "I'm sorry, folks, I try my best for you, but there's no guarantees in this life," he said at last. "We gotta learn to be grateful, you know?"

But the tourists were not grateful, especially when he admitted that no Louisiana alligators had ever been known to kill a human being. They were not content with blue herons and water snakes, or a fifteen-hundred-year-old cypress, and even when he rounded up the tour by taking them to the SITE OF MIRACLE sign and narrating his rescue from drowning by the God-sent appearance of the full moon, they were unimpressed. When they had driven off in their various SUVs, Pitre saw that there was only seventy cents in his tip jar.

Monday was wet and chilly, but on Tuesday the sun came up strongly again. Pitre sat by his boat all morning, squinting into the distance. His throat was dry. At noon a group drove up in a Dodge Caravan.

"Over here," he called to them hoarsely, "Pitre's Tours, that's me."

"No, I think we're booked on the other one," a lady told him brightly.

He was about to tell her that there was no other one, when a motor started up behind him with a flamboyant roar and he turned and saw Bunch, wearing a fresh white T-shirt that said BUNCH'S ENCHANTED SWAMP TOURS, CHIEF GUIDE VIRGIL BUNCH.

"This way, ladies, gentlemen!" cried Bunch.

Pitre just stared.

"What's enchanted about this swamp?" asked a fat man, looking up from his guidebook.

"Wait and see."

Once his party was on board, Bunch roared out into the middle of the lake as fast as the motor could go, then headed into the flooded woods and ducked in between the stumps. He bumped into a floating log to make the boat jump and the tourists yelp. Then he cut the engine and said, "My friends, welcome to paradise! This just happens to be the only Enchanted Swamp in all of Louisiana."

He had paid the older man's techniques the compliment of extensive study and had decided that the whole experience needed a little bit of personality and pizzazz. Bunch began the tour by claiming ancestry from every culture that made up the tasty gumbo of present-day Acadiana: the Cajuns; the Creoles, black and white; the *gens de couleur libre,* as well as slaves; even the Chitimacha Indians, "who took what they needed and left the balance at peace, you know?" He assured his party that the twenty-foot, flat-bottomed aluminum skiff they were sitting in had been personally designed by him to reach the parts of the swamp where other boats just couldn't go.

"Has this boat a name?" asked one Frenchwoman.

"Sure does," Bunch improvised; "it's called the *Zydeco.*"

Another of his tricks was to present everything in the best light. Instead of telling his tour party that blue herons were very common in this part of the river system, he instructed them to keep an eye out for any flash of blue in the trees, because they just might be lucky enough to spot the rare blue heron, who brought ten years' good luck to anyone who glimpsed him. Finally, catching sight of the head and shoulders of a little gator basking on some driftwood, Bunch made his eyes bulge with amazement and told the tourists that this fellow must be fifteen feet long.

"No!"

"No way!"

"Mr. Bunch? Virgil? Did you say fifteen?"

"They're just like icebergs, that way," he hissed, paddling the boat near enough for them to take photographs. "For every inch you see, there's a foot underneath the water. Not too close!" he told one little girl. Rolling up his jeans, he showed them an old scar on his shin from one time he'd had too much rum and fallen over someone's guitar case: "Gator bite."

One lady took a picture of his scar.

"The only sure way to keep them from attacking," said Bunch, taking out a squashy paper bag, "is to give them some snacks." And he started lobbing lumps of rancid chicken at the alligator, who snapped at one or two before sinking beneath the surface.

On the way back, he gave his happy party the rundown on good ole Cajun humor and *joie de vivre,* not to mention *laissez les bon temps rouler* on the bayou, winding up with a dirty joke about a priest. Finally, he produced his tip jar, which had an alligator jaw glued on top, and they crowed with delight and stuffed their notes through its wicked teeth.

That night Bunch was eating steak and listening to the Breaux Bridge Playboys at Mulate's when Pitre walked in. The older man took one look at him across a crowd of Canadian college kids, then turned and walked back out the door. So that's how it was now, Bunch thought. He wasn't hungry anymore; he pushed away his plate.

The summer turned hot, and there was more than enough business to keep both men busy. Old Pitre didn't alter his methods. He turned up at nine every morning and sat there in the sun waiting for custom, pretending his former friend was invisible. The sun cooked him to red leather; you could nearly hear him sizzle. That was the downside of being a hundred percent pure white Acadian, Bunch thought wryly, but a crack like that wasn't so funny unless you could say it out loud. Ah, to hell, this was none of Bunch's doing; blame the Spirit of the Lord.

He himself had bought a cheap cell phone so tourists could book their tours with him direct. He got his sixteen-year-old daughter to make him a Web site with ten pages of photographs of alligators, and linked it to every listing on Louisiana tourism. "*See local indigenous wildlife in its natural ecohabitat which makes it*

a photographer's dream. Fishing also available." Bunch's real
stroke of brilliance was finding a medium-sized gator with a
stubby tail and feeding it meat scraps daily, until it would come
when he called. After a few weeks he scrawled *"Performance of
Live Cajun Music Included"* on his leaflets, threw a small accor-
dion into his bag, and upped the fare from twenty dollars to
twenty-five.

Whenever he felt his spiel was getting a little flat, he'd spice it
up with a tall tale about a six-foot catfish or a ghost. He took great
pleasure in transforming Pitre's near-death experience into a tale
he called the Swamp Man. "My grandpère used to say the Swamp
Man was a crawfisherman, stayed out too late one night, crashed
his boat into a tree in the dark and drowned in no more than two
feet of water. What's he look like? Well, kind of decayed, you
know—holes for his eyes, and dripping weeds all over him . . ."

Pitre overheard that story, one day, as he was drifting along
with his own tour. He listened in, but didn't look in Bunch's direction. As their boats floated past each other, the tourists waved
in solidarity. Pitre pulled down a tangled clump of grey Spanish
moss and explained in his hoarse monotone that this was an air-
borne plant that did no harm to the trees it hung from.

He kept on telling it how it was. He didn't think the Spirit
wanted him soft-soaping things. He broke it to his tourists that the
trees in Mudd Swamp were slowly dying because the government's levee kept the water at an artificially high level all year
round. Yes, the birds were pretty, but their waste was poisoning
the trees from the top down. And a nutria was no relation to a
beaver; it was more of a rat.

What bugged him the most, as the first summer of his new
saved life wore on, was that his customers were always asking him
where the restroom was—as if an open skiff or a knot of trees
could be hiding such a thing. He wrote at the top of his leaflets,

"NO RESTROOM FACILITIES," but the tourists didn't seem to take it literally. One of them, when Pitre had explained the situation at the landing, said to her husband, "Let's go, hon. I've never been anywhere that didn't have a restroom."

One July afternoon, after the dust of the departing cars had settled, Bunch walked over to Pitre. "I was thinking of renting a Port-o-Let," he remarked, as if resuming an interrupted conversation.

Pitre slowly shifted his gaze from the cypress forest to the man in front of him.

"But they cost a bit, you know, because the company has to drive all the way out here to empty it. What say we go halves?"

"What say nothing," said Pitre through his teeth.

"Oh well, *cher,* if you're going to be like that," said the younger man with a shrug. "Though I don't think your heavenly friend would like your attitude . . ."

Pitre's face never flickered, but the remark had got under his skin. He headed out to the swamp that evening, on his own, to see if it was any cooler than the land. When he got to the Site of Miracle, he cut the engine. He squinted up at the willow tree, but it looked much the same as all the others: a swollen base, tapering to a skinny top. He tried to feel again what it was that had touched him that moonlit night when he'd come within an inch of drowning. A sensation of being marked out, prodded awake, as distinct as a fingertip in the small of the back. He'd been so sure about his new calling at first, but now it seemed as if he'd mistaken some small but crucial marker a while back and gone astray.

A few days later there was a Port-o-Let standing in the shade of a live oak by Bourdreaux Landing. It looked like a grey plastic alien craft. Pitre pretended not to notice. At noon, he was emptying his boat of one group and filling it up with another when a girl ran over. "Uh, I wanted to use the restroom?"

"No restroom," said Pitre automatically.

"I tried the one over there, but it's, like, locked! It says, 'For use of Bunch's Enchanted Swamp Tours only.'"

Pitre's teeth clamped together, and his bad molar started to throb. "That's a mistake," he muttered. "Very sorry, ladies and gentlemen. You'll just have to wait."

"I can't wait two hours," wailed the girl.

"That's the trouble with you kids nowadays," Pitre told her. "Nobody's got any self-control of themselves."

Her family drove back to the hotel, and he didn't get any tips that day, either.

In August it was hitting a hundred by ten in the morning.

Bunch bought a cap with a visor to keep the glare out of his eyes. He took to claiming that his name was authentically Acadian. "Sure is, ma'am. Used to be Bonche, you know, back in Canada, but when the British kicked us out at gunpoint back in 1755, my ancestors had to change to Bunch to avoid persecution."

The young man varied his tall tales to keep himself from getting stale. He always took his tours past a duck blind in the middle of the lake, but sometimes he said it was a man-made nesting sanctuary for orphaned cormorants, and other times he called it a shelter for canoeists caught out on the lake in a lightning storm. Once—just to see if he could get away with it—he claimed it was a Dream Hut for young Chitimacha boys undergoing spiritual initiation.

"The Swamp Man? That's a terrible story," he said towards the end of all his tours, lowering his voice as if he was almost afraid to tell it. "This crawfisherman, back in old-time days, it was a long hard season, and he was desperate to know where the fish were biting, so he did voodoo. You know voodoo?"

Fervent nods all round.

"I bought a how-to book on it in New Orleans," confided one old lady.

Bunch darkened his tone. "So this guy, he conjured up this spirit, and he didn't know it, but it was the devil. This guy struck a bargain that his crawfish cages would always be full, you know? So now the devil had a hold of his soul. And the very first time the guy went out fishing, it was in the evening, getting dark, and he bent down to pull up his first cage, and it was so full, it was so heavy that it pulled him right down into the water."

The tourists looked into the oily sheen, shuddering.

"Did he drown?" asked a small girl.

Bunch nodded. "Only he never really died. The flesh rotted off his bones, that's all. And if you ever come out here in the evening, just when it's getting dark, well, all I'll say is, don't put your hand into the water, because the Swamp Man might grab hold of it and pull you in!"

Two women moaned theatrically. They weren't really afraid, Bunch knew; in this day and age it was hard to really scare anybody.

As trade fell off a little in the worst of the heat, he couldn't have done without his cell phone. It meant he could sit around in the shade at the Lobster Shack, drinking homemade root beer, till he got a call to say there was a group wanting a tour. Whereas old Pitre squatted in the dust at Bourdreaux Landing every day like some kind of scarlet lunatic, under a limp banner that said PITRE'S HOLY SPIRIT TOURS ANYTIME.

One morning Pitre turned up at Mudd Swamp at eight; he'd had a pain in his jaw all night that had kept him from sleeping. His stomach wasn't right, either. He sat down in his usual spot and tried to pray. The problem was that he'd never got the knack of it in his childhood. And now he was a man of the Spirit, he still didn't know quite what to say, once he'd got beyond *Oh Lord, here I am, like you told me.*

By noon not a soul had turned up. Pitre's tongue was stuck to the roof of his mouth. He'd forgotten to bring any water. His jaw was hurting bad now; he blamed his molar. His boat floated motionless beside the landing, not ten feet from the other man's, which had a duck decoy glued on the prow and a freshly painted name: *Zydeco*. Pitre narrowed his eyes at the dirt track that led down from the road. There was no shade; the sun bored into his head through his eyelids, his ear holes, his cracked lips. In the long grass he saw a sledgehammer and recognized it as his own; he must have left it there after banging in a sign. He lurched to his feet at last, feeling the old break in his leg. His body was just a collection of bad memories. But there was something he could do, anyway.

He picked up the sledgehammer and staggered under the weight of it. He cradled it against his shoulder like an old friend. At the landing, he climbed down into the *Zydeco;* the skiff skittered under his feet. His heart was sounding strangely. He hoisted the hammer over his head and brought it down with all he had.

Pitre was lying in the bottom of the boat. He couldn't tell if he'd managed to hole it. The light was behaving like water. He seemed to have stopped breathing. He couldn't tell whether something had gone wrong with the whole world or whether it was just him; he felt like he was under some kind of dreadful enchantment.

At the hospital the nurse was a big black lady from Lafayette; she got pissy with him when he tried to pull the oxygen tube out of his nose. Kept saying, did he know he could have died?

"So could we all," said Pitre balefully. A phrase floated back to him, and he pointed one unsteady finger at her: "You know not the day nor the hour."

They let him out on the third morning, just to shut him up, according to the nurse. "You take it easy now," she growled, "because nobody gets three chances."

When he got back to the Landing, Bunch was sitting on the side of the *Zydeco*. The boat seemed unmarked, Pitre noticed with a slight pang, and the sledgehammer was nowhere to be seen.

He was obliged to speak. "Understand you called me an ambulance on that cell phone of yours."

"That's right," said Bunch, as if they were chatting about the weather.

Pitre stared past him, at the cypresses, their heavy greenery. "I received a message," he said, jerking his chin upwards.

"Another one?"

He ignored that. "We don't want another Cain and Abel situation. In a spirit of brotherhood," said Pitre, then paused to clear his throat, "I propose that we unite our tour companies."

Not a smirk from Bunch.

"No use both doing six trips a day when we could each do three."

"Whatever the Spirit says, my friend," said Bunch, letting his teeth show when he grinned.

Baggage

Niniane Molloy had never been anywhere like the Los Angeles Neverland. They sold melatonin for jet lag and chromium picolinate for sugar cravings. There was chocolate-free chocolate and honey-pickled ginseng. In the next aisle, two huge young men debated whether powdered pearl would help them achieve definition. There were trays labeled JUICE-YOUR-OWN WHEATGRASS; Niniane stroked the tender stalks with one finger, then moved away in case she would be seen and made to pay. Sacks of one hundred percent unbromated flour weighed down a shelf. She had never known that flour was bromated before. She wondered what harm she'd been done by thirty-four years of bromate. Or was it bromide? Or brome?

Arthur used to drink echinacea, even though their mother called it one of his fancy American habits. It made him retch, but he swore he never got colds.

Now Niniane was studying the little rolls of homeopathic tablets. One was for travel sickness and general nausea, another for sleeplessness and irritability. She hadn't slept since the night

before last. Or was it only yesterday? It tired her to keep adding
eight to everything. If it was blazing sun outside the Neverland
Health Store in La-La Land, then it must be pub-closing time
back in Ireland. EXHAUSTION DUE TO FEAR, said the next label.
Niniane thought maybe what she needed was Fear Due to Exhaustion. Did the tablets know the difference?

In the end she didn't buy anything. She couldn't find a remedy for partial deafness due to having the dregs of the cold to end
all colds and flying halfway round the world anyway, because it
was a free ticket from a supermarket competition, no changes, no
refunds. And anyway, she couldn't bring herself to stand at the
Neverland's counter, holding up the queue while she peered at
dimes and nickels like a visitor from another planet.

It was hard to cross the road in this town, she found; cars saw
only each other.

Back at the Hollywood Hills Hotel, Niniane sat in the single
chair, its metal tubing impressed on her thighs. She thought of
Doris Day's motto for decor—"Better to please the fanny than the
eye"—and it almost made her smile. The room was bare as a stage
set. A woolen jumper, glasses, purse, a three-pack of knickers she'd
bought at the airport when she realized her bag wasn't going to
come down the carousel no matter how long she waited; they'd
turned out to be thongs. And a broken-spined copy of Marcel
Proust's *Remembrance of Things Past,* volume one. It wasn't being
read that had worn the book out, but being carried. Niniane had
found it in Arthur's room at home in Limerick, years ago, after he
left for good, on the shelf in between *How to Get a Green Card* and
Complete Poems of Walt Whitman. She always took it on holiday in
the hopes of getting into it. Not that this was a holiday, exactly.

She took the creased card out of her pocket again. *"LA Self-
Storage,"* it said; *"The No-Fuss Solution."* Below the address, what
had to be a room number, scribbled in red: *2011.* Someone had

stuck the key to the back of the card; the tape was brittle with dust. She'd found it at Christmas in the ashtray in the drawer, the ashtray Arthur wasn't supposed to have had in his room, because as their mother always said, no child of hers would be stupid enough to smoke. Niniane had kept it in her purse for months now. What did it mean that her brother had left the key in the ashtray? That it didn't open anything anymore, didn't matter at all? Or that it just wasn't worth coming home to Ireland for?

Later. Later would do.

Niniane lay diagonally across the brown and orange coverlet. The slatted blinds made a bright shadow on the wall. She considered taking her tights off, but she had no socks with her, and her heels would be sure to blister as soon as she went out for a walk. She lifted her head off the bed for a moment to contemplate her black nylon legs. Her tights were all that were holding her together; if she peeled them off, the skin might come, too.

It didn't seem to her that she had slept, only that the next time she looked at the wall it was the colour of ashes, and the clock said ten to midnight.

There was a phone beside the bed, but she couldn't hear a dial tone. Had her ears stopped up completely? She sniffed and yawned like a goldfish on dry land. "Hello," she said into the mouthpiece. At least she could hear herself. Then she noticed the sign on the table: EXTRA CHARGE TO PLUG IN PHONE.

Niniane went around the corner to the Five and Diner and rang the airline. It always slightly embarrassed her to give her name. Arthur used to call her Ninny. Her mother had got them both out of some trashy novel about Merlin. Doris Day always hated her name, too; she had her friends call her Clara, or Susie, or Eunice, or even Do-Do. In America you didn't have to stay what you were. You could change your name or your nose or just get in your Chevy and drive away.

The airline told her that her bag might have gone to Cincinnati.

Niniane's mouth still tasted of sour orange juice from the plane. She sank into the bulging plastic of a corner booth and ordered the All-Day Pancake Special. She picked out new words from the conversation in the next booth: *brewskis,* she heard, and *high colonic,* and *that's bitchin'.*

She sat up in bed reading Proust with watering eyes till half past two, while a moth charred itself against the bulb. Then she switched on the Weather Channel with the sound turned down and fell asleep watching a tornado inch its way up the East Coast. In her dream Niniane had the strangest sense that Arthur was nearby, maybe in the shower or parking his yellow convertible on the street below her window.

How long had it been, she wondered when she woke up. Five years this summer since her brother's last trip home, she was sure of that. He'd told them he was living in Dallas, but was very vague about his job, something to do with sales. And when was that slightly peculiar phone call from San Diego, the time he didn't sound happy enough to be drunk?

One Christmas, early on, she remembered, her mother had been loud in complaint. "Nothing but a card!" The postmark was from LA, no address on the back of the envelope. Dark inked words inside, scattered like seeds across the printed message. *Happy Christmas folks, hope you're all well*—was that it? Or *Take care of yourselves, love A.*? If Niniane had known it was going to be the last message, she'd have read it more carefully.

A year later, there was no card, and her mother said the American postal system was known for its deficiencies. But Niniane suspected Arthur had forgotten. Men without wives were notoriously bad at keeping in touch.

The following year, no card, no comment.

A friend from the office, waiting by the photocopier, asked

after that handsome big brother of Niniane's she'd gone to a college ball with. "My god, how long has it been?" And then, brutally, "Don't you miss him?"

Niniane had felt an immense weariness and walked away.

On the rare occasions Arthur came up in conversation at home these days he was like a figure in a children's book, frozen in time. When neighbours asked, her mother always said that her son was on the West Coast and doing very well. But after tea one New Year's Eve, alone with her father in the kitchen, Niniane had finally asked it, that question without a verb: "Any word from Arthur?"

Her father had said nothing, just kept drying his hands on the dishcloth. The dishwasher was pumping and he was slightly deaf these days. She liked to tell herself that he hadn't heard what she said.

There were some people splashing round in the motel pool already. As soon as Niniane was dressed she walked out to the railing and squinted down. She didn't have anything to swim in, and besides, the pool looked so small, it would be like floating in a petri dish. These toffee-coloured girls and boys with their candyfloss hair would flinch from her pale Irish body.

The man at the desk asked where her car was; she really should have rented a car. "I can't drive," she told him, smiling placatingly. It was obviously a sentence he'd never heard before.

Back home in Limerick, Arthur had been the one who was always borrowing the Fiat to drive to godknowswhere and leaving the seat pushed too far back. Niniane was the one who had stayed in with their parents and made tea and toast in the intervals of *The Late Late Show*. If there were only two of you, things got divided up that way.

She walked out into the shiny street. The morning sun was strange on her skin. She considered buying a clean T-shirt from a stall, but they all had palm trees on them, or Elvis. She'd never known heat like this, so thick you could slice it, so heavy the streets seemed to waver. But she looked up at the glassy sky and for a moment caught that feeling. Songs with the word *California* in them wandered through her mind. If ever a place was the polar opposite of Limerick, this was it. Once you got here, how could you ever go home? Which reminded her of the key, back in the hotel in the ashtray. But it could wait a few hours more. She had come here for herself, really, for a break from ordinary life. She could be a tourist like anybody else.

Only Niniane didn't look like anybody else, as she sat at the very back of the Stars' Homes tour bus. Her skirt was three feet longer than anyone else's, hot on the back of her knees. Her jumper was knotted round her hips. Her black vest revealed tufts of hair at her armpits, which was just about as unacceptable as leprosy in this town; she kept her elbows clamped by her sides. She sang grimly in her head: *Take me back to the Black Hills, the Black Hills of DA-KO-TA.*

As the bus wormed its way up a steep avenue, she was pressed back in her seat. She'd stopped listening to the commentary a while back, after Boris Karloff and Marlene Dietrich. Most of these mansions looked the same, anyway: lush trees protruding over twenty feet of security fence. She tried to imagine Arthur behind one of these shaded windows, sipping wheatgrass juice.

Niniane tried to follow the little red stars on the map, but they danced before her eyes like chicken pox. It was too hot to sit still.

The speaker behind her head crackled. "That was Vincent Minnelli's and now look to your left, you'll see coming up at 713 North Crescent Drive, the lovely home of Miss Doris Day."

She pressed her cheek to the glass, but there was a eucalyptus tree in the way. The prickling air was closing in around her. She couldn't bear this any longer. She lurched to the front of the bus.

"Take your seat, ma'am," the driver said. "No standing while the bus is in motion."

"Would you stop the bus, please?"

"We gotta respect the privacy of the stars."

"Let me off, I can't breathe," she bawled. She had never shouted at a stranger before.

As the bus drew away from the curb, leaving her standing on the shoulder, Niniane felt almost wonderful. The grass under her feet was unnaturally plump. The sun went behind a cloud for a moment and the air seemed a little cooler. There wasn't another human being in sight; only high walls and hedges, and the soft whirr of sprinklers, and the bark of a pedigree dog. Maybe Arthur was a gardener. Any minute now he would stroll along the path with a sack of clippings in each hand.

She walked back as far as No. 713. It looked like all the others. The light bounced off the sidewalk like a chorus line. Maybe Doris would come out in a minute, wearing yellow, with that toothy smile. Niniane had a look at the plush lawn and sang in a whisper: *"Please, please, don't eat the daisies."* Then, all at once, she was so tired she had to sit down on the curb. Her face cream was melting into her eyes; she seemed to be wearing false lips made of paper.

When she looked up, a police officer was getting out of his car. On his hip was a huge gun, the only one she'd ever seen in real life. Niniane stood up so fast that everything went black before her eyes.

"I was walking," she said in answer to his questions. "Just walking, and I got tired."

He put away his notebook and opened the car door for her.

"I wasn't going to hassle her or anything," she repeated as she fastened the seat belt.

The police officer asked who she meant.

"Doris Day."

"Miss Day hasn't lived in that house since 1975, ma'am."

He drove her all the way back to the Hollywood Hills Hotel. There was one moment, when they paused at a red light, when she thought of asking how long a person, a family member, would have to be gone before he could be reported as missing. But then the lights changed.

She apologized for putting the officer to the trouble and asked him to let her off anywhere, she could walk, but he told her this was not a walking kind of city.

Such an odd word for it, *missing,* she thought as she sat on the thin hotel mattress. Maybe Arthur wasn't missing them at all; maybe he was incommunicado. Now there was a grand phrase. Maybe her brother was alive and well in his condo, just around the corner from the Hollywood Hills Hotel, and living such a wonderful new life that he couldn't be bothered to write home about it. Selfish bastard.

A shriek, outside in the street. The window was dusty above the air conditioner; she pressed her face to it. On the street two young men on Rollerblades were greeting each other with loud cries. The black guy had short white hair. They kissed on both cheeks, then slid off in opposite directions.

That wasn't it, was it? Not enough of a reason to never come home. Niniane had always known Arthur wasn't the marrying kind, even though it had taken her nearly thirty-five years to put words on it. She had tried to bring it up once, but he'd changed the subject, which was fair enough. And their parents must have known, too, in their way. Nothing was said, but they never nagged him with questions about girlfriends.

Maybe Arthur had somebody over here. Maybe that was enough for him. *A chosen family*—that was the phrase, she'd read it in a magazine. But he was kidding himself because you couldn't unchoose your old family. You couldn't just walk away, not when they'd never done anything to deserve it.

Niniane had always thought her brother liked her. But how little he knew of her anymore. He'd been away for her breakup with Mark, and her promotion, and that time she had the ovarian cyst and for a month thought she was dying. Whereas, to give them their due, her parents had always been there. Sunday after Sunday. Always on the same sofa in the same front room in the same terraced house on the same street in Limerick, the same sofa both she and Arthur had clung to when they were learning to walk. Her father getting balder and more taciturn, her mother rather more irritable since her hip operation, but both still there, in their places. And so was Niniane. Her own job, her own flat, but a daughter still, a daughter till the end.

She put her few possessions in her bag and went outside to hail a taxi.

The worst pictures always came when she was only half awake, or stuck in traffic. Arthur in prison, crouched in the corner of a cell. Arthur shooting up in an alley, his hairless arms pock-marked with holes. Arthur hawking himself on a street corner, bony with disease. What was it, his mystery? What was so bad that he couldn't lift the phone?

It occurred to her for the first time that he was dead. Doris Day's only brother died of epilepsy when she was thirty-three. These things happened. Was that relief Niniane felt, that curious surge in her throat? It couldn't be. She felt sick with shame. She pressed her face against the sweaty glass of the cab window.

Light-headed, she walked through the white corridors of LA Self-Storage. Fluorescent strips crackled overhead. The only sound was the pant of the air-conditioning. She thought if she turned a corner and bumped into a stranger she might scream. But who else would come here on a Sunday evening? She whispered the chorus of "Hotel California" to give herself courage. This place was like a prison for misbehaving furniture.

She came to 2011 at last; it looked like all the other doors. The key was in her hand. What could furniture tell her? Arthur always had good taste, but there wouldn't be some vault of treasures. There wouldn't be a film of the missing years.

For a moment, as she slid the key into the door, she hoped it wouldn't open.

Niniane felt for the light switch and flicked it on. The locker was about ten by ten by ten feet of nothing. She stepped in, as if to search the bare corners. Nothing at all. She shut the door behind her back and for a moment feared she'd locked herself in. She was more alone than she'd ever been. There weren't even gaps in the dust to hint at whatever Arthur had once kept here; not even the marks of his size-thirteen feet from the day he must have taken it all away.

Niniane let herself slide down the door till she was sitting on her heels. She began to cry, slow and grudging, like loosening a tooth. The hard walls multiplied her breath. In between sobs she kept listening for footsteps.

At the pay phone, various options ran through her head as the receiver played "Greensleeves" in her ear, but each seemed more improbable than the last. If she missed this flight home, she had no way of paying for another. If she went to the police, they would look embarrassed for her and tell her to come back with some evidence that a crime had been committed. No known associates. No last address.

"But I'm his sister, I swear," she told the voice at the other end of the phone. "You must still have his address, because he's paying for one of your storage lockers, he must be, or else you'd have changed the lock, wouldn't you?"

The voice sounded computer-generated.

"Will you at least take my address in Ireland?" she butted in. "Just in case. I don't know, in case he ever stops paying or something. I'm his sister," she repeated, like a bad actress from a soap. "He'd want me to know where he was."

Which was a lie, she thought, as she jammed the phone onto the hook. She had no idea what Arthur wanted. Most likely she would never find out if the empty locker meant that he was dead, with his bank account slowly draining, or that he was living high on a hill with all his chairs and lamps around him, rich enough not to mind paying for an empty locker, too careless to remember where he had left the key.

"The airport, now, please," she repeated to the taximan, who was barely visible behind the smoked glass. Niniane lay back against the sticky leather and let the traffic draw her into its slipstream. LIVE NUDE GIRLS, said a neon sign, NOW HIRING. Now there would be a quick way to change her life.

The sky was full of planes, crisscrossing like fireflies. In the far distance she caught a glimpse of the famous white letters lit up on the hill. If she hadn't known they said *Hollywood* she would have had no idea: *No Food,* she would have read, maybe, or *Hullaballoo,* or *Home Now.*

At the airport, Niniane was told that her bag had just arrived from Pittsburgh. She stood in line to pick it up, then queued again to check it in for Shannon. In Duty Free, she bought her parents a $19.95 gilt Oscar that had a hopeful, dazed expression. She would bring it over next Sunday. It would give them something to talk about so they wouldn't have to talk about Arthur. She would see it on the mantelpiece every Sunday for the rest of her parents' lives, and someday she would have to decide whether to give it to Oxfam with the rest of their stuff or take it home and put it on her own mantelpiece.

She had a window seat. All night she stared out at darkness or

read Proust. When the sun came up over Shannon, hurting her
eyes, she had finally got as far as the bit about the madeleine.

The American pilot announced that they would be landing
momentarily. Niniane's head shot up out of her doze; for a second,
she misunderstood his use of the word and believed him, thought
the plane was only going to dip down like a bird onto the runway,
gather strength for a moment, then wing away to somewhere else
entirely.

When she emerged from Customs there were people waiting
with cardboard signs held against their chests like X-rays. None of
them had her name on. Trunks and totes spilled along the conveyor belt, climbing over each other at corners. She edged into the
crowd, watching the procession of bags. A sign over the conveyor
belt said in red letters, ALL BAGGAGE LOOKS THE SAME. BE SURE YOU
HAVE YOUR OWN.

Necessary Noise

May blew smoke out of the car window.

Her younger sister made an irritated sound between her teeth.

"I'm blowing it away from you," May told her.

"It comes right back in," said Martie. She leaned her elbows on the steering wheel and looked through the darkness between the streetlamps. "You told him to be at the corner of Fourth and Leroy at two, yeah?"

May inhaled, ignoring the question.

"Fifteen's way too young to go to clubs," observed Martie, tucking her hair behind one ear.

"I don't know," said May thoughtfully. "You're not even eighteen yet and you're totally middle-aged."

That was an old insult. Martie rolled her eyes. "Yeah, well Laz is so immature. Dad shouldn't let him start clubbing yet, that's all I'm saying. When I heard Laz asking him, on the phone, I said let me talk to Dad, but he hung up."

May flicked the remains of her cigarette into the gutter. Somewhere close by a siren yowled.

Martie was peering up at a dented sign. "It says 'No Stopping,' but I can't tell if it applies when it's two a.m. Do you think we'll get towed?"

"Not as long as we're sitting in the car," said her elder sister, deadpan.

"If the traffic cops come by, I could always drive round the block."

May yawned.

"I guess Dad was feeling guilty about being away for Laz's birthday, so that's why he said he could go clubbing," said Martie.

"Yeah, well the man's always feeling guilty about something."

Martie gave her big sister a wary look. "It's not easy," she began, "it can't be easy for Dad, holding everything together."

"Does he?" asked May.

"Well, we all do. I mean, he may not do the cooking and laundry and stuff, but he's still in charge. And it's hard when he's got to be on the road so much—"

"Oh, right, yeah, choking down all those Texas sirloins, I weep for him."

"He's not in Texas," said Martie, "he's in New Mexico."

May got out another cigarette, contemplated it, then shoved it back in the box.

"Are you still thinking of giving up the day after your twenty-first?" asked Martie.

"Not if you remind me about it even one more time." May combed her long pale hair with both hands.

Silence fell, at least in the old Pontiac. Outside the streets droned and screamed in their nighttime way.

"Actually, I don't think Laz gives a shit that Dad's away for his birthday," remarked May at last. "I wouldn't have, when I was his age. Normal fifteen-year-olds don't want to celebrate with their parents, or go on synchronized swimming courses or whatever it was you did for your fifteenth."

"Life Saving," Martie told her coldly.

"The boy wants to go to some under-eighteens hiphop juice-bar thing where they won't even sell him a Bud, that doesn't seem like a problem to me, except that he better get his ass in gear," said May, slapping the side of the car, "because I've got a party to go to."

"I said you should have called a cab."

"I'm broke till payday. Besides, Dad only lets you use the car when he's away so long as you give me and Laz rides."

"You could use it yourself if you'd take some lessons," Martie pointed out.

"There's no point learning to drive in New York," said May witheringly. "Besides, next year I'll be off to Amsterdam and it's all bikes there."

"Motorbikes?"

"No, just bicycles."

Martie's eyebrows went up. "What are you going to do in Amsterdam?"

"I don't know. Hang out. It's just a fabulous city."

"You've never been," Martie pointed out.

"I've heard a lot about it."

Martie tapped a tune on the steering wheel. "It'll be weird if you go."

"Not if. When."

"When, then."

May yawned. "You're always complaining I never clean up round the apartment."

"Yeah, but when you're gone, there'll still be Laz, and his mess will probably expand to fill the place."

"Oh, admit it," said May, "you love playing Martyr Mommie."

Martie gave her elder sister a bruised look. Then she scanned the street again, on both sides, as if their brother might be lurking in the shadows. "This thing you're going to tonight," she said, "is it a dyke party?"

Her sister sighed. "It's just a party. With some dykes at it. I hope."

"Is Telisse going?"

"I don't know. She's not really doing the dyke thing anymore, anyway."

"Oh."

"Why," her sister teased her, "did you like Telisse?"

"No, I just thought you did," said Martie stiffly. She checked her watch in the yellow streetlight. "Come on, Laz," she muttered. "I bet he's doing this deliberately. Testing our limits."

"God, you're so parental," May hooted. "No wonder Laz hates you."

"He does not."

"He so does! He's always telling you to get off his case. 'Get her off my fuckin' case, May!' he says to me." May's imitation of her brother's voice was gruff with testosterone.

"He doesn't mean he hates me," said Martie. "He doesn't actually hate any of us."

May groaned and shifted in her seat, leaned her head back, and shut her eyes. "G'night, Ma Walton . . ."

The minutes lengthened. Martie stared into the rearview mirror. A truck went by slowly, picking up garbage bags. "We could call Laz on your cell phone," she said, "except he probably wouldn't hear it over the music. Maybe I should go in and look for him," she added under her breath. "Or no, I can't leave the car, in case it needs to be moved. Maybe you should go."

Her sister gave no sign of hearing that.

"There he is." Martie threw open the door in relief. "Laz!"

The boy was stumbling a little, head down.

"Come *on,*" she cried. "We've been waiting. May's got a party to get to."

"What do you know, the boy is wasted," said May in amusement, turning her head as Laz struggled to fold his long legs into the backseat.

"He couldn't be," Martie told her, "it was a juice bar."

May giggled. "Now there's a first. *Teens Gain Access to Alcoholic Beverage!*"

"Okay, okay," said Martie, starting the car with a rumble. "Laz, are you in? Your seat belt." She waited.

"Can we just drive?" asked May.

"Anyone who doesn't wear a seat belt is a human missile," Martie quoted. "If I had to slam on the brakes suddenly, he could snap your neck."

"Oh Jesus, I'll snap yours in a minute if you don't get going. Laz!" snapped May, turning to face her brother. "Get your belt on now."

He grinned at her, his eyes drowned in his dark hair. His fingers fumbled with the catch of the seat belt.

The car moved off at last. "Good night, was it?" May asked over her shoulder at the next traffic light.

The only answer was the sound of retching.

"For god's sake," wailed Martie, taking a sharp right. "Not on the seat covers!"

But the noises got worse.

"That's really vile," said May, breathing through her mouth as she rolled down her window as far as it would go.

"Are you all right now?" Martie asked her brother, peering in the mirror. "Do you want a Kleenex?" But he had slid down, out of sight. She wormed one hand into the back of the car, grabbed his knee. "Sit up, Laz."

"Leave him alone for a minute, why can't you?"

"May, he could choke on his own vomit."

"You're being hysterical."

Martie twisted round again. "I said sit up now!"

"OK, pull over," said May, for once sounding like the eldest.

"But—"

"You're going to crash. Stop the car."

Martie bit her lip and braked beside a fire hydrant.

May got out and slammed her own door. She opened the one behind and bent in. "Laz?"

No answer.

She pulled him upright, wiped his mouth with his own sleeve. "He stinks." After a long minute, she said, in a different voice, "I think he may be on something."

"On something?"

"Laz? Wake up! Did you take something?"

"Like what? Like what?" repeated the younger sister, her hands gripping the steering wheel.

"Oh, Martie, I don't even know the names for what kids are taking these days. Laz!" May shouted, trying to lift his left eyelid.

The boy moaned something.

Martie let go of the wheel and started scrabbling in her sister's bag. "Where's your phone, May? I'm going to call 911."

May climbed over her brother's legs and wrenched the passenger door shut. "Are you kidding? Do you know how long they take to respond? We'll be faster driving to Emergency."

"Which? Where?"

"I don't know, try St. Jude's."

"You'll have to navigate for me," stammered Martie.

"I'm busy holding Laz's head out of this pool of vomit," said May, shrill. "Just go down Fourth; there'll be signs on Thirtieth. Move it!"

Martie drove above the speed limit for the first time in her life. Laz didn't make a sound. May gripped him hard.

"You should be talking to him," Martie told her, at a red light. "Keep him awake."

"I don't think he is awake."

"Is he asleep? He could be asleep."

"He's out of it; he's unconscious," snapped her sister.

"Is his windpipe open? Check his pulse."

"I can't tell." May was gripping her brother's limp wrist. "There's a pulse but I think it's mine."

The light was still red. "Let me." Martie burst open her seat belt, squeezed one knee through the gap between the seats. "Laz?" she shouted, pressing her fingers against the side of her brother's damp throat.

"Shouldn't you—"

"Shut up. I'm listening."

Silence in the car, except for a little wheeze in Martie's breathing. She put her ear against her brother's mouth, as if she was asking for a kiss. Then the car behind sounded its horn, and Martie jerked back so fast she hit her head on the roof. "He's not—"

"What? What?"

More horns blared. "Green," roared May, blinking at the lights, and Martie slammed the car into drive.

"I think it fucked him up when Mom went off," said May. The sisters were sitting on the end of a row of orange seats in the Emergency waiting area, their legs crossed in opposite directions.

"They say the younger you are when something like that happens, the more it messes up your head."

"That's garbage," said Martie unsteadily, examining her cuticles. "Laz was too young; he wasn't even three. He doesn't remember Mom being at home; he doesn't know what she looked like apart from photos."

"He must remember her being missing," May pointed out. "You do."

"That's different. I was five." Elbows on her knees, Martie stared up at the wall, where a sign said UNNECESSARY NOISE PROHIBITED.

"That first couple of years, when all Dad fed us was out of cans—"

"She had postpartum depression that never got diagnosed," Martie put in. "That's what Dad says."

After a second, May shrugged.

"What does that mean?" Martie imitated the shrug.

"Well yeah, that's what Dad *would* say," said May. "He'd have to say something. He couldn't just tell us, 'Hey kids, your mom took off for no reason.'" May pulled out her cigarettes. "I mean, we could all have something *undiagnosed*," she added scornfully.

Martie pointed at the NO SMOKING sign.

"I know. I know. I'm just seeing how many I've got left. What's taking them so long? You'd think at least they could tell us what's going on," barked May in the direction of the reception desk.

Her younger sister watched her.

"At the hotel, did they say where Dad was?"

Martie shook her head. "Just that he wasn't back yet. They'll give him our message as soon as he comes in."

"He's probably boinking some Texan hooker."

"He's in New Mexico," said Martie furiously, "and you can just shut up. You don't know why Mom left any more than any of us—you were only eight," she added after a second. "I think it makes sense that she was depressed."

"Well sure, it must have been pretty depressing pretending to be our mom if all the time she was longing to take off and never see us again."

"I hate it when you talk like that," said Martie through her teeth.

No answer.

"You think you're so savvy about the ways of the whole, like, world, when really you're just bitter and twisted."

May raised her eyes to heaven.

The woman behind the reception desk called out a name, and Martie jumped to her feet. Then she sat down again. "I thought she said Laurence. Laurence Coleman."

"No, it was something else."

"I forgot to get milk," said Martie irrelevantly. "Unless you did?"

May shook her head.

"Laz didn't eat any dinner. I kept some couscous for him to microwave, but he didn't want it; he said it looked gross." Martie put her face in her hands.

"Take it easy," said her sister.

"They say if there's nothing lining the stomach . . ."

"He probably got some fries on the way to the club. I bet he had a burger and fries," said May.

Martie spoke through her fingers. "What could he have taken?"

"Nothing expensive," said May. "He's always broke."

"I just wish we knew, you know, why he did it."

"Oh, don't start the whole eighth-grade lecture on self-esteem and peer pressure," snapped May. "Look, everyone takes some-thing sometime in their life."

"You just say that because you did. Do," added Martie, her cheeks red. "It just better not have been you who gave it to him."

"For Christ's sake!" barked May. A woman with a child asleep on her stomach stared at them, and May brought her voice down. "I would never. I don't do anything scary and if I did I wouldn't give it to my moronic kid brother."

"You can't know what's scary," said Martie miserably. "People can die after half an ecstasy tablet."

May let out a scornful puff of breath. "They said he was fitting. Having fits, in the cubicle. E doesn't give you fits."

Her sister sat hunched over. "You know when she asked us about our insurance provider?"

"Yeah. Thank god Dad's got family coverage in this job, at least."

"No, but I think she was calling them, the insurance people. She picked up the phone. Why would she call them right away?"

May shrugged.

Martie nibbled the edge of her thumb. "Do you think maybe they won't cover something . . . self-inflicted?"

"It's not like he jumped off the Brooklyn Bridge," said May.

"But if he took it—"

"Shut up! We don't know what he took or what he thought it was. Get off his case!"

There was a long silence. "I care about Laz as much as you do," said Martie. "Probably more."

"Fine," said May, her voice tired.

Martie got up and walked off. She dawdled by the vending machines, and came back with something called Glucozip.

A girl had come into the waiting area, arm in arm with her mother. The girl had a deformed face, something red and terrible bulging between her huge lips. Martie looked away at once.

May whispered, "I didn't think that was possible."

"Don't stare," said Martie, mortified.

"She's put a pool ball in her mouth! I tried it once, but no way."

Martie looked over her shoulder. So that's what it was. "You tried to do that?" she repeated, turning on her elder sister. "Why would you do that?"

"I was thirteen or so; I don't know. It was a dare."

"That's not a reason!"

Her sister shrugged.

Martie sneaked another look at the girl with the ball in her mouth. The mother was scolding loudly. "Where's your so-called friends now, then?" The girl twisted her head, made a small moan in her throat.

Martie turned away again and offered her sister some Gluco-zip. "You should, even if you don't feel thirsty," she urged her. "We're probably dehydrated. Unless we're in shock, in which case they say you shouldn't drink anything, in case they have to operate."

May stared at her sister.

"Are your extremities cold?" Martie persisted.

"What do you know?" said May, harsh.

The younger sister looked away, took another drink. Her throat moved violently as she swallowed.

"One crappy First Aid for Beginners course, and suddenly you're an expert?"

Martie took a breath, paused, then spoke after all. "I know more than you."

"Like what? Like what do you know?"

She spoke rapidly. "For instance, if someone's got no pulse and he's not breathing, he's dead. Technically."

"He fucking isn't!"

"Technically he is. That's the definition of death," Martie told her sister shakily. "It's not brain death but it's technically death, until they get the heart started again."

"It's you who's brain-dead," growled May.

"I just—"

"I don't want to hear it!"

Silence. Martie, eyes shining, read the back of her can.

"They've probably infibrillated him," May told her, "and now they're just letting him rest."

"I think you mean defibrillate."

"I don't think so," snapped May. "And also, they've got chemicals they can use. There was that scene in *Pulp Fiction,* when Uma Thurman snorts heroin by mistake, and they stick an adrenaline needle in her heart."

"I can't stand that kind of movie," said Martie. "They're totally unreal."

"No, they're too real," her sister told her, "that's what you can't stand." She let out a long breath. "When are they going to tell us something?" she said, leaping to her feet. "I mean, Jesus!"

"Could you keep your voice down?" whispered Martie. "Everybody's staring."

"So?" roared May. "I mean, what the fuck does that mean?"— throwing out her arm at the sign that said UNNECESSARY NOISE PROHIBITED. "What the hell is unnecessary noise? If I make a noise, it's because I need to."

"You don't need to shout."

"Yes I do!"

Martie seized her elder sister by the hand and pulled her back into her seat. May went limp. Her head hung down. The people who had been watching looked away again.

"Do you think," Martie asked May half an hour later, "I know this probably sounds really stupid, but do you think it's any use, do you think it's any help to people, if you're there?"

"Where?" asked May, eyes vacant, taking a sip of Glucozip.

"Near them. Thinking about them."

"Like, faith healing?"

Martie's mouth twisted. "Not necessarily. I just mean, is it doing Laz any good that we're here?"

"I think maybe we're irrelevant," said May, without bitterness. "He never liked either of us that much in the first place."

"You don't have to like your family," said Martie uncertainly.

"Just as well," said May under her breath. "Just as well."

"Laurence Coleman? Laurence Coleman?"

They both registered the words at last and jerked in their seats. "He's not here," said Martie confusedly to the man in the white coat, whose small badge said DR. P.J. HASSID. "They took him in there," pointing vaguely.

"If you would come this way—"

They both scurried after Dr. Hassid. May plucked at the doctor's sleeve. "Is he alive?" she asked, and burst into tears.

Martie stared at her elder sister, who had tears dripping from her chin. One of them landed on the scuffed floor of the corridor.

"Just about," said Dr. Hassid, not stopping. There were dark bags under his eyes.

Laz, lying in a cubicle, didn't look alive. He was stretched out on his back like a specimen of an alien, with tubes up his nose, machines barricading. May wailed. Martie took hold of her elbow.

"Laurence will get through this," said Dr. Hassid, fiddling with a valve.

"Laz," May sobbed the word. "He's called Laz."

"It doesn't matter," said Martie.

But Dr. Hassid was amending the clipboard that hung at the end of the bed. "L-A-S?"

"Zee," gulped May.

"L-A-Z, very good. It's better to use the familiar name. Laz?" the doctor said, louder, bending over the boy. "Will you wake up now?"

One eyelid quivered. Then both. The boy blinked at his sisters.

ACKNOWLEDGMENTS

"Touchy Subjects" was first published as a self-contained chapter in *Ladies' Night at Finbar's Hotel,* devised and edited by Dermot Bolger (Dublin: New Island, and London: Macmillan; San Diego and New York: Harcourt, 1999).

"Expecting" was broadcast on BBC Radio 4 in 1996, and first published in *You Magazine/Mail On Sunday,* 8 October 2000.

"Oops" was first published in a shorter form in *Sunday Express* (Summer 2000).

"Do They Know It's Christmas?" is adapted from a short radio play, part of my *Humans and Other Animals* series (2003), produced by Tanya Nash for BBC Radio 4.

"The Cost of Things" was first published in *The Diva Book of Short Stories,* edited by Helen Sandler (London: Diva Books, 2000), and then adapted into a short radio play as part of my *Humans and Other Animals* series (2003), produced by Tanya Nash for BBC Radio 4.

"Pluck" was first published in *The Dublin Review* (Autumn 2002); before publication, I adapted it into a ten-minute film of the same name, directed by Neasa Hardiman and produced by Vanessa Finlow (Language, 2001).

"Good Deed" was first published in *Rush Hour,* edited by Michael Cart (Volume 1, 2004).

"The Sanctuary of Hands" was first published in *Telling Moments,* edited by Lynda Hall (Madison: The University of Wisconsin Press, 2003).

"Team Men" was first published in *One Hot Second: Stories of Desire,* edited by Cathy Young (New York: Knopf, 2002).

"Speaking in Tongues" was first published in *The Mammoth Book of Lesbian Erotica,* edited by Rose Collis (London: Constable/Robinson; New York: Carroll & Graf, 2000).

"The Welcome" was first published in *Love and Sex: Ten Stories of Truth,* edited by Michael Cart (New York: Simon & Schuster, 2001).

"Enchantment" was first published in *Magic,* edited by Sarah Brown and Gil MacNeil (London: Bloomsbury, 2002).

"Necessary Noise" was first published in *Necessary Noise,* edited by Michael Cart (New York: Joanna Cotler Books, 2003).

I'd like to record my gratitude to Sinéad McBrearty for providing all the soccer knowledge for "Team Men," to Dermot Bolger for editing "Touchy Subjects," to Tanya Nash for her work on the radio version of "Do They Know It's Christmas?" and to Vanessa Finlow and Neasa Hardiman for their work on the film version of "Pluck."

For inspiring these stories, on the other hand, I want to thank Maria Walsh for "Speaking in Tongues"; Helen Stanton for "Oops"; Sharon Switzer and Claire Sykes for taking me on the trip to LA that lies behind "Baggage"; Helen Donoghue for the one in Belgium that led to "The Sanctuary of Hands" (and also Catherine Dhavernas for her conference on The Hand which was the story's occasion); Denis Donoghue for proposing I take a fresh look at Martha, Mary, and Lazarus in "Necessary Noise"; all my former housemates at Paradise Housing Co-operative in Cambridge for "The Welcome"; Wen Adams and Nairne Holtz for "Do They Know It's Christmas?"; and Emma our late great cat for "The Cost of Things."